Praise for Colin Kers‹

C000280755

This is a stunning first novel for C
rousing supernatural thriller as memoraᴅɪᴇ ɑ⊃ ᴜᴜⱴⱴ ⱴ⁻ ⁻
and Stephen King. Kersey promises to be one of the strongest voices
in the genre for years to come.

TULSA WORLD

Colin Kersey's *Soul Catcher* is the best kind of first novel, a fast-
paced thriller absolutely overflowing with riches. Open it and enter
a fascinating world of Northwest lore, heartfelt characters, and one
very smart dog. Get comfortable, because once the spirit wind
launches its reign of revenge on Seattle, you will not be able to put
it down.

JO-ANN MAPSON, AUTHOR OF *HANK AND CHLOE*
AND *BLUE RODEO*

Exciting, eerie, with excellent characterizations and a fast pace, this
is a believable thriller.

ELLENVILLE PRESS

Chilling and ravishing. This author has a wonderful ear for the
language and a profound insight into the sounds of silence.

S.P. SOMTOW, AUTHOR OF *VANITAS* AND *JASMINE NIGHTS*

First time novelist Kersey melds elements of the Indian curse story
and the disaster novel in the fast-paced horror tale set in
contemporary Seattle. Kersey shows an aptitude for bringing
characters to life.

PUBLISHERS WEEKLY

Colin Kersey's first effort is a mature and auspicious debut.

WASHINGTON POST BOOK WORLD

SWIMMING

WITH

THE

ANGELS

COLIN KERSEY

atmosphere press

for Vicki

PART I
PHOTOGRAPHS

You can look at a picture for a week and never think of it again. You can also look at a picture for a second and think of it all your life.

-Joan Miró

CHAPTER ONE

The first time a camera saved my life, I was newly married with big dreams and a terrifying level of naivete.

I left my boots and an accusing fragrance of hawthorn, cypress, and chicken shit in the entryway. It was late on a Friday evening and I was relieved to find Heide was home making dinner. Tonight, she wore only an apron and a pair of blue panties. Some people insist on their food being cooked by people wearing clothes. I am not one of them.

I kissed the back of her neck while I admired the penne pasta being tossed with chicken, capers, onions, peppers, and olive oil.

"Looks tempting," I said as I ran my hands up over her belly to her breasts. "The food looks tasty, too."

She snorted and kissed my cheek. "How was work?"

"Oh, you know how it is with landscaping. Lots of dirt, and then some more dirt. Very dirty." I tweaked her nipples and continued nuzzling her neck. "How was yours?"

She spanked the pasta solidly with the wooden spoon, turned off the burner, and swiveled to throw her arms around me. "You are a naughty man."

"Dirty."

"And I like it."

A long kiss followed. Very long.

"Is the pasta ready?" I asked afterward.

"It can wait." She grabbed my belt buckle and pulled me toward the bedroom. Dinner would be delayed.

***

"Seriously, how was your day?" I asked later as she stroked the hairs on my chest.

"Have I ever told you how much I love your furry chest?" she asked.

"Once or twice."

"My day was great." She paused. "Incredible actually."

I lifted her chin so I could look into her green eyes. "Did you win the lotto or something?"

"Something like that," she said coyly.

"Tell me."

She put a finger to my lips. "Why don't you shut up and get me some wine?"

When I came back, she was frowning as she held up my mud-caked jeans from the floor where I had discarded them. "You weren't kidding about the dirt."

"You didn't seem to mind earlier." I held out her glass of wine. "By the way, what happened to dinner?"

"Dinner can wait. Put down the wine and come back to bed. I'm not through with you yet."

Some nights we skipped dinner. This was evidently going to be one of those nights.

***

"I have no problem living with a man who likes to get his hands dirty," Heide said later. "Actually," she purred, "I kind of like it."

She reached for the glass of wine on the nightstand. "But I have a problem living with a man as talented as you are and

4

whose vocabulary is limited to four-letter words and a few foul Spanish phrases."

"Well—" I managed to swallow an obscenity. Heide was right. The dialogue of a landscaping crew made up of several day workers and a couple of full-timers like me was not exactly Masterpiece Theater repartee.

"Your photographs are better than some of the stuff I see in art galleries. When are you going to get serious about your career?"

"Someday." I brushed a lock of hair the color of a rusty nail from her face. It was a great face. Freckles plentiful as stars.

"'Someday' is not an adequate answer. I need a plan. Now." She poked me in the chest. "Either give me a date, or I'll make one for you. I am not planning to spend the rest of my life in a crappy one-bedroom apartment while my amazingly gifted husband breaks his back putting in lawns and fences for rich assholes."

During our first year of marriage, my career—or lack thereof—was one of the few things we argued about and, lately, the discussion was becoming tedious. I felt trapped with a capital "T."

I finished my glass of wine and wished I had thought to bring the bottle back to the bedroom.

"Most photographers make even less than I do," I countered. "An art director job for an advertising agency in L.A., on the other hand, would not only pay the bills, but leave us with enough for a down payment on a condo. Or maybe even a house with a yard for the kids in a couple of years."

"Kids as in baby goats, right?" she asked.

"Yeah, those too," I said. "But I can't get a job as an art director if I don't have a book of experience, and I can't get the experience without finishing my degree and getting an internship working on recognized brand names."

I had managed to finish my third year at Otis College of Art and Design before getting married and running through my savings. Thanks to a trillion or two of unpaid debt, college loans were now harder to get. And call me old-fashioned, I did not like starting off a marriage in deep financial distress. At least not more than the sinkhole we were already in danger of drowning in.

"We're talking at least 50K to finish school and that ain't going to happen anytime soon. Not with this landscaping job."

Heide was silent for a bit as she sipped her wine. Then she said, "I might be getting a raise soon."

My pulse rate rose an octave. "I'm probably hallucinating from starvation, but did you just say you were getting a raise?"

"Big raise."

"Really?"

She leaned over to kiss my nipple. "Would I lie to you?"

A shimmer of hope crept under my normally suspicious radar. I might have asked why a wire transfer associate merited a big raise, but then she looked at me with that impish grin that had enraptured me on our first date. As my mother told me more than once: "Dev, you're a sweet boy but you're missing one important thing: it's called 'horse sense.'"

I had fallen for Heide at least twelve minutes before the first moment I had seen her. Like so many Match.com subscribers, we met face to face in a coffee shop. Over iced lattes, I learned she had never been married, was not anxious to start a family, was bored with her job at the hedge fund, and wanted to see the world "before it gets too expensive, or there's another pandemic." As I recall, no one mentioned money.

Our second date was on a Friday night. After too many glasses of wine, we went back to her place, made love like it was the Super Bowl of sex and we were on opposing teams, and woke up ready to go again. From that moment forward, we never spent another day apart.

Yeah, I know it sounds foolish. But it worked. Until that day it didn't.

I was so enthralled by her body and the way she laughed that I totally overlooked whatever did not fit my view of her as the ideal partner. Like binge-watching old horror movies until four in the morning. Or the temper that could come out of nowhere.

For Christmas, she bought me a Canon camera with a telephoto lens that we were still paying for. Among other things, I liked taking cameo photos. I had zero interest in posed photos, or worse—selfies. I preferred capturing the real person, hemorrhoids, and all. Often, the best way to do that was to catch them off guard. Heide did not mind me clicking away while she was taking a shower or getting dressed. If not in a hurry to get somewhere, she would sometimes put on a little exhibition. Taking photos while she was eating, however, was a no-no.

Later that night, I woke up ravenous and discovered her missing from bed. A light shone from the kitchen. Thinking I might catch her in her nighty or less, I grabbed the camera from where it hung by a strap on the doorknob and tiptoed down the hallway. Shadows dappled the contours of the pale skin of her back as she stared at the bright screen of her laptop. When she heard the soft click of the camera, she slammed the laptop shut and whirled to face me.

"What the fuck are you doing? Jesus!"

"What's with you?" I asked, taken aback.

"You scared me."

"Sorry."

"I couldn't sleep," she said.

"You're going to be dead tired in the morning," I warned. We were scheduled to meet her boss and his family for a ride on their boat to Catalina Island.

Later, I would realize how sadly prophetic my comment would turn out to be.

CHAPTER TWO

Heide's friend, Jeff, the head of IT at the hedge fund where she worked, had invited us on the boat. We planned to join his wife and daughter for drinks at their waterfront home on Lido Isle in Newport Harbor followed by a cruise to Catalina Island. Although they were only seven or eight years older than us, we lived on different planets financially. From the way we gawked, you might have thought we were astronauts setting foot on the moon for the first time. As I watched Jeff strut about in his floppy Panama hat, a large Cuban cigar in one hand and a glass of hundred-dollar tequila in the other, I could see how some people—such as my wife, I suspected—might feel jealous. I was reminded, however, of something my father once said. "We have a saying in India: 'Money hides in the tiger's ear.' Do not go envying them with more than us. You don't know what they had to do to get it."

My father has been in America for nearly 40 years, but to listen to him talk, you might think he just stepped off the plane from Bangalore. He often uses Indian proverbs when he speaks to me. Many of these colorful platitudes refer to tigers. I am not sure what this says about him. Or me.

Newport Harbor is the picture-perfect place to live in Southern California. It is the largest pleasure-boat harbor in the country with more than ten thousand boats of all sizes from eight-foot dinghies to 150-foot luxury yachts. There are at least a dozen colorful bars and restaurants for people-watching and weather that is always at least ten degrees cooler than the rest of Orange County. Property is outrageously expensive, of course, which is why Heide and I were living two miles inland in a "charmingly petite" one-bedroom apartment. But you could enjoy an evening stroll or morning run on our hilltop bluff with a panoramic view of the harbor and the Pacific Ocean for free.

It was the perfect place to live unless you must often drive to distant jobs on one of the many freeways. As I did with a million other drivers, many of them texting on cellphones, interspersed with the occasional lane-splitting daredevil motorcyclist. Travel time could easily double or more if a texter and daredevil crossed paths.

Water lapped at the pier where I stood as the green-fringed fingers of California fan palms whispered secrets in the mild breeze. A slender line of clouds lay to the north while twenty-six miles to the west, the usually smog-obscured Catalina Island sat. It gleamed as if detailed in one of the car washes that Southern Californians frequent to rinse away the grit and grime from their cherished vehicles. With the Canon camera I captured a burst of photos as a brown pelican of prehistoric design swooped low, and then, wings tucked tightly against its sides, plummeted into the harbor in search of breakfast. Two docks away, a German shepherd gave chase, barking and leaping into the saltwater. A large sailboat glided by followed by a couple of young women paddleboarders wearing bikinis, their tanned leg and arm muscles taut as bowstrings.

Each house snuggled up against its neighbor so that the view from the waterfront was of docks populated by electric Duffy boats with their trademark blue canopies, or by large sail or motor yachts, many of them outfitted with fake owls to scare away seagulls. Perched a few feet beyond the water's edge and up short stairways were small but elaborate patios.

They displayed explosions of potted red geraniums and expensive outdoor furniture posed on travertine flagstones circumscribed by immaculately groomed boxwood hedges leading to multi-million-dollar homes, each one striving to appear as prosperous as its neighbors.

I noticed all this because my photography-trained eyes are accustomed to observing such details and, as part of a landscaping crew, I know how to spot thousand-dollar pots.

Back at the nearly all-glass house a mere twenty feet from where I stood, Jeff's wife, Debbie, and their young daughter, Christy, were carrying dishes of fruit, cheeses, and other munchies to their boat, a 30-foot-long bolt of cadmium-yellow fiberglass that appeared lightning fast just sitting there. A pirate flag hung from the rear stanchion like a one-finger salute to all those less fortunate.

I was annoyed to see that Jeff had slung his drink-carrying arm around Heide, their heads bent close together. Occasionally, I would arrive home to find Heide missing. When she arrived home an hour or two later, she would often be slurring her words while apologizing for working late or having a drink with co-workers. Although still February, it was a gorgeous day in the mid-'70s. Heide had insisted on wearing a sundress which showed off her legs to advantage but would provide minimal protection from the sea breezes once we were out of the harbor and sprinting across the ocean waves with nothing but a low windscreen for protection.

"What was that about?" I asked when we were seated together in the rear of the boat a few minutes later. Jeff had exchanged his floppy hat for an Angels baseball cap to protect his prematurely bald head and was busy flipping switches and topping off his drink while Debbie untied the lines.

"Oh, that was nothing." She smiled and waved her arms. "Just work stuff. Isn't this just amazing?"

"Spectacular," I said. "Gives me chills right here." I pointed to the wallet in my rear pocket. That earned me an elbow in the ribs.

"This could be you and me one day," she said.

"Even with a job someday as an art director, I don't see a 30-thousand-plus monthly mortgage payment in the cards. Not in this lifetime."

"Frankly," I said. "I'm a little surprised a young guy like Jeff, can afford this." He was a smart guy, educated at Wharton, but still on the low side of thirty-five. "Who are all these people? Hollywood stars, pro athletes, Google founders?"

"Honey." She smiled again and this time her eyes were so large, I thought she was high on something. "You'd be amazed how much money people make where I work. It's insane."

Coming from my humble background growing up in a small town in western Texas, son of an immigrant father and mother, "insane" sounded like an understatement. But if Heide and I were beggars at a waterfront banquet, we could at least enjoy it for a day.

The twin V-8 inboard engines started with an angry growl, one after the other, followed by a throbbing burble. A seagull floating nearby squawked and departed in alarm. Debbie untied the last line, climbed on board and we backed out into the main channel.

"All righty then," Jeff swiveled his captain's chair around to face us. "Let's get this party started. We'll be docking in Avalon in less than an hour."

"Aye, aye, captain." Christy climbed into the forward passenger seat with her mother.

Jeff put the boat in gear, and we rumbled forward. I took advantage of the calm water and slow speed to snap a few more photos, using the telephoto lens to get up close and personal with a great blue heron posing on a weathered piling.

We had just reached the legal harbor speed of five knots when the camera's viewfinder settled upon a solitary figure standing at the end of a neighboring dock, pointing something at us that looked a lot like a gun. So much in fact...

"Wait," I shouted over the engine noise. "What is that guy—"

I didn't finish the question before bullets began splintering fiberglass and shredding bodies with popping sounds followed by screaming.

I threw Heide to the floor with me. "Stay down!"

The boat was still moving forward, but the awkward tilt of Jeff's head told me he was no longer driving it. Christy lay screaming on the floor while Debbie writhed and shrieked hysterically from the passenger seat, "Oh my God, oh my God, oh my God."

I snuck a quick look over the side and spotted the shooter removing a magazine and inserting another. Staying low and trying not to step on Christy, I scrambled to the front of the boat and jammed the two throttle levers forward. The sound of bullets erupted from behind us as we rocketed forward, engines roaring. Bits of vinyl seats, fiberglass, and bloody body parts peppered me as we blasted past the paddleboarders, swamping them in our wake. I barely avoided running down a man and his dog in a kayak. People stared from boats, docks, and patios as we thundered down the normally placid channel.

When I thought we had outdistanced the bullets, I dropped the engine speed to idle, stood, and reached for the cell phone in the pocket of my shorts, thinking to call 911. It was all I could do to control my shaking and dial.

"This is Orange County Emergency Dispatch," said a calm voice. "What is the nature of your emergency?"

Boom! A blow like that of a hammer struck me in the ribs and knocked me on my ass. I lay partially on top of poor little Christy as I struggled to get my breath back. Bullets continued to smack into the boat and its passengers, narrowly missing me.

From somewhere beneath Christy's body, I heard a faint voice repeat, "I'm sorry, what is the nature of your emergency?"

I reached for the phone and got a handful of something mushy instead.

"Jesus, lady!" I yelled. "I'm on a boat full of dead and injured people in Newport Harbor and everyone on the planet is trying to kill me!"

I pulled Jeff down from his captain's chair to the floor beside me and noticed he was missing one eye and part of his skull. I climbed just far enough into his captain's chair to see a woman with a ponytail wearing a baseball cap, reflective sunglasses, and blood-red lipstick standing in a smaller speedboat and using a two-handed grip to fire a large gold-plated handgun. She continued firing methodically as if in no hurry, exchanging magazines as needed, the bullets striking Debbie, the windshield, and the boat. I rammed the throttles forward again and steered toward the boat traffic in the main channel. Just ahead was the ferry crossing between Balboa Peninsula and Balboa Island. As we charged toward them, passengers laughed and cheered as if we were filming a movie.

I glanced back at Heide and was stunned to see her lying in the bottom of the boat, her legs splayed to either side, one bloody hand cupping her right breast. Her skin was a deadly white, and she was choking, foamy blood spraying from her mouth. I had to stop the boat.

I cradled her head in my lap.

"Sorry, Dev," she rasped, her spittle spraying my face. "I fucked up."

I leaned in close to hear her. "What do you mean? This isn't your fault."

She managed to grab the front of my shirt with a bloody hand. "There's a hundred million in a bank in the Cayman Islands." She began to shiver, and I knew she was going into shock. "They want it back."

My mind raced back to her comment the night before about getting a big raise. "You stole? Why?"

13

"For you. To finish school. For us. Jeff said...couldn't be traced. Guess he ...wrong."

"But we have everything we need!" All I ever wanted was you, my heart shouted.

She looked at me with tears running down her cheeks. "I—" Then the light in her eyes died, and her breathing stopped.

I shook her as if that might bring her back. A tear fell on her face. "Don't leave me, Heide. Please!"

I heard another engine approaching. I peeked over the side of the boat hoping it was help coming. Instead, it was the fucking red-lipped woman with the gold handgun coming back to finish the job. A bullet clanged off the chrome deck railing by my head. Another punched through the side of the hull, missing me by inches. I reached down to find my shirt drenched with blood from the earlier wound, and now Heide's blood, too.

"Where the hell is the Harbor Patrol?" I shouted, hoping the voice on the missing cell phone could hear me.

Then I glanced at my watch and realized that probably less than ninety seconds had elapsed since leaving the dock. Help likely was not coming for several minutes at the earliest and there was no place to hide on the boat before red lips came in for the kill. The decision was simple: I could close my eyes, give up and die here with everyone else, or I could fight back.

"Hang on, honey," I coaxed a comatose Christy as I crawled over bodies on hands and knees through blood, piss, cheese, soggy crackers, and tequila toward the bow, trying not to gag on the smell. I pushed the throttles forward and spun the boat in a tight arc, so tight that I nearly capsized us and had to cut the engines to prevent water from pouring in over the stern. The instant the boat righted itself, I hit the gas again, the huge engines launching us straight toward the other boat. The shooter's face went from a smug smile to surprise. She fired again and again, bits of plexiglass from the windshield tearing at my face and arms as the short distance between us closed rapidly. I did not care. I have this unwritten rule: nobody gets to kill my wife and just walk away.

What happened next is unclear. I recall a thunderous, screeching crash as the boats collided and being thrown upwards and over the bow. The crazy part (real or imagined) was seeing the body of the shooter fly over me in the opposite direction and I heard a scream that was less human-sounding and more like that of an incensed cougar in a wildlife documentary that missed catching its prey. Then my body crash-landed on the other boat and the lights went out. Until I woke up in a hospital room with a massive headache and a guy in a suit sitting there studying me as if deciding whether to cook me or eat me raw.

CHAPTER THREE

You can feel the night. It is alive with sound, smell, touch, taste, and mystery. A living, breathing thing electric with possibilities and danger. It is all I know.

It's called ROP, short for Retinopathy of Prematurity. I weighed just two and one-half pounds when I was born thirty weeks into Momma's pregnancy. It was common back then for hospitals to use high levels of oxygen in incubators to save the lives of preemies like me. Unfortunately, they think that is what burned up my retinas and left me permanently blind.

Mama, are you watching what is going on down here? Today, Vonda asked me why I never smile. Said she was tired of looking at my face with its permanent frown. Then her good-for-nothing husband Stu said, "She don't realize how good she's got it."

If my life is so good, why am I lying awake every night thinking of slitting their throats while they sleep? How about a little respect for a change?

I would like to see them try to do the housework and cook the meals every day, blinder than a bat, and getting no thanks for it. Instead of complaining about the fried chicken being too dry, how about just once inviting me out to dinner? When was the last time, they asked me to come along with them? Try never!

It ain't right what I have to deal with, Mama, and it is making me crazy. No one cares about how I feel—not even Daddy. I am just their slave girl.

I wear long-sleeved tops and Farmer John overalls every day so no one can see what I have done to myself. Otherwise, they would lock me up instead of just calling me "looney tunes" like they do now. And then I really would go crazy from the bad music in my head.

You said a man would come for me when the time was right, and I believed you, Mama. But you also said God promises in the Bible that he only has good plans for us and that was a lie. Because how could letting you die and taking you away from me possibly be "good?"

I have given up believing there is really a God. If there is, he does not care about people—at least not me. It has been ten years since you said you were going to heaven. If you are really up there, can't you say something? Maybe get one of the angels to get off their lazy ass and do something? The truck delivering "our daily bread" appears to have broken down somewhere.

I wiped away tears with an old towel.

Listen, whoever you are, wherever you are, if you are out there, you best be getting a move on pronto. Momma said you would be coming someday to take me away from this place, but I may be running out of time. I only know one way to deal with the pain and loneliness and it ain't working like it once did.

If you are out there, please come soon. Before I lose control.

I heard Patsy whimper softly.

CHAPTER FOUR

"How much do you know about the Sinaloa Cartel?" FBI Agent Catania leaned forward in his chair.

A dark blue, tailored suit emphasized his lean physique. I caught the glint of an elaborate cufflink on one sleeve. Who in Southern California still wears cufflinks? I did not even own any long-sleeved shirts.

Earlier, I had thumbed through a thick binder of mug shots which now lay at the foot of the hospital bed. I certainly could not have missed the photo of the female shooter. It was like she wanted to be identified. Ramona Gutierrez was said to be the head of Los Antrax, the armed enforcement wing of the cartel. A newspaper clipping called her the "el Angel de la Muerte." Angel of Death. Her image was engraved in my memory and would be until the day I died. Of course, no one was taking bets on my living for more than a couple of days. A week at most.

"Look, I realize you're still hurting and probably groggy from the drugs, but you need to accept the cold hard facts. There is no place you can hide where they will not find you. You just witnessed firsthand what they do to people who steal from them." He sat back. "What do you suppose they're going to do now that the news media has posted your photo everywhere?"

I searched for the button that would release more oxycodone into my IV. My bandaged side made even moving an arm painfully difficult and whoever was barbecuing my ribs had just turned up the gas.

"This what you're looking for?" Catania held up the control. "You can have it back when we're done."

I waved my hand with the pink glow of a blood oxygen monitor clipped to my forefinger.

"Like I already told you," I said. My throat was still raw from the tube they had stuck down it on that first day when I was out cold. "I know nothing about the money. Believe me, I would tell you if I knew. My wife said she was working late with her manager on an important project. It never occurred to me they were up to something like this."

Catania replaced the cap on his fountain pen and put it and the small leather-covered notebook in the breast pocket of his suit. He leaned back in the chair.

"Then, to put it bluntly, you're fucked." He smiled. With his dark suit and whitened teeth, he reminded me of a shark.

I shook my head to clear the fog that dulled my ability to think. "What can I do? Can you hide me?"

"Hide you?" Catania smirked. "You want the U.S. government to hide you?"

"Don't you have a..." In my muddled state, I could not think of the right words. "A program for people—innocent people like me?"

"You mean witness protection? WITSEC is for political prisoners and people of value. It appears that our clever friends in the cartel have figured out how to launder their drug money in millions, and maybe even billions at a time, using your wife's hedge fund and legitimate SWIFT bank transfers. Unless you can explain how your wife and her associate managed to siphon a hundred million dollars from the cartel and where exactly that money is located, you have zero value as a witness." Catania straightened the lapels of his suit jacket.

"Actually, zero might be on the high side."

"But what if I don't have the money?" Then I remembered Heide's last words. "My wife said it was in a bank in the Cayman Islands. Does that help?"

"Lots of banks in the Caymans." Catania shrugged. "Unless you know which bank, the account name, and password, you're out of luck."

He sat forward again. "Let me explain something to you. If you are like most people, you probably think they are some little ragtag gang of Latinos with bad teeth who never made it through junior high, let alone college. I hate to burst your bubble, but these guys are way more sophisticated than you think. They have got jets, helicopters, computers, all manner of weapons and people who know how to use them. They can afford to pay their best people ten or twenty times more than what our government pays us. Which means that if we can find you, they can find you."

"From what our team has learned so far," he continued, "it looks like your wife's friend in systems admin had been skimming money in relatively small amounts for more than a year that didn't raise a red flag. His monthly debt load, however, had finally reached a level that required his recruiting help within the firm to make a big score. Your wife probably had no clue who she was stealing from—just spin the dial and collect your winnings. Unfortunately for her, they ripped off the wrong people."

"But why kill everyone?" I asked. "Don't they want their money back?"

"In case you have not noticed, these guys don't play by the rules. Matter of fact, there are no rules," Catania said. "I'm guessing they'll eventually recover the money. What matters most to them right now, however, is avoiding further losses. That and making a statement in case anyone else gets crazy ideas. The last thing they want is someone else trying to rip them off. They would rather lose the money and have no one left alive to explain how it was stolen. Killing people is their way of putting a damper on anyone having similar thoughts."

"Yeah, I could see how that might work," I said.

"To you and me, a hundred million is a lot of money," Catania continued. "But to them, it's small potatoes."

He paused. "There's one last bit of information our forensics team discovered from reading the emails and text messages between your wife and her partner in crime that I thought you might want to know. They may have been thieves, but from what we can tell, they weren't lovers."

A tear raced down my cheek before I could hide it. The knowledge that Heide was plotting behind my back was excruciating, even minus the infidelity.

"What happened to the girl, Christy? She going to be okay?"

He shook his head no.

There was a large clock on the wall, but I was having difficulty reading the time. "How much time do I have?"

"I'd guess twenty-four hours. Maybe forty-eight tops. Based on the amount of damage to both boats, you may have managed to injure the female shooter. From what I hear, you better hope she is dead. Regardless, they will have replaced her by now. The Newport Beach cops are watching your place, but they'll probably move on by tomorrow." As Catania stood, he handed me the pain medication controller. "Here. Knock yourself out."

He started to leave, then stopped. "Listen, if you're telling the truth, then I'm sorry for you. Your only hope is to go off the grid and hope they get tired of looking for you someday. Because otherwise, they're going to hunt you down and kill you."

CHAPTER FOUR

Not long after Catania left, a nurse showed up with a tray of food.

"How are you feeling?" She reached for my wrist. She had a nice accent and freckles. Her name tag read Ximena, which she had conveniently written with a pronunciation key, "she-men-ah," in large, neat letters on a nearby whiteboard.

"I could use some aspirin, a Diet Coke, and a facelift," I said. "Otherwise, great."

She frowned with concern as she took my pulse.

"I really need to get out of here," I said.

"You need to eat. Besides, your pulse rate is too high to be going anywhere. Eat then rest," she ordered.

"Listen to me, Ximena: the people who shot me and killed my wife may still be hunting for me. The man who was just here from the FBI warned me that I'd be putting everyone at risk if I stay."

That got her attention. She dropped my wrist like it was radioactive. "El cartel narcotraficante?"

In her dialect, every word carried a few extra calories. I nodded.

"These are very bad people. Trust me. They kidnap innocent people and cut off the heads of their enemies."

Her eyes darted to the doorway as if they might be

standing there even now. "Where will you go so they won't find you?"

"I don't have a clue. All I know is that I don't have much time."

"You need to disappear," she said. "Don't go to your family or friends. You will put them all in danger. I know because this is how I lived before coming here from Colombia as a little girl."

She looked like she wanted to disappear, too. Maybe run to an administrator, call the police, something. Anything but stay here with me. And who could blame her? I was bad news on steroids.

"Help me find my clothes and I'll be out of here before trouble arrives."

She retrieved my clothes from a plastic bag in the closet. The shorts and shirt were caked with dried blood. She threw them in the trash.

"Wait here," she said. "I'll borrow a set of scrubs from one of the male nurses."

Changing clothes was not easy. Fortunately, Ximena was eager to help me.

"I'm sorry, but you need to hurry," she said. "We are all in danger while you are here."

"How do I get out of here?" I asked when I could breathe again.

"The hospital will not be happy about your leaving, but I think I can make them understand your special situation." She frowned again. "You will need to sign consent forms, of course, and then you can go."

Ximena was evidently quite persuasive. Less than ten minutes later, she wheeled me downstairs to the exit where an off-duty security cop was waiting for me.

"Thank you," I said.

She squeezed my hand. "Vaya con Dios, my friend."

The security cop drove me home and helped me out of his

car. In my haste to leave, I realized I had forgotten to ask Ximena for a prescription of pain pills. I stepped into the sunlight and swore from the stabbing pain in my ribs. I could already feel the oxycodone wearing off. A headache bloomed behind my eyes.

A Newport Beach cop sitting in his cruiser in the parking lot of our apartment with the engine running and air conditioner howling let me into the apartment after I showed him my driver's license.

"Not going to find much left," he said as he followed me inside. "The FBI confiscated your laptops, cellphones, and whatever else they could find. You want them back, you just need to hang around for six months and file a request with the court."

"Of course, by then I'd be dead," I said.

"More than likely."

I realized that I could not have kept the electronic items anyway. Anything with Wi-Fi or GPS could be tracked.

The apartment was a disaster. It was obvious that not only the police and the FBI, but possibly the cartel had been there, too. Not only were my MacBook and Heide's Dell laptop missing, but it looked like the closet and every drawer and cabinet had been thoroughly examined.

I spotted a hundred-year-old Kodak camera that had once belonged to my great grandfather in India, with brass gears and fittings and a wooden frame. What had until today been one of my few treasures now lay in pieces, scattered in the middle of the living room floor.

"Shit."

"Funny ain't it?" the cop said. "One day, you're you. The next day, it's like you're suddenly a fuckin' nobody. I have seen people end up homeless, living on the streets, all because they got sick and did not have insurance, or caught a run of bad luck and had no family or savings to fall back on. Sad."

I stared at him, the realization that I was now alone was

overwhelming. Stripped of everything I had loved and worked hard for, including my wife, my identity, and my dream of a career in marketing. My life was gone, stolen from me in a matter of hours.

Nor was I feeling at the top of my game physically. I almost did not recognize the unshaven, haggard, pale face of the pitiful wretch who stared back at me as I searched the medicine cabinet for aspirin.

"I'll be downstairs in the cruiser for another twenty minutes," the cop said as he reappeared from the living room. "If I were you, I'd try to be out of here by then. We'll do a drive-by later tonight, but that ain't going to protect you if the cartel wants to kill you. I hear stories all the time of the crazy things they do to people who try to rip them off."

I nodded. The fact that I was an innocent bystander was unimportant to the sociopaths who kept their money and secrets closely guarded against threats real or imagined.

The question of where to go suddenly loomed large. Family and friends were out. According to Catania, anyone found with me would likely be executed, too.

Changing from the borrowed scrubs into a shirt and jeans was a painful ordeal that took longer than it should have. Taking the laces out allowed me to slip my feet into my boots without bending over.

Before preparing to leave, I checked the "whatever" drawer in the kitchen. Everybody has one. It's for whatever isn't easily categorized or comes in too small a quantity to deserve its own space. Loose change, business cards, miscellaneous screws, old restaurant matchbooks, phone numbers for people you have not talked to in years scribbled on wrinkled Post-It Notes, cheap pens from hotels, keys to things you cannot remember, rubber bands you will never use, et cetera. And there it was—the size and thickness of a thumbnail and so small it was easy to miss. But this was a 64GB memory card containing over a thousand photos: our wedding, honeymoon, birthdays, holidays, my best shots, and a hundred more memorable events. I might never again look at the now-painful highlights of my life taken over the past several months. But there was that one photo taken of Heide working on her laptop on our last night together that I wanted to examine carefully. I stuck the tiny card in the change pocket of my jeans.

Then I heard the front door squeak and nearly croaked from a heart attack. Still foggy from the pain medication, I was not sure if the cop had come back, or if I had left the door unlocked. I grabbed a butcher knife from the knife block and tiptoed into the front room to investigate. Sunlight now streamed through the gaping doorway, an imprudent invitation to the cartel killers sent to blot out the sole survivor of their carnage.

"Who's there?" I shouted as I gripped the knife tighter.

No one answered. Then I felt something brush against my leg. It was the neighbor's cat, the one who thought he owned the place.

"Don't scare me like that, Mister Tibbs."

He jumped onto the sofa and purred while I scratched between his ears.

Moving to the bedroom, I was bludgeoned by self-pity. Heide's robe lay on the floor. I pressed it to my face, drinking in her smell. My favorite photo of her smiled shyly up at me from the dresser. I stared for a minute at her glass-protected visage, considering whether to take it with me. Then, as tears began obscuring my vision, I laid it gently face down in a half-opened drawer of her underwear. In the same drawer, I spotted an unsigned birthday card, a reminder that I would be twenty-three years old in a few days. If I lived that long.

Part of me wanted revenge, to lie in wait with a baseball bat and see who showed up. But nothing I could do was going to bring my wife back, and picking a fight with a Mexican drug cartel would not be "astute," as my father had liked to say.

According to Catania, my only hope was to disappear without a trace before they found me and resumed their lethal vengeance.

A half-hour later, I closed the door behind me, carrying only a large gym bag into which I had stuffed a handful of shirts, jacket, a spare pair of jeans, shorts, a few toiletries, and the bottle of aspirin from the bathroom medicine cabinet. In my present condition, it was all I could do to drag the bag to my Ford pickup and crawl in.

The truck presented yet another problem I was unprepared for. I could not very well drive a vehicle licensed to me and hope to remain incognito for very long. Even with different plates and the GPS turned off, it would still be possible to track. I had no choice but to get rid of it.

Less than a mile from home, I spotted a gardener mowing a lawn while a battered white Toyota pickup waited by the curb. He inspected me incredulously as I explained that I was ready to trade him my five-year-old F150 for his twenty-year-old rust bucket. He kept turning from me to stare at my truck as he stood with crossed arms over his broad chest while I sweated in the hot sun trying to convince him that it was paid for and that I had not stolen it.

Fifteen minutes later, I was headed north on the 405. I had no idea where I was going. I just needed to get away. Thinking would come later.

As I quickly learned, the Toyota had no air conditioning or radio. It squeaked and squealed like a creature was being tortured beneath the floorboards, and top speed was under sixty-five miles per hour. There were a lot of things in hindsight I might have done better, but with a mushroom cloud forming in my head and the pain in my ribs growing incrementally with each mile, it was all I could do to keep one foot on the gas pedal and steer.

Traffic is never light in L.A. Even in the bowels of the night, the freeways and arterials are alive with the lights of cars scurrying somewhere. Fortunately, it was late morning, there were no accidents and traffic was as light as it gets in this over-populated part of the world.

Sometime after transitioning to I-5, my brain began functioning again, albeit at half-speed. Against a vibrant blue sky, thin tendrils from wispy clouds and the contrail from a military jet led me north. I needed a new name and a job and money. Stopping at a bank, however, would leave a trail marker for the cartel to follow. Catania said they were good at tracking. Maybe as good as—or better than—the FBI, which was a daunting thought to consider.

My mother liked to mix truths, half-truths, and outright fiction into stories she told me as a child. One of them was about a great-great-something-or-other of mixed race, the son of a lieutenant in the Scottish Highlanders and an Indian princess. She spoke proudly of this distant relative being a Risaldar in the 2nd Bengal Lancers who fought with distinction during World War I, earning an Indian Order of Merit. I always liked the sound of his name. From henceforth, I decided I would be Grayson Reynolds.

Without identification or a social security number, finding a job—even as a dayworker—would not be easy. As my previous employer had learned the hard way, both the federal and state governments were only too happy to seize assets including cash, vehicles, and even homes if they found you were paying workers under the table. More than income, however, I needed a place to stay that was "off the grid" as Agent Catania had suggested. Having witnessed their savagery firsthand, I had no doubts about what would happen if the cartel found me.

The anger at Heide's killers that had helped me overcome the pain of my injury, as well as the physical and emotional loss, was wearing off. I had not even begun to sort out all the ramifications. The sudden shock of not only losing my wife and partner, but my identity and future was devastating.

"Fuck." With money running low and killers possibly on my trail, there was no time to grieve.

I spent a few of my precious dollars on lunch at a Denny's Restaurant. A server directed me to the Bakersfield city library where, for a dollar an hour, I was able to get on a public computer.

Searching for jobs was more difficult than you might guess. I could not risk a background check that could trigger a pursuit by the cartel which eliminated 98% of employment opportunities. Within the remaining 2%, I looked for something off the beaten track, something remote that did not require a lot of experience. At the end of the hour, I had found one possibility that sounded promising.

CHAPTER FIVE

In my overwrought state caused by delay and pain, I drove right by it the first time. The second time, I spotted the gravel parking lot and ranch-style home, half-hidden behind a thick row of rain-stooped evergreens that separated it from the road, and the small wooden sign with "Trout Fishing" in hand-painted letters. I sat for a moment, listening to the rain drumming on the Toyota pickup's hood. It was a long way from L.A. Three days, fourteen hundred miles, four quarts of oil, and a large bottle of aspirin had transported me to a remote location in the foothills of the North Cascade Mountains, two hours north of Seattle.

Unfortunately, my appointment had been scheduled for noon and it was now after three. Difficulty getting showered and dressed, followed by getting stuck in outrageously bad Seattle traffic—and I thought L.A. was bad!—had contributed to the delay.

I had just begun to ease myself down from the driver's seat toward the ground when a brilliant flash lit up the sky. Thunder, majestic and heavy with reproach, boomed a moment later, echoing off the nearby mountains. My left foot, numbed by the long drive, slipped on the wet door sill. Unable to recover, I pitched to the ground. Pain erupted in my left side where the bullet had shattered a rib. Rain pelted me. As if that was not humiliation enough, I heard the screen door bang.

I struggled to stand, using the truck door to pull myself up, but had succeeded only in getting to my knees when a golden retriever began snuffling determinedly at my crotch.

Anger and frustration added to my sour mood. "Get away, pervert."

The dog backed off and tilted her head as if questioning how crazy someone must be to be kneeling on a gravel driveway in the pouring rain. After staring at me for a good thirty seconds and deciding I was no threat, the dog barked and wagged her tail.

With Fido's encouragement, I made a desperate effort to stand. The combination of the loose gravel and the Velcro bandage wrapped around my damaged rib cage left me gasping with pain. I held onto my side and surrendered to the rain. When it rained in Southern California, the sky opened with a blitzkrieg of watery bullets. Knowing the propensity for mudslides and flash floods, people ran for their lives. Here in the foothills of the North Cascades, as I was learning, the rain was a persistent, monotonous thing that you could not escape.

The dog pressed her nose into my wet hand. "All right then. Friends?"

The retriever moved quickly toward the house, eager to gain shelter from the rain, and I followed a good deal more slowly. I climbed the porch and found the screen door partially closed, but the door was open, and the dog was already inside. Loud arguing came from inside the house. I knocked. There was a shriek followed by a crash.

"Hello?" I called out anxiously. When no one answered, I opened the screen door and peered inside. Something whirled toward my face. I jerked my head back just as a plate shattered against the door jamb. Shards littered the floor.

A hand caught my arm and pulled me down behind a couch. I found myself staring into the green eyes of a blond woman, a few years older than me. "Do you have a death wish or are you just feeble-minded?" she asked.

Very possibly true on both counts, I realized.

"Who are you talking to?" a second female demanded from the other side of the room.

Ignoring the question, the woman with green eyes smiled and stuck out a hand. "I'm Vonda. What's your name?"

"Gray."

She ducked as another plate sailed over the couch. "You missed!" She giggled.

"Tell me who's there or the next throw I make will be for you," the voice called out. "I'm warning you: I don't miss."

"Says his name is Gray," Vonda replied. I noticed she wore only a man's plaid flannel shirt.

"What? You've never seen a woman's legs before?"

I admit I might have been staring. Between the pain and anxiety, I was not sure of anything.

"Grayson Reynolds," I answered the other woman.

***

I recognized his voice instantly. He was the one who had called from a public phone three days earlier. Said he had found the job posted on the internet. From the strain in his voice and the noise in the background, it had sounded like he was near a busy street.

"Where are you?"

"I'm just north of Los Angeles, but I can be there in two days."

I thought about this. I have never driven a car, but this did not sound right based on what I knew about geography.

"Hello? Are you still there?" he said.

"Are you flying, driving, or taking the bus?"

"Driving."

"Isn't that a long way to drive in two days?"

"Yeah, it is. But I don't want the job to go to someone else

while I'm on my way there." He sounded nervous and a bit desperate. But he also sounded intelligent and very different from the low life's around here.

And now, here he was—three hours late. Daddy had long since given up and gone to town. Vonda and I were fighting— something we did with tiresome regularity—when he came to the door.

"You're so late, we figured you came to your senses and decided not to show," Vonda said.

I could smell the rain in his hair and clothing which helped to mask a faint odor of sweat and medicine. Having spent a lot of time at Momma's hospital bedside, I recognized the betadine smell instantly. I might not be able to see, but I can smell and hear all kinds of things—even things people are thinking, but do not say. There was a roll of distant thunder and I shivered in delicious anticipation.

***

"Hold your fire." I used the couch to stand and grunted from the effort.

"Did I hurt you?" The plate thrower was younger, brown-haired, and wore a long-sleeved top and overalls over a petite figure that was at least five inches shorter than the blond woman. Her alert posture reminded me of a hummingbird, ready to fly away in a millisecond.

I moved closer and stuck out my hand by way of introduction. "You must be Valerie, the one I spoke to."

Ignoring my extended hand, she cocked her head in the same way the dog had. Large violet eyes swept the ceiling as if they were searching in another realm and I wondered if she was blind. If so, her aim was downright scary. Supernatural even.

We were standing at the entrance to the family room. Beyond it, separated by a dining room table and chairs, was the kitchen. The sound of a car in the driveway caused everyone to turn. Through one of the rain-streaked picture windows that framed the room, I saw an older Cadillac roll by on its way toward the larger of the metal-roofed outbuildings.

"Oh, crap," Vonda said. "Just when we were having fun."

"That will be Daddy," Valerie offered.

Vonda hurried to the kitchen. She returned a moment later with a broom and dustpan. Valerie hovered near a gleaming spinet piano where she began carefully rearranging several framed photos and knickknacks. "Don't forget to put away the wine bottle," she said. "It's on the countertop by the refrigerator."

"Thanks, Val." Her sister left the broom leaning against the couch while she located the bottle. When she determined that it still contained a small amount of wine, Vonda raised it to her lips and downed the last swallow. Then she winked at me and tossed the empty into the trash pail under the sink with a crash and wiped her mouth with the back of her hand.

There was a noise behind me. The door opened, and a middle-aged man entered. He glared at me in surprise.

"Who're you?" he asked, hanging his coat on a hook by the door.

I hesitated just a second. "Grayson Reynolds." I put out a hand and the other man shook it with a look of suspicion.

"Virgil Van de Zilver." He squinted. "Weren't you supposed to be here three hours ago?"

"He had a flat tire," Valerie said. Vonda and I both looked at her in surprise.

Virgil was an inch or two shorter than me and a good deal thicker through the middle, though he was not fat. He wore a plaid wool shirt like the one Vonda wore, khakis, and a pair of Rockport walking shoes. Beneath a red Case IH cap was an honest Dutch face, lined by sun and age.

"You could have called."

"Lost my cell phone." Lost my everything, I could have

added.

"Where's Stu?" Virgil asked, looking over one shoulder at his daughters. "I didn't see him or his car."

"Probably down at the Skooner having a beer," Vonda said.

He glanced at his watch. "It's still working hours. He forget that Saturdays are his responsibility around here?" He set his wet cap on the piano where Valerie had earlier straightened up. Then he spotted the several shards of the plate that still littered the floor. "What happened here?"

"Nothing," Vonda said.

"She hid my..." Valerie blushed. "My woman things!"

Vonda chuckled. "'Woman things'? Is that what you call tampons?"

Virgil stared at Vonda. "Now why on earth would you do that?"

She shrugged. "Can't we ever just have fun now and then? Act like a normal family?"

"As the oldest, you have a responsibility to look out for your sister. And, by the way, where are the rest of your clothes? The day is two-thirds gone and you're still half-naked."

"It's the weekend, Daddy. Besides, my toes needed painting." She grinned at me. "Like 'em?"

Each of her toes sported a green, gibbous moon. Personally, I prefer pink, but I have always admired women for their attentiveness to their nails.

Virgil pulled out the captain's chair at the head of the table. "Spiritual guidance, that's what you both need." He sank down heavily. "Your poor mother must be rolling over in her grave."

Vonda rolled her eyes, but Valerie's pale face had turned red and blotchy. Vonda took a seat on one side of the table and Valerie, the other. Embarrassed to be listening in and unsure what else to do, I wandered over to the piano to inspect the photos on its top.

None of the photos appeared to be recent. In one of them,

two young girls, the smaller one dark-haired and serious, the other one blonde with a smile that held a hint of mischief, clutched the hands of a fair-haired woman whose piercing dark eyes held my own. I could almost hear her speak: "Don't be bringing your troubles here."

Valerie nervously stroked her dog whose head rested in her lap. Virgil reached into his back pocket and withdrew a large kerchief that he used to clean and dry his metal-framed glasses.

He sighed at last. "Is it too much to ask, or can I get a cup of coffee?"

Although Vonda was closer, Valerie sprang up to get it. She put out her hand briefly to locate the countertop.

"You ever done any maintenance work?" Virgil asked. "I saw the California plates, but even without 'em, you don't look like you're from around here."

"Are you referring to my skin color?"

Silence crashed into the room.

"Kind of exotic looking, if you ask me," Vonda said after a long pause.

"I don't care if he's purple like a plum," Valerie said from the kitchen.

"Sorry, sis, but he ain't plum purple, banana yellow, or raspberry red. Not even lime green. More like Hershey's milk chocolate brown." She smiled at me. "Sis only knows the colors you can eat."

"What on earth are your girls gabbing about?" Virgil exploded. "I'll have you know that I don't care what color a man is as long as he's honest and works hard. I was simply referring to the fact that he looks a bit scruffy for someone applying for a job—even in an off-the-beaten-track place like this."

From what I had seen of my reflection in the Toyota's rearview mirror, Virgil's comment was an understatement. It had been a week since that fatal day in Huntington Beach and, in my haste and with limited finances, I had not done much to keep up appearances. In addition to the bruises and several small cuts that still marked my face, I had not bothered to shave. I looked more like a refugee from a war zone than someone applying for a job.

Then I felt my passion rising and realized that, during the past few days, I had forgotten what it was to feel anything except the pain that was both deafening and defining. I stood up straight, squared my shoulders, and took a step toward the three of them. It was showtime.

"I'm from West Texas by way of Southern California, but I know how to work hard."

Virgil squinted. "Ever drive a tractor?"

"I did some haying as a kid."

Valerie touched her father's arm and placed a mug down in front of him. He stirred the coffee absently and stared at me for an uncomfortable twenty seconds or so. "C'mon then." He stood up. "Let's find out what you can do."

Virgil removed a jacket from a wooden wall coat rack. I shuddered in anticipation of the damp cold as I thought about the test I was about to face. Driving a tractor is about as easy as it gets. Just put the transmission in gear—any gear—and go. But I was not in the best physical condition. In fact, I may possibly have been in the worst condition for a job interview in the history of North America.

"Wait," a voice called. The way we pirouetted in tandem, you might have thought we had been practicing.

"You need something on your head." Vonda plucked a tattered Sedro Woolley baseball cap with a lopsided brim from one of the other coat pegs.

Our hands touched briefly as I accepted the proffered hat. "Quite a relic."

"That hat's seen better days," Virgil said. "It belongs to Stu, my son-in-law." He opened the door and held it. I pulled the venerable cap on over hair that was a little longer and shaggier than my normal buzz cut, and we stepped out into the rain.

We walked toward the back of the house, shoes crunching on the gravel driveway. The rain continued to fall, harder now: a slow, steady, ceaseless downpour, the drops making a *thwocking* noise as they struck the hat.

CHAPTER SIX

Coming from Southern California where lawns, if they existed at all, were often smaller than the swimming pools they surrounded, I was unprepared for the expanse of green that now greeted us. Acres and acres of grass, lush as a golf course and nearly as plentiful, extended before us, descending gradually before disappearing down the hill. Close by the house were rows of rose bushes, not much more than crippled stalks at this point, separating the backyard from the park-like grounds. Halfway down the slope, a stand of cedar trees were surrounded by a low, rock wall. They soared up like giants, guarding what lay beyond.

"You walk like you were walking on glass instead of grass," Virgil said. I noticed him studying me out of the corner of one eye. "And pardon my saying so, but you don't look much like a maintenance man. Leastwise, not the ones from around here."

"Really?" I was attempting to watch where I stepped while surveying the entirety of the farm which was not easy. The descending ground was uneven, and each step required a reach that sent little jolts of pain through my damaged ribs. "What do I look like?"

"I dunno," Virgil replied after a few seconds of careful consideration. "But too smart by at least half, I'd say. And a good deal too thin."

I realized that my appetite was yet another thing I had lost since Heide's death. A list of all my losses would likely fill a small notebook and lead to some serious couch time with a shrink if I allowed my mind to go there. Which I could not. Not now and maybe never. In my extremely limited experience, I had discovered that the only way to deal with sudden, unexpected loss was either to give in to it or block it. I chose the latter as the only viable option.

Some two hundred yards below, the white, split-rail fence gave way to a line of trees, shrubs, and ferns. The naked limbs of alder trees and cottonwoods stood out in stark contrast against the darker evergreens. Near the base of the slope and beyond the cedars, I spotted the nickel-glint of a pond, pockmarked by the rain. A heavy mist clung sinuously to the hills above, leaving a jagged, snow-crowned mountain peak exposed. The monochrome sky looked as if someone had drawn a feather through it. Where they caressed the hills, the clouds were wisps of smoke.

Virgil directed me toward the larger of two metal buildings. "When did you say you drove a tractor?"

"In high school. For three summers."

"And when was that exactly? Hard to tell, what with your beard, how old you might be."

"About five years ago, I guess."

The beard had been Heide's idea. "All the guys are wearing them," she had said. At the time, I thought having a beard was not worth the trouble but grew it to please her. Now, I no longer thought about appearances or pleasing anyone, for that matter.

We passed through a large, double doorway into a cavernous barn with a spotless concrete floor. There wasn't a spec of hay or tack in sight. It smelled of oil and fertilizer and was cold enough inside that our breath was visible. The rain drummed steadily on the metal roof. Otherwise, the barn was still as a cathedral. Virgil hit a row of switches and light hissed, flickered, and exploded from rows of fluorescent tubes high overhead. Lining the barn's walls was an assortment of hardware, from old bicycles to farm implements. Beyond the Cadillac stood a green John Deere, rear tires as tall as a man, hooked up to a hooded piece of equipment that I did not recognize.

"That's the hammerknifer," Virgil explained. "Take a look."

With difficulty, I managed to get down on my knees to inspect this strange-looking contraption more closely. Hundreds of double-edged blades dangled from an axle. I touched one that looked like it might have been replaced recently and determined that it was razor-sharp.

"It'll chop through just about anything: two-by-fours, beer bottles, soda pop cans, and bones if you happen to fall in its path. Do not ever stick your hand in there to clear it when it is turning. It will suck you in faster than you can holler for help. And one more thing: the hood is designed to prevent stuff from flying out the back, but not the front. Stay away from rocks. They'll wreck the blades, not to mention smack you in the head if it picks up a stone and flings it at you."

"Sounds dangerous," I said. Driving around L.A. is scary, but at least you do not have to worry about your vehicle throwing rocks at you.

"It's all business. Never for one, little, bitty moment forget that fact." Virgil reached over, pulled the choke out, and turned the ignition switch on the tractor. The engine fired with a metallic rattle. "Go ahead. Get on. Let's see you take it for a spin." He nodded toward the grounds outside.

"In the rain? Won't it ruin the grass?"

"The hammerknifer don't care one way or the other," Virgil said. "It will cut just fine, rain or shine."

Here it was then—the moment of truth. I approached the tractor slowly, searching for a step of any kind to make the climb up onto the seat easier, but, on this model at least, there wasn't one. I looked around for a step stool, or maybe even a ladder.

"What're you waiting for?"

I took a breath, held it, and, using the steering wheel for leverage, hauled myself up. Halfway up, something—a stitch probably—gave in my side. The next several seconds felt like someone was holding a blowtorch to my ribs. The tractor seat, a concave metal shell with no padding, was as hard and unyielding as granite, but I barely noticed while gasping from the exertion and pain. Grimly, I recalled the doctor explaining that there was a bullet fragment too close to the aorta to be removed and was still moving around. If it nicked the artery, I could bleed out before help arrived. The way this occupational test was going so far, I was starting to think that death might not be so bad. My parents had converted from Hinduism to Christianity before leaving India, but reincarnation suddenly sounded like a fine idea.

"Something the matter?" Virgil asked. "You move slower than molasses on a cold day."

Let's smash one of your ribs and see how you do, old man, I thought. Unable to breathe much less respond, I searched beneath the seat for the lift lever, found it, and shoved it forward. Behind me, I felt the hammerknifer rise into the air. Without so much as a rearward glance—something I could not have managed anyway—I shifted the transmission into second gear and gave the engine some throttle. The tractor lurched toward the open door.

Once outside, I tilted my face up into the rain and felt a little revived. When I could breathe again, I lowered the hammerknifer and shoved the blades into gear. A violent humming, thrashing noise immediately came from behind me. I was able to stand up and shuffle my feet around the tractor's small floor space far enough to confirm that the grass was indeed being chopped into a uniform height by the hundreds of whirling razor blades. I steered the John Deere for the opposite side of the greensward. When I had made a wide oval and covered most of the distance back, I glanced over at Virgil who motioned for me to return.

So far, so good. Now came the interesting part. After shutting off the blades and raising the hammerknifer, I had to reverse the tractor back into its previous location in the barn. Looking over my shoulder felt roughly akin to having a pair of scissors thrust into my ribs. After numerous minor course corrections, I succeeded in parking the tractor back in its original resting place. I lowered the hammerknifer, turned off the engine, and wiped the rain and sweat from my face with a damp sleeve.

Virgil had already walked over to a stubby, orange vehicle with four wheels in the back and two smaller ones in front like the tugs they use to move the luggage carts around at airports. Above the grill appeared the brand name, Payloader. I slid to the ground from the John Deere with only a small grunt of pain. Behind the orange Payloader were three big gangs of mower blades that could cut a ten-foot swath in a single pass.

"Meet the Bull. It has got a straight-six Chrysler motor producing a hundred and seventy horses and it will mow the entire forty acres in less than a day when the grass is dry. The only problem is keeping the blades in adjustment. Too close and you will hear them chatter up a storm. Then they slip and slide more than cut the grass and you end up with an ugly mess. Too loose and they won't cut anything. But do it right and they'll sharpen themselves."

He upended the mug to finish the last of his coffee. "It's a bit like dealing with women," Virgil added. "You've got to give them some attention now and then to keep 'em happy."

I looked to see if he was smiling, but he was not.

The final stop on the tour was a green and yellow John Deere riding mower that looked positively toy-like by comparison to the other mowing machines.

"This is for up around the house and the playground area

we maintain for the children of our customers," Virgil said. "Vonda likes to drive it sometimes in summer. She calls it 'Little Deer.' Let's go outside. I'll show you the ponds."

"What else have you done besides drive tractor?" Virgil asked when we were back outside, headed down the hill in the rain. My feet were now soaking wet, my teeth were beginning to chatter, and I realized I had had nothing to eat since a hamburger the night before. Hello, hypothermia.

"I worked in a warehouse for a couple of summers while I was going to college. Before that, I delivered newspapers, mowed lawns, did some haying like I said earlier. For the last two years, I worked for a landscaping firm in Orange County, California."

"Orange County, huh?" Virgil nodded as if this geographical detail explained something important. "What made you come up here?"

Flash. Boom.

It was probably only a trick of the imagination, but I could almost see the muzzle flash and hear the crack of the gun as the bullet struck me. I stared at Virgil for a moment, unable to speak. Remembering Heide's death caused acid to rise in my throat, scalding it. Confessing that I had fled Southern California for this remote location to avoid being hunted down and killed by the Sinaloa Cartel was not likely going to improve my employment outlook. I waved an arm, anxious to jump-start my lips, say something—anything at all—to get past this moment.

"This. The trees. The mountains." Nearby, I spotted two large rabbits with red eyes watching me from their hutch as they chewed on lettuce. "Look at these big guys." I bit the inside of my cheek. I half-expected the man to frown, maybe even laugh. Fortunately, he did neither. This would be my first insight into Virgil Van de Zilver and it was refreshing to learn that, unlike people in Southern California, Virgil was not a man who agonized over the subtext of conversations and, for this, I was extremely grateful.

"That's Thelma and Louise," Virgil said, nodding toward the rabbits. "Daughters named them."

Which one is Geena Davis? I wondered.

We came to the first pond where thousands of random craters appeared with every second, then rippled away, silently, on its surface. Except for the rain striking the grass and our clothing, it was unbelievably quiet. A drop stuck the back of my neck and I turned up my jacket collar as an arctic chill passed through me.

"Any fish in there?"

"A thousand more or less," Virgil answered.

"Really?"

Curious, I peered into the pond's depths for a sign of fish but could see nothing except our reflections and that of the trees, hills, and waterlogged sky. "How big?"

"Not very." Virgil held up a large hand with thumb and forefinger perhaps three or four inches apart. "They grow faster during a mild winter like this last one. By the time summer rolls around, they should be legal size up to maybe eight inches." He paused to spit. "There's two of these man-made ponds. The second one is further down the hill. We use 'em for raising trout, not for fishing. The natural pond I'm about to show you is where our customers fish."

"What do trout eat?" I had fished for trout as a kid using nightcrawlers, but that did not seem practical for feeding a thousand or more fish.

"Each other, unless we feed 'em. Rainbow trout are cannibals. You drink?" Virgil asked suddenly.

"No." Which was true if you were talking strictly about the present and not the past. Like yesterday, for instance, when I needed a pint of Jack Daniels to anesthetize my pain—mental and physical.

"Take drugs?"

"No."

"Been in jail?"

"Never."

Virgil paused, appraising me. "What exactly do you do?"

"Try to stay alive" was probably not going to get me the job.

"Try to get by mostly," I said.

"'Try to get by,'" Virgil repeated. "That's one I haven't heard before."

He started walking again. "You ever been to church?"

"Sure."

"And?" He gave me that sideways look again.

I shrugged. "Didn't work for me."

"Didn't work?" Virgil frowned.

Yeah, I thought. Me and God got an understanding: He doesn't give a damn about me and I don't either. I swallowed. My frustration rose as we walked in silence.

"You consider maybe you were the one who didn't work?"

I had to look away from his stare.

The final pond was at least an acre or two in size and even had its tiny island where a moss-covered cherub raised his hands skyward amid a half-dozen hemlocks. A small wooden shack stood on the far side of the pond, its porch extending out over the water.

Virgil stood, hands in his jacket pockets, staring at it.

"My wife's studio," he said at last. "She used to draw, paint some, before she got too sick from the cancer. I am not sure the medications did her one bit of good. Just made her more ready to go, I expect."

I waited silently, uncomfortable with where the conversation was headed, but curious, too. I was still a rookie when it came to mourning the loss of a spouse, but I was certain that a long goodbye was better, no matter how sad and painful the ordeal, than no goodbye at all.

The rain continued to *thwock* upon my hat and sneak inside the collar of my jacket. A sudden swirl in the dark water seemed far too large for some trout. I half-expected to see a beaver or muskrat appear.

"I used to carry her down here," Virgil said. "She would sit there bundled in a chair on the deck for hours at a time. She would read, sleep, read some more. Mostly just sit there, staring at her island. She called it 'Isla Mujeres' after some place down in Mexico she visited in college."

He looked off in the distance where the rain-shrouded mountains sat silently watching. "Don't get down here much anymore since she died." Virgil's lined and weathered face had become so white, I could almost see the network of capillaries just below the skin.

Bereavement gripped my heart in its heavy, calloused hand. "I'm sorry."

"The job doesn't pay much," Virgil said. "But it's year-round. Six hundred a month, plus room and board. That there's the room." He nodded toward the shack. "If you were expecting a mansion, I expect you'll be disappointed. It has a bed, a small space heater, a sink, a toilet, and a shower. That's about it. You still interested?"

While grateful for the offer of employment, I was stunned by the small sum. Seventy-two hundred a year? It was now obvious why the job remained open. Other than gasoline and the occasional meal out, I did not foresee the need for much in the way of money. On the other hand, six hundred a month for full-time work had to be either a mistake or a joke.

I attempted a smile. "You're kidding, right?"

Virgil scowled. "Did you not hear me? I said six hundred, take it or leave it."

Uh oh. I tried to amend for my blunder with a nervous burst of arguments. "We're talking no health care benefits, am I right? And no retirement plan, social security, or income tax—correct me if I'm wrong."

"Think you're pretty smart, do you?" the other man said, his cheeks now flushed. He kicked a divot in the sodden turf with the toe of his Rockport. "Fine. You don't want the job, you can get off my property."

"Wait. Let me explain."

But Virgil pressed on, head down and hands in his pockets, toward the house. Meanwhile, the rain continued unabated as if it might never stop and the entire world would once again be drowned in a vast and merciless sea.

CHAPTER SEVEN

From the moment I heard Daddy stomping up the porch stairs, I could tell that something was wrong.

"What happened?" I asked.

I heard him hang up his coat and hat. When he didn't immediately tell me, I knew it was bad.

"We don't need his kind around here. Got an attitude, that one. Already got more than enough bad attitudes to go around here. Don't need another one."

I heard a vehicle start up in the parking lot and the angry squeal of springs as it drove away.

"What'd you do, Daddy?" *I tried to sound normal, but secretly boiled with fury. Men! Such fragile little egos that they must protect at all costs!*

"Can I get some more coffee?" *I heard him sit at the table in his usual spot.*

"How come you two argued?"

"He seemed to think the pay was beneath him."

"Even after you explained the job included a place to stay and meals?"

"Must have looked around and thought we were rolling in dough." *He sipped his coffee with a loud slurp.* "We don't need his kind. Not here anyway."

"What kind of money did you offer him?"

"Same as the last one. Six hundred."

From the news programs I listened to, I thought this sounded low. "Maybe you should have asked him what he thought was fair, Daddy?"

"Don't matter now what he thinks. He's gone for good. I chased him off."

I hoped he was wrong. Because I seriously doubted that I could continue the charade of Daddy's little girl and being treated like the family's slave much longer.

Lately, while the others slept, I counted sheep. And dreamed of slitting their furry little throats.

***

"Idiot!" I pounded the steering wheel as I drove back the way I had come earlier, the sky growing darker by the minute as evening approached and the rain continued its unremitting assault. The narrow, tree-lined road serpentined along the hillside, occasionally revealing a farm with cleared acreage and a few marooned outbuildings. All too soon I would be back in Mount Vernon with the busy I-5 slicing through it and the decision clamoring to be made: where to go? I drove as slowly as I could and dumped the last of the aspirin bottle out onto my lap, gulped the few remaining pills, and tossed the empty container on the floor among the empty plastic water bottles and fast-food wrappers. At this point, neatness no longer counted.

Don't ask me why I argued with the old man. A difference of a few hundred dollars a month—or even several thousand— was inconsequential to my survival. The problem was not money, after all. It was staying alive.

According to Catania, the FBI agent who had interviewed me in the hospital, my only hope was to disappear so thoroughly that I could not be found by the cartel who wanted their money back and me dead. With its remote location and lack of background checks or employment forms required for new employees, the trout farm was as close to being ideal as I had been able to find with limited resources and on such short notice.

Now what? As poorly as the interview with Virgil had gone, I might as well have stayed in Southern California and saved myself three days of driving. The drenching cold combined with the preposterous—not to mention illegal—compensation level offered had shocked me so greatly that I had simply reacted instead of nodding in agreement. I had been within minutes, possibly seconds, of taking possession of the tiny cabin Virgil had offered me and able to lay my head down to sleep without the constant stress of worrying about where to go. Now the moment was gone, and I needed a do-over.

I felt the familiar swelling in my heart from Heide's death, but there was anger, too. Of all the thousands of banks, governments, and other legitimate financial entities to steal from, my wife had chosen a Mexican drug cartel notorious for cutting off the heads of their victims! Based on the ginormous amount of money changing hands every day at the hedge fund where she worked, Catania suggested that she could have stolen a million or two and possibly gotten away with it—a premise which Jeff's previous lifestyle supported, before he got too greedy. No one might have noticed or taken the time to sort it out if they had. Just a rounding error. An inadvertent lapse by two employees digitally lobotomized by the billions of dollars rushing past their eyes on high-definition monitors and morally impaired by the Lambos, Ferraris, Bentleys, and Aston Martins glinting in the deep shadows of the executive parking lot.

If I had known about Heide's plan, I could have stopped her, explained the risks, and pleaded for sanity. She would still be alive, and we would be together right now, relaxing over a glass of wine or a margarita, watching the boats go by on a

Saturday evening. Instead, I was soaking wet, hungry, and suffering from hypothermia in the cab of a rusted hunk of junk with no direction and no future.

My mind returned to our last night together and her outburst when I had photographed her from behind. What was that all about? With my pain and anxiety level in the red zone these past few days, I had totally forgotten about the tiny photo memory card residing in the change pocket of my jeans. Now I was curious to learn what I might have missed that day. Curiosity returned once again to anger.

"Dammit, Heide! Why the fuck did you do it?"

Whether it was the moisture in my eyes or the poor performance of the defroster, I needed to wipe the condensation from inside of the windshield with the saturated sleeve of my coat to see where I was going.

Less than a mile from the I-5 entrance I spotted the electronic reader board for a bar called the Beersheba with the slogan, "Where the beer is always cold and the women are hot." It was time to regroup and consider the options, meager as they might be.

CHAPTER EIGHT

"What the hell happened to you?" the guy sitting at the bar next to me asked. He wore a watch cap above a deeply lined face. I saw him eying me and the puddle of water forming beneath the bar stool suspiciously. "You look like someone shot your dog and stole your wife. Or maybe it was vice versa. Either way, you need a drink. Bartender," he called out, "better get this man a drink before he expires."

It was a typical sports bar so that without turning your head, you could simultaneously watch hockey and at least three basketball games.

"What can I get you?" the bartender asked over the din of the crowd.

"Black Jack neat," I replied. My teeth were chattering, making it hard to talk clearly.

"Well?" the old guy asked after I had had the first sip. "What was it? Dog or wife?"

"I had a job interview that didn't go well," I said.

"Let me guess: was you trying out to be a lifeguard, or maybe a deep-sea diver?" He chuckled. "Or maybe a fisherman on one of those Alaskan trawlers?" He cackled. "I swear I never saw someone looking so drowned and depressed in my life."

I tried to smile, but my face was still so frozen I am not sure how it might have looked. I took another swallow before answering.

"Maintenance job on a farm."

He took a drink from a long-necked beer bottle and burped before adding, "What was the problem, if you don't mind my asking?"

"Problem?" I considered. "I guess it was me."

"That goes without sayin', young man," he said.

"I didn't realize how low the compensation was."

He turned around on his barstool so he was facing me. He took another long pull on his beer. "There was this Cherokee fellow from Oklahoma I rode with years ago. He had more colorful expressions than you could shake a stick at. 'Keep the shiny side up.' That kind of thing. He once told me that the difference between homeless and hopeful is a job, whether you are living on the rez or in Manhattan. Said we need to be doing something every day, no matter how menial or low-paid. It's in our DNA."

I savored the whiskey. In my current weary and waterlogged state, it was warming, comforting.

"If you were looking for advice, I'd recommend you get some warm food and get dried out some before giving that job another shot." He clapped me on the shoulder, then dried his hand on his jeans.

I grimaced. "I don't think there's any going back. Not after the owner told me to get his property."

"Ran you off, did he?" The old guy frowned. "Of course, another thing that crazy Indian said was, 'Never look a dead horse in the mouth.' I have no clue what that means, but I believe it may fit the present occasion."

"Ready for another?" the bartender asked.

"Just my check," I said.

"Give it to me, Bob," the old guy said. "And bring me some more stale nuts when you got a second."

He nodded at me. "Your turn next time."

"Thanks," I said. "For the drink and the advice."

"Listen," he said. "Long as we are talking advice, look for an open door, one that ain't been slammed shut in your face. I hate to say it, but you are shit out of luck on that other one. Time to cross it off your list and move on to something new." He waved his beer bottle at me. "That's just me talkin'. Not the Indian."

***

Tapping on the pickup truck's window woke me from a miserable sleep. I pushed up from the well-worn seat where I had spent the past hour or so curled in a tight ball and rubbed my eyes. It was after ten p.m. according to my watch. As I rolled the window down, I was surprised to see Valerie huddled under an umbrella, looking tiny as a woodland faery in the moonless night, and the dog crouched beside her, trying to avoid the rain.

"Heard someone drive up a while back and, seeing how late it was, figured it must be you." She held out something wrapped in tinfoil and a blanket. "Made you a sandwich and here's something to help you stay warm."

"Why are you doing this?"

"Depends." She wiped a wet strand of dark hair away from her face. "You stayin' or goin'?"

"Your dad says he won't hire me, but I thought I'd ask him to reconsider in the morning. I don't exactly have anywhere else I need to be."

"Breakfast is at six," she said. "Daddy insists on bacon and eggs every morning. Come up to the house and be ready to make your case by then." She stroked the dog between the ears. "Come on, Patsy. Let's go in where it's warm and dry."

"Hey, before you go. Is he serious about six hundred dollars a month?"

"Oh, Daddy is serious about everything, but that doesn't mean you can't ask for more." She smiled. "I figure you're worth at least six-fifty."

The dog grinned happily as she led Valerie back to the house.

CHAPTER NINE

It took several seconds to get my bearings when I woke. A robin chirped from somewhere nearby. The heavy wool blanket that Valerie had brought smelled of mothballs but had kept me warm. I had to wipe the condensation from the glass before I could see out the pickup truck's windshield. Although the sun remained hidden behind the mountains, the rain had stopped, and the sky was clear. I touched my bandaged ribs. They remained tender, especially in the area where I had felt something give the day before when climbing up onto the John Deere tractor.

The pain was a constant reminder of my situation which was becoming more desperate by the day. I needed the job, but I also needed this place. The trout farm was as unlikely a place for someone on the run from a Mexican cartel to hide out as I was likely to find—especially on such short notice. Disappearing completely was the only hope I had of staying alive, but maintaining my invisibility was not entirely self-serving. If the killers managed to track me down, I could also be putting whoever I was with at risk of injury or worse.

I saw by my watch that it was nearly six. I thought about changing my shirt and decided it was not worth the pain. I figured this final attempt to convince Virgil to give me the job would have less to do with the shirt I was wearing and more with my humility and his willingness to accept my apology.

I opened the truck door and was immediately refreshed by the crisp air. I could see my breath as I labored up the gravel parking lot to the house.

I was about to knock when the door opened.

"Right on time," Valerie said.

Even half-closed, her eyes were noticeably large and framed by long lashes. Once again, she wore denim coveralls over a long-sleeved shirt. Patsy, my new best friend, swished her tail against me happily as I followed them into the dining area.

Virgil frowned as I entered. He was seated at the head of the table. A tall, lean man wearing khakis and a blue plaid shirt looked up from his plate. He had short, brown hair, blue eyes, and was good-looking in a Nordic sort of way.

"Sit down," Valerie said. "Have some breakfast. I made plenty for everybody."

I sat down across from the other man.

"I thought I told you to get off my property," Virgil said.

"Before I left, I wanted to apologize if I said something to upset you and to ask if you'd reconsider."

"Stu," Virgil turned to the other man, "this is the guy I was telling you about. Calls himself Gray. Says he's from California."

"Whereabouts?" Stu asked. "L.A.?"

"Orange County."

Stu nodded. "I know the place."

Valerie set a plate of scrambled eggs, bacon, and toast in front of me. "Coffee? Stu's been just about everywhere. Haven't you, Stu?"

I thought I detected sarcasm to which Stu did not bother to reply. Valerie placed a cup of coffee carefully before me and sat down on my right. Patsy stuck her nose in Valerie's lap and she offered the dog a strip of bacon which Patsy inhaled.

I sipped the coffee. "Hazelnut?"

Valerie smiled. "I had some stashed away for a special occasion. Like it?"

Stu sniffed his coffee before shoving his mug aside. "Can I get some real coffee?"

Valerie ignored him, and Vonda chose that moment to enter, wearing a charcoal suit, white silk blouse, and high heels. A strand of pearls draped her throat. It was the first time I had seen her wearing anything other than a smirk and a man's shirt. Now she was wearing makeup and her blond hair was carefully brushed. If she did not look quite like she belonged on Santa Monica or Sunset Boulevard, where Armani and Burberry were the uniforms of choice among young career women, she also did not look like she belonged with the Walmart crowd wearing jeans and parkas on the outskirts of the decidedly un-metropolitan Sedro-Woolley.

"Hi, Daddy." She stooped to kiss Virgil's forehead before sitting down next to Stu. "Morning, sweetie. Where is my coffee, Val?"

"Coming right up," Valerie said.

"I can help," I offered, but Valerie ignored me and everyone else gave me a look that said I had just committed a major faux pas.

"Have a seat, darlin'" Virgil said to Vonda. "Ain't you running a little late this morning?"

"It sounded like we had a guest." She studied me. "I swear whatever else you are, you are a much-needed intrusion in our morning gatherings. You can usually hear a pin drop." She stole a strip of bacon and a slice of toast off Stu's plate.

"That's rude," he grumbled.

"I thought it was impolite of you not to offer me some," Vonda said. She winked at me. Valerie returned with a mug of coffee cradled in two hands which she delicately placed in front of her. "Thanks, Sis," Vonda said over a mouthful of food.

"Can I get some real coffee, Val?" Stu said.

"It's Val-er-ie and I didn't hear you say 'please.'"

Stu laid his fork carefully on his plate. "I'll get it myself." His chair scraped the floor loudly as he stood.

"Valerie," Virgil said. "Get the man some decent coffee."

"He knows where it is."

Uncomfortable to be watching and listening to the bickering between Stu and Valerie, I remained silent.

Vonda pecked Stu's cheek. "How's my man this morning?"

"Same as every other damn morning," Valerie said.

"Strong and mean as a bear. That's why I love him," Vonda said.

Stu smiled at his wife's flattery.

Vonda studied me for a moment while sipping her coffee. "I see you're wearing a wedding ring. Where's your wife?"

In my hasty travel and preparations for the job interview, I had forgotten about my ring and the questions it might raise. I managed to swallow. "My wife died."

Their chewing stopped, and three faces watched me with interest. Valerie's half-closed eyes made it look as if she were looking at the table, yet her posture was one of intense alertness, as if she could hear not only the words that were spoken but those that were not.

"Recent?" Virgil asked.

I wiped my mouth with a napkin to buy a moment before nodding. Here it comes, I thought, the real test. Driving the tractor had just been the appetizer.

"Looks like we got a handyman with a few skeletons in his closet," Stu said.

"Stu!" Vonda scolded. "I apologize for my husband's bad manners. How did she die?"

I had to think about this. Under their stares, I studied my plate, as if the answer might be hidden there among the scrambled eggs, toast, and hash browns. The coffee jiggled in my cup as my right leg quivered beneath the table.

"Illness?" Virgil asked.

"No, not an illness."

Flash. Boom.

I heard a cough. It might have been Virgil. I did not think it was Stu.

"Oh, my." Vonda set down her coffee.

I took a breath. "A car accident. She was killed by a drunk driver."

"Criminy," Virgil said.

"They catch him?" Stu asked.

"He died, too," I adlibbed. A famous president, or maybe it was a quarterback, once said that a lie was as good as the truth if you can get away with it. The number of people killed on Southern California highways—even in a single week—was high enough that I did not figure anyone would bother checking up on my story.

"That's Southern California for you," Stu said.

Vonda punched his arm. "Can't you show a little sympathy for once?"

"Are you sure you're up to working?" Virgil asked.

"I'm sure."

The silence that followed seemed to stretch for minutes but was probably only a few seconds.

Finally, Valerie spoke softly. "I think you should hire him, Daddy."

Virgil sipped his coffee and made a face. "Opening day is less than two months away. With all this rain and the warmer temperatures, the grass is going to get too tall to mow if we don't get control of it now. We better see how much we can mow today with the hammerknifer. If the weather clears later in the week, Gray can go over it again with the bull, then hit it with the sweeper to clean up the dead grass before it kills the lawn."

"No problem," Stu said. "The John Deere is lubed, fueled, and ready to go. What about you?"

He looked at me. "Ready to start earning your grub?"

I nodded, too relieved to have a job to speak.

Vonda stood and smoothed her skirt. "Sorry, Gray, but I'm going to be late for work if I don't move my ass."

She pecked Stu on the cheek a second time. "Go easy on Gray his first day."

"I'm headed to town," Virgil added, standing up. He drained his coffee. "Lordy, this is awful. Can we please go back to the regular stuff?"

"Sure, Daddy," Valerie said. She began clearing plates and silverware.

Stu stood up and smiled good-naturedly. "I've got to hand it to you. You really know how to break up a party." He picked up the newspaper lying near his plate. "Meet me in fifteen minutes down at the barn."

As the last one remaining at the table after Stu left, I finished my coffee and what remained of breakfast, then began clearing dishes from the table. The dog ambled over to an old mat near a heating vent, circled the wagons once, and plopped down.

"You don't need to do that," Valerie said from the kitchen. "I'm in charge of the cooking and cleaning around here."

Ignoring her, I gathered up the dirty dishes and carried them to the kitchen where she was loading the dishwasher. Her organizational skills, I noted, were far different than Heide's haphazard loading. All the cups were in one row, glasses in another, separated by a row of bowls. Plates were arranged by size while silverware was by type. Spoons and forks were pointed up, knives down.

"My mom taught me to be polite," I said. "When you eat with strangers, you offer to help clean up."

Valerie gathered another handful of dishes from the sink and continued loading the dishwasher.

"I appreciate your politeness, but please don't try to help. You will just confuse me. I know exactly how many plates and cups and utensils are on that table—or at least I did, until you started clearing them." Valerie went on working as she spoke.

"Vonda once pocketed a spoon. I spent half the day down on my knees, crawling around the house looking for it."

"Why on earth would she take a spoon?"

"How the hell should I know?" She straightened up to face me, her pale face flushed. "Because she can be a jerk and enjoys making my life difficult, what else?"

I recalled the hidden tampons. "I'm sorry. I thought I was helping."

Valerie went back to loading dishes. I grabbed a pan and began to scrub. I have always admired the handicapped. Based on my admittedly limited experience, they often work harder at succeeding and feel less sorry for themselves than many of those people born far more fortunate. But this was the first time I had worked side-by-side with a young, blind woman. As I studied her, I saw that even without makeup, plucked eyebrows, or hair coloring, she was unnaturally beautiful. Ethereal. Add to this the fact that she had brought me a sandwich and blanket the night before and had spoken up for me at a critical moment at the breakfast table and I was ready to help clean dishes, wax the floor, or anything else she might require.

"Are all men so stubborn?" she asked.

"Pretty much."

There was a large dollop of dishwashing soap on her right breast that I resisted the impulse to brush off.

She sighed. "If you insist on washing the pans, I'll dry and put them away."

"That was the best breakfast I've had in a long time."

"Did you get enough to eat?"

"More than enough." I rinsed a heavy, cast iron frying pan.

"Are you fat or skinny?" She pinched my side and I let out an involuntary, "Ouch."

"What in God's name is that you're wearing?"

"Nothing."

"C'mon, Gray. I may be blind, but I'm not stupid."

"It's a back brace for heaving lifting."

She felt around my shirt, eyes closed beneath her heavy brows, until I twisted away.

"That's no back brace. It is a bandage. Do not try to lie; I can smell the betadine. You're dinged up, aren't you? You can't work like that."

"I'm fine," I protested. My voice sounded too loud in the small kitchen.

"Don't worry," she said, as if reading my mind. She picked up the frying pan and began drying it. "I won't say anything. How'd you get hurt?"

"The accident."

"The same one that killed your wife?"

I nodded before realizing she could not see my response. "Yes."

Several seconds went by and I thought—hoped—Valerie would let the subject drop, but I was wrong.

"I'm sorry about what happened to your wife," she said. "How old was she?"

"Would have been twenty-four in May." I handed her another pan to dry.

"Was she pretty?"

I faced the window over the sink where condensation from the dishwater veiled the view of the outdoors. "Very."

"I bet she was smart, too."

I felt the familiar swelling in my heart from the bitter sting of betrayal. *"Sorry, Dev. I fucked up."*

This would not do. My eyes searched the room for something to anchor against the riptide of despair. "I noticed the piano. Do you or your sister play?"

"My mother did. I play the viola." She placed a soap pod in the dispenser, then closed the dishwasher door.

"I bet you're very good.

She paused before turning on the dishwasher. "Why do you say that?"

"Just watching the meticulous way you work."

A smile flirted with the corners of her lips and she shrugged. "I was the featured soloist with the state high school orchestra."

Can I hear you play sometime?"

"Really?" Her violet eyes swept the ceiling. "You'd like to?"

"Absolutely."

She frowned. "Stu will be waiting for you down at the barn. You better go."

I glanced at my watch. It was two minutes after I was supposed to meet Stu.

After putting on my still-damp jacket and opening the door, I looked back to where she was wiping the stovetop. "Seriously. I'd love to hear you play sometime."

CHAPTER TEN

I found Stu viewing a spreadsheet displayed on a large computer monitor in an office tucked into a front corner of the barn.

"Let me welcome you to the brains of our little operation." He leaned back in the metal office chair. The padded armrest was missing from one of its arms. He sipped from a mug. "Mr. Coffee is hiding behind the door there. Just Folgers on tap, I am afraid. You want hazelnut, peppermint tea, or engraved napkins, you'll have to round that up yourself."

"Folgers is fine." I poured coffee into a mug that still contained the stain from the last time it had been used. Once you have been shot, as I had discovered, drinking from a less than pristine mug no longer generates the same misgivings.

"That Valerie is a scrappy little bitch, isn't she?" Stu said.

I managed to scald my upper lip and spill a tablespoon or so of the hot liquid onto my leg. Stu chuckled.

"In case you had not noticed, she tends to bring out the worst in me. Then again," his face grew more serious, "her constant pecking wears thin day after day. I don't remember the last time she had a kind word for me." He shrugged. "Not that it really matters, I suppose."

"She's just a kid," I pointed out.

"Turned twenty, I believe it was, in January," Stu said,

nodding. "But don't worry too much about Miss Valerie or any of the Van de Zilvers for that matter. They are tough as a flock of leghorns. Pick on one and you have started a war with all three. Ol' Virgil's a pretty fair guy, but don't get between him and his daughters or you'll need a surgeon to remove his Rockport from your backside. Believe me, I found out the hard way. And more than once." He smiled.

"That your investment portfolio?" I pointed to the screen.

"That's one way to describe it. These are the hatches." He ran a finger down a column. "I can tell you how many fry we bought and when, how much we paid for 'em, what it cost to feed 'em, and how many were caught and sold. The difference is how many we got left, with an allowance for predators like raccoons, the occasional blue heron or eagle, and the trout themselves."

I was impressed. Who would have guessed that a small trout farm in the foothills of the North Cascades would be so high-tech? "I guess you have to keep track of everything to know what your return on investment is."

Stu nodded. "ROI. That is what matters, all right. Look here." Deftly using the mouse to close one document and open another, he selected an item from a pull-down menu. A moment later, a line chart materialized across the screen. "This program tracks weather conditions and fry growth. See this?" He pointed to a hill in the graph line. "This was a mild winter. A mild winter usually means bigger fish. Bigger fish means more money. Looks simple, but it's more complicated than you might think."

Stu closed the spreadsheet and opened a new screen. "While I was waiting for you, I did a little research. This you?"

Up popped a faded daguerreotype of a turban-wearing man with a full beard who was dressed in a cavalry uniform with a holstered pistol on one side, a saber dangling from his belt on the other while also holding a rifle.

I stared in surprise at the distant relative whose name I

had stolen.

"My sword isn't that long," I managed to say.

"No doubt your wife was disappointed," Stu said. He tapped the screen. "Says he died fighting Germans." He swiveled to face me. "I'm guessing with a name as uncommon as Grayson that you might be his descendent?"

My left eye began to twitch as I considered how a genealogical trail might lead to my parents and eventually me. Damn Google anyway. The last thing I needed was for Stu to learn that the Sinaloa Cartel was looking for me.

"Frankly," Stu said, "I do not give a damn who you are related to, or where you are from. I just find it kind of odd that there is nothing about you online." He stared at me. "Nothing on Facebook, Instagram, or LinkedIn. Nothing on Google except a guy who has been dead for over a hundred years. It's like you are a fucking ghost."

"Never had the time or the inclination for social media," I said. "I always thought those websites and apps were about as useful as playing computer games when you could be outside doing something productive or fun." Like shooting photos for instance.

Stu nodded but looked less than satisfied. "What happened when your wife died? Didn't you have a job, friends, or family? Why did you leave there and whatever you were doing to come up here?"

"Can I let you in on a secret?" I asked. "I started to drink. AA meetings were not doing it for me, and a counselor said I might need a change of scenery."

The problem with lies as everyone knows is that a little one leads to a bigger one and so on. Next, I would be saying I had joined the circus and had a falling out with the lion tamer.

Stu stared at me for an uncomfortable ten seconds or so. "Enough of this." He closed the computer down. "We've got lawns to mow and fertilize, fences to mend and the driveway needs some holes filled before we can open. It's time for you to get to work." He stood up and zipped up his jacket. I followed him outside.

On the downhill side of the barn where they could not be seen from the road were two large fuel tanks.

"The John Deere uses diesel, and the Bull and everything else takes gasoline. Make sure you don't mix them up. Got it?"

"Got it."

"There is a lot of money tied up in all of this," Stu gestured to include the barn and the land. He studied me for a moment. "What would you guess this place is worth?"

"No idea."

"Take a guess."

"A million? Maybe two?"

"Not bad," Stu said. "A tad on the light side. You probably passed a housing development or two on the way up here. Raw land's going for one hundred thousand an acre. We got over forty acres here. That is four million just for the land. Throw in the view and the ponds and you got maybe another half a million."

"Want to know the really sweet part?" Stu smiled. "There isn't a lick of debt. Not one dime."

I did not know what to say. Much as I might have found the topic of money interesting once, under my current circumstances, I now found it depressing and even nauseating.

"Virgil owned an old Skagit Valley tulip farm handed down from his grandfather through his father," Stu offered. "But it was Louise—the girls' mom, bless her bones—with the cash. He spent some of her money on fixing up the place. Added two ponds and this barn. Then put the rest into mutual funds."

I tried to change the subject by pointing to the clouds that piled high and blocked the view of the mountains. "Think it will rain?"

Stu stared at me like I was an idiot. "Around here, you don't bother to ask a stupid question like that. The sky could be blue as robins' eggs and it could still rain cats and dogs within thirty minutes."

He led the way back inside the barn. "You Californians are all alike," he added. "You move here during spring or summer, everything warm, dry, and hunkey-dory. Come November, you will be bitching night and day about the rain. A year from now, you'll wish you were back in California. I've seen it a million times before."

"Not me," I said. California was now the last place I wanted to be.

"Yeah," Stu said. "We'll see." Then his face grew serious again. "The grass is too high and wet for the bull. You need to get it all today with the hammerknifer. I see where you had it out yesterday, so I assume you know how to drive it."

"I think so." I waved an arm at the sprawling green expanse. "What's the best route?"

Stu shrugged. "Start up at the road and work your way down. Or you can start at the ponds and work your way up. It's the same amount of grass, either way. Be careful around the roses. They were Louise's special varieties, something she fretted over and talked to like they were kin. And don't fall asleep and drive into one of the ponds. I don't want to be the one to have to fish your butt out."

***

I drove in second gear, poking along, the hammerknifer chopping a nice, even wake in a sea of green. As a teenager, I had found driving a tractor to be the most incredibly boring and monotonous work. It was the same now with one important difference: I desperately needed the solitariness, the symmetry of the long, geometric rows, the comforting thrum of the engine vibrating up through the seat and floorboards. For the moment at least, I was the captain of my life once again and the John Deere was my ship. My mind, so burdened of late, was free to wander among the evergreen-bearded hills beneath a scudding armada of clouds driven eastward by winds launched far out in the Pacific toward an as-yet-vaguely-glimpsed fortress of formidable mountains. And in the sweet-smelling fragrance of newly mown grass, I rediscovered something as simple and rare as peace of mind.

After working my way up the driveway from the barn, I turned east along the road. Heeding Virgil's warning, I kept one eye out for rocks or other debris. Fortunately for my ribs, I only had to stop once to retrieve an empty beer bottle.

When I finished the first pass along the road, I started down the tree line that separated the Van de Zilver property from its quarter-mile distant eastern neighbor, then made a wide turn back toward the driveway. Overhead, a flock of Canadian Geese arrowed north.

I had nearly finished a second, football-field-sized oval when I spotted Stu driving a white Mustang slowly up the drive. Stu stopped and waved me over. I dismounted from the idling tractor and approached the car on foot. Now what, I wondered.

"Got a reason for going so slow?" he asked. "The grass is growing faster than you're cutting. If you plan on finishing sometime this century, you'd best get a move on."

"Okay." I watched the Mustang ease leisurely out the

driveway and onto the highway.

Back on the John Deere, I slipped the transmission into third gear and resumed mowing. The great thing about a tractor is the enormous torque. You can start in any gear and be at full speed in no time without the need to shift. The clamor behind me was louder, the ride rougher, and it seemed to me that the mown grass looked more ragged, but progress was now at least fifty percent faster.

I completed the first oval and began another that overlapped the first. That was followed by yet another, each one a milestone of accomplishment and satisfaction. I made it a point to drive with caution as I neared the row of roses. Plastic identifying tags fluttered in the breeze. Fresh bark surrounded their roots to protect them from frost, and the canes looked to have been carefully pruned. Meanwhile, the clouds had gradually dissolved into a colorless, uniform ceiling that descended until it seemed to nearly meet the ground. Then it began to rain. Over the thrum of the hammerknifer, I heard the hiss of rain striking the earth.

If I had let myself, I could have easily drifted into a pit of depression over losing everything. Instead, I used the pain of physical exertion and the beauty of my surroundings to help heal my emotional wounds.

There was one more thing: every time I started to think about Heide or feel pity for myself, I would focus on the red-lipped monster who had shot me, killed my wife, and trashed my life. It was a cruel face, devoid of mercy.

Flash. Boom.

According to Catania, the cartel had virtually unlimited resources. Such that they would likely find the trail of the money and locate where it was hidden. Unless I found it first.

CHAPTER ELEVEN

In the steady downpour, I did not see the two figures waiting beneath the tall Douglas fir until I was nearly beside them. Valerie held up a brown bag with one hand while the other held Patsy's halter. She wore a yellow rain slicker with the hood pulled back. I parked near the tree, shut off the John Deere's engine, and climbed down to join her.

"Ready for some lunch?" she asked.

I checked the time; it was nearly one-thirty and I was suddenly starving.

"I am now." I took a bite of the sandwich she offered and began to chew. "Strawberry jam and cheddar," I mumbled through a mouthful of bread. Patsy licked her lips and wagged her tail in appreciation.

"Like it?"

"It's great."

"Liar."

Once more, I was struck by her ability to hear beyond the words that were spoken and without the benefit of being able to see body language or gestures. "I admit, I've never had it before."

"Cheese is boring by itself, don't you think?" she asked. "I hate boring sandwiches. How are your ribs doing?"

I shrugged, embarrassed that she might feel pity, then

remembered that she could not see. "Fine. Just fine."

"Good." She scratched behind the dog's ears. "I'm glad. Well, it's time to get back, I guess."

She turned to flutter off toward the house, but I was not quite ready for her to leave. "What's for dinner? Trout?"

She stopped, tilted her head up toward the underside of the tree, and barked a short laugh as if she saw something funny up there in its naked limbs. "Daddy doesn't like fish. Mostly, he likes me to cook red meat. Occasionally, I will roast a chicken or ham. We're pretty much a meat-and-potatoes family."

"No spaghetti? Or maybe some ravioli, fettuccini, tortellini, or lasagna?"

"I don't even know what all of those are. Are they all noodles? Occasionally, if there's leftover hamburger for meatballs, I manage to sneak some spaghetti in."

"How subversive. What about stuffed eggplant?"

She pressed her lips together and shook her head. "Nope. Vonda usually does the shopping, unless I have the food delivered. One time, we decided to experiment with fajitas."

"'Fah-hee-tahs,'" I corrected.

"I had a hunch I didn't have it right." She smiled, her eyes half-closed.

"I like your way of saying it better. Just be careful if you ever visit La Jolla."

"Anyway, you would have thought we had served up garbage. Daddy made us throw it out."

"Sounds positively dull. Don't you ever get a craving for salmon or swordfish, maybe some squid?"

Her nose scrunched up. "What's squid taste like?"

"Rubber."

"Ewwww. Just what I always wanted for dinner: Goodyear radials."

We both laughed. I realized that I had not laughed since Heide had died. It felt good. Together, we listened to the rain falling all around us. Dead needles and fir cones carpeted the ground and gave off a clean, pitchy smell. Under the tent-like protection of the tree, it felt like we were standing in an enormous cathedral surrounded by the quiet rustlings and murmurs of the congregation.

"I better go. If Daddy gets home early, he'll wonder where I am." Valerie waved her fingers. "See you later, alligator."

She pulled up the hood of her raincoat. "C'mon, Patsy."

I watched her and the dog walk back toward the house, then climbed onto the tractor and resumed making soggy ovals in the sea of green.

***

"He came!" I was so excited, I needed to tell someone. "He's just like you said, Momma." After all these years of waiting, I had nearly given up. But now Gray was here, and he was just like Momma said he would be.

I was chopping vegetables by the sink while I talked to Momma like I did when I was a little girl. "Ever since you died there has been no one to talk to, no one to take me places, and no one to make plans with. He has only been here a few hours and we have already talked twice! Three times if you count last night when I took a sandwich out to his truck."

"He was so pleased and thankful for the sandwich I made him today. We stood beneath a fir tree and it was so still and quiet in the rain. My hands were sweating, even though it was cool, and I could hear my heart beating so fast I thought I might die.

"He even said he wants to hear me play the viola. I think he likes me, Momma!"

"Jesus Christ, Valerie." Vonda startled me. "You talking to yourself?"

"What are you doing home?"

"I wasn't feeling well."

75

I heard her open the refrigerator and take out a bottle of wine. "Kind of early to start drinking, ain't it?"

"Just a small glass to settle my stomach. Where's Gray?"

"Working. Why do you care?"

"Just asking. You talk to him?"

"He misses his wife. Said she was pretty and smart."

"Yeah?" I heard her pouring wine into her glass. It sounded like a tall glass.

"He's just like Momma said he'd be," I blurted. I could not help myself.

"'Like Momma said?' I hate to be the one to tell you this, Valerie, but Momma has been dead for ten years. And, far as I know, she did not tell fortunes. Least not to my knowledge."

"She said Gray would come. She even described him. A sensitive man. Intelligent, not full of pride and self-importance."

"Did she also say he was brown-skinned?"

"I don't care what color he is."

"Got it all planned out, don't you?" Vonda said. "Poor Gray. Arrived here just twenty-four hours ago and he's already spoken for."

I could not see my sister, but I recognized the snarky tone in her voice.

"Don't mess this up, Vonda. I'm warning you."

"Why should I care what you want?"

"You're married!"

"Well, ain't you the observant one."

Without thinking about it, I realized I had chopped the vegetables up into smithereens. I began twisting the knife in my hand. "I swear, Vonda. You don't know what I'm capable of."

"Yeah? What are you going to do? Cry? Stab me with a potato peeler? Tattle on me like you used to do when Momma was alive?"

She snickered as she left the room. I gripped the knife

tightly in my hand and, for the hundred-millionth time, thought about how much I wanted to kill her.

CHAPTER TWELVE

The wind swept in late in the afternoon, bringing with it a precipitous drop in temperature. The rain slanted heavier and, although sundown was still officially a good way off, the sky darkened to a dreary charcoal. Unfortunately, the John Deere had no lights, either to read its fuel gauge or to illuminate where I was going. I was now shivering so hard that I could hear my teeth chattering above the engine noise. I fastened the snap of my coat collar as I peered through the gloom, trying to decipher firm land from the quagmire. My jeans, cotton pullover and nylon jacket had long before given up any pretensions of water-resistance. The muscles of my arms and legs were stiff and my ribs screamed their displeasure. There remained a good amount of area yet to mow, however. Stu had advised me to finish today and I was determined to try.

Call it stubbornness or its evil twin: stupidity. My father had told me so many times that I was good for nothing, that I had spent most of my life trying to prove him wrong. The only professions he considered worthy were a doctor or engineer. The uncle who had tried and failed to become a professional photographer was considered the black sheep of the family. More than the bruises my father had given me, his words were the reason I had left home two days after graduating from high school and never looked back.

Hunched over the John Deere's rain-slick steering wheel, I worked my way down to the ponds where the rain had made the ground wet and treacherous. Even with their enormous tread, I could feel the tractor tires beginning to slip. I looked back toward the barn hoping to spot Stu, but there was no welcoming light or sign of life. Was Stu watching me now to see what I would do? Perhaps he had already knocked off for the day. On the other hand, he might think me a coward—"afraid of a little rain"—if I quit now. For better or worse, I was on my own. I decided to proceed further downhill and finish the less challenging mowing first. I would save mowing around the ponds for later, unless Stu showed up and offered to call it a day.

Something like an hour later—it was too dark to read my watch—I finished mowing the lower reaches of the property and motored slowly back up to the smaller of the three ponds. I glanced once more toward the barn—where was Stu?—then geared down into second. I was nearly abreast of the oblong pool of black water when the wheels found too little substance to grab onto and began to spin. Abruptly the tractor careened to one side as the right wheel began to dig itself into the mud and the left tore gouts of sod from the ground, pitching them toward the blades of the hammerknifer.

"Shit!" I stabbed the clutch to the floorboard. I disengaged the hammerknifer, then lifted it clear of the ground before trying to ease the tractor forward out of the grave it was digging for both of us. Slowly, I released the clutch. The tractor bucked like a stallion as the wheels dug deeper into the soft soil. I put the clutch in again, this time shifting into reverse.

"C'mon. You can do it," I pleaded.

Again, the tractor surged, but could not free itself. I climbed down to inspect the damage. The ground was so soggy that my footsteps made sucking noises. To my horror, I saw that the huge tires had torn deep troughs into the earth, destroying the lawn.

Briefly, I considered drowning myself in the pond and getting it over with. It being my very first day on the job, my mental state was somewhat less than ideal.

"Fuck!" I kicked a tire in frustration, slipped in the mud, and, quicker than the blink of an eye, landed flat on my back. Rain pelted my face.

I tried sitting up, but could not because of my damaged ribs. I had to roll over onto my knees. I pounded the saturated earth with a fist in frustration, angry at Heide, the cartel, Stu, myself, and the world in general.

Because isn't that the way of it? Just when you think there might be a reason for hope, a chance that something good could still happen, that there might be a God who cared about his people, the bogeyman jumps out of the bushes and rabbit-punches you in the back of the head and then stands over you, hee-hawing.

***

Vonda answered the door wearing a pink sweatsuit and white socks. Her initial surprise changed quickly into a look of alarm.

"Holy crow."

"I need to speak to your dad."

Her eyebrows shot up. "Come in."

Patsy came close enough to sniff, then backed away, wanting nothing to do with me. I could not blame her. I was soaking wet, bespattered with mud, and unfit for company—human or hound.

"Who is it?" Virgil called from the living room.

Valerie appeared at her sister's side. "Are you okay?"

"I don't want to mess up your floor," I said.

"Oh, the hell with the floor," Vonda said. "Get your ass in here where it's warm."

She dragged me by the coat sleeve. "It's Gray," she said.

"How come you're so late?" Stu growled from the other room.

"He needs to see you, Daddy," Vonda said.

I walked past the piano to the edge of the indoor-outdoor carpeting that marked the border between the family room and the living room. Virgil reclined in a La-Z-Boy near the television, which was showing CNN. Somewhere on the planet, the sun was shining. Probably Southern California.

Stu looked up from the couch. "You decide to go for a swim?"

"More like a mud bath."

Virgil raised the remote control he was holding and hit mute. "Let's hear it," he said in the silence that followed.

"I'm bogged down by the lower pond. I've tried everything I can think of but can't get out."

It was so quiet that I could hear Virgil exhale through his nose.

"I'll pay for the damage to the lawn."

"Dammit!" Stu threw down his newspaper. "First damn day on the job. I told you he was a fuck-up."

"Watch your language." With his lips pressed tightly together, Virgil stared at me. "How come you didn't quit when you saw the ground was getting saturated? Didn't anybody tell you about the ground around the ponds being soft?"

"I figured he was a smart boy." Stu glared at me. "What am I supposed to do, hold his hand? Maybe I should have sent Patsy out there with him. The damn dog has more sense."

"It was my fault. I could feel the tires starting to slip but kept going until it was too late."

Virgil nodded. "Meet me by the tractor tomorrow before breakfast. Stu, you bring the bull and some logging chain."

Stu shook his head. "I knew you were a piece of work the first time I saw you."

Virgil picked up the television remote. "I am taking the cost to repair that sod out of your paycheck, Stu. Next time—well, there better not be a next time."

***

"Spartan" was the first word that came to mind when examining the one-room cabin. A thin mattress rested on a metal cot that sat snugly against one of the rough-sawn and sweet-smelling cedar plank walls. Light came from an overhead bulb and a small reading lamp from a nearby desk and chair. What looked to be a closet proved instead to be a miniature bathroom, not unlike the head on a sailboat. It included a shower area barely large enough to stand in and draw the curtain around your body, and, in a nod to efficiency, a toilet and sink were set in such close proximity that it was possible to sit on the john and brush your teeth over the sink at the same time. A clothes rod ran a short distance along the wall over the bed and, above it, a shelf for clothes or books. In my current mental state, where extraneous clutter was not an easy thing to sort through, the cabin seemed virtually ideal. The exceptions were the lack of a driveway and the small, plastic heater which produced an odor of cooked dust when I turned it on high to combat the pervasive, damp chill.

With the first hint of heat, I felt exhaustion overtake me. It was all I could do to walk back to the truck and lug the bag with my clothes down the hill. I forced myself to shed my dripping clothes and Velcro bandage to take a hot shower, the hard spray like tiny arrows attacking my tender ribs and muscles. Then I wrapped a large towel around me, turned off the light, and lay down on the unmade bed.

As I curled into a ball, I recalled lying next to Heide, the satiny feeling of her skin, her scent as I kissed the back of her neck. That life, with all its simple pleasures and silly dreams, was gone. My last thought before falling into unconscious slumber was that I had found a refuge from the violence and imminent danger that stalked me and would do my best to hang on to it, no matter the cost to my body. Or soul.

***

Listen. You can hear the rain falling on the cabin roof, the deck, and the pond. Beneath that, there is the sound of his breathing, soft and regular.

My body quivered with excitement and fear, my heart beating so loud in my ears that I had to wait for it to quiet. I smelled the cedar walls and floor, the rain and sour sweat smell of his clothes, and the clean, soapy smell of his body.

I crouched beside him where he lay on the narrow cot. I reached out to touch him lightly. He was sleeping on his stomach, exhausted by the long day. I did not think he would wake. His skin was cool. He was naked, covered only by a damp towel. The wool blanket I gave him the night before when he was sleeping in his truck was probably still there in his truck.

His skin was smooth, covered by fine hairs. He had taken off the bandage he was wearing around his middle. I played with his hair. I drew my knife from its pouch and used it to cut off a lock to take back with me.

Vonda said his skin color is brown like a Hershey chocolate bar. I do not know what color is exactly, but Momma taught me that there are some colors you can taste, like blueberry blue, orange orange, and vanilla white. It makes me wonder what Gray tastes like. I licked his shoulder then jerk back when he moaned.

When I was sure from his breathing that he was still sleeping, I let my nightgown fall to the floor. It was cool in the cabin and my nipples were hard as cherry pits, but down there, I was moist and warm. After a while, my breath came quicker. I did not think he would hear me, but I no longer cared.

You were right, Momma. You said he would come.

CHAPTER THIRTEEN

I woke from an uncomfortable position on the small cot, startled by the angry pain in my ribs. I discovered a spring in the thin mattress pad I had not noticed the night before. Behind the frayed edges of the window blind, dawn emerged silent and colorless. The wool blanket I had forgotten in the truck was now covering me. Someone had evidently visited me during the night.

I was brushing my teeth when I was surprised by a knock at the cabin's front door. "Rise and shine, sleepyhead. Ready for a cup of coffee?"

"You bet," I mumbled through a mouthful of toothpaste. I struggled to climb into jeans and a flannel shirt and cursed my lack of a robe. Dressing in haste proved difficult, however, and donning footwear was next to impossible "Hang on."

Some few minutes later, still barefoot and with my shirt buttoned just enough to cover the bandages, I opened the door to find Valerie standing outside holding a mug of coffee in one hand and Patsy's harness with the other.

"Jeez Louise," she said. "I've known dead people who move faster."

I wiped beads of sweat from my forehead. "Sorry."

"I might have spilled a little." She handed me a half-filled mug. Like the previous days, she wore a long-sleeved top under denim overalls. Today, however, she had added a pair of gold hoop earrings. Her pale face displayed a blemish that reddened her chin, yet failed to detract from her delicate features.

"We missed you at dinner last night. You're probably starving."

"Ravenous." I knelt stiffly to pet the dog and had my face cleaned in return.

"How about giving me your dirty clothes, and I'll wash them for you."

I stared at her. "Really? You'd do that for me?"

"Hand them over," she demanded. "You're meeting with Daddy and Stu in fifteen minutes. Don't be a minute late. I'll have breakfast ready when you're done."

"I'll see you then."

"Not if I see you first."

It was a stale joke when I had first heard it in grade school, but, coming from a blind woman, it stopped me cold.

"C'mon, Patsy," Valerie said. "We've got eggs to fry."

I watched her walk back up the hill, carefully skirting the pond, able to traverse the uneven terrain without a cane. It now appeared more than likely that it had been she, rather than Vonda, who had been my nighttime visitor.

***

"If that was a horse, we'd probably shoot him and bury him right there," Virgil said.

The three of us were standing, hands in pockets, by the John Deere. Virgil wore a red nylon vest over a blue plaid flannel shirt and a pair of dark green chinos stuffed into a pair of black, unbuckled galoshes.

"Nothing sadder looking than a tractor mired in the mud." He sipped coffee from a ceramic commuter mug with a Cadillac logo emblazoned on it.

Stu wore jeans and a plaid flannel shirt under a jacket. I had on my spare jeans and shirt, but my parka and boots were still damp from the previous day even though I had carefully hung them on the chair in front of the tiny heater in the cabin.

The rain had stopped and the kind of dazzling, virgin sky that Southern Californians experience only by getting on an airliner and climbing to thirty thousand feet emerged from among towering cumulus clouds. Above the green hills, sharp-toothed mountains had been freshly dusted with snow. The air was invigorating. My stomach let out a groan.

After unhooking the mower blades, Stu had driven the orange Payloader, nicknamed the Bull, down from the barn. I held one end of a logging chain with the other end wrapped around the John Deere's front axle, while Stu backed the Bull up. I put up a hand to indicate when he should stop, but Stu did not quit backing until the rear of the stubby vehicle rested against my legs.

"Say when," he joked.

I looped the chain over the Bull's trailer hitch and climbed onto the Deere.

"Put it in third gear," Virgil ordered. "When you feel the Bull begin to tug, let out the clutch real slow. Make him pull you out. Don't try to force it."

I did exactly as I was directed, and within seconds the tractor was free.

"That wasn't so bad," Virgil said. He laid an arm over my shoulders. "Let me offer you a bit of advice, son, lest we have to repeat this sorry business with even worse consequences. Next time it starts to rain hard, you park whatever you are riding on. If the equipment don't need maintaining, or the barn need sweeping, you can clear underbrush around the tree line or weed up around the house. When you get a chance, the parking area could use some fresh gravel. There's a pile of it out behind the barn." He nodded in that direction. "When we finally get dried out, it will be time to see to the fence. Stu can show you where we keep the lumber and the paint.

"Later today, the two of you take a shovel and rake and see what you can do to get this sorry-looking patch of earth back into shape. Come mid-April, I do not want there to be any trace that this area was ever torn up. Am I clear?"

Embarrassed by the damage I had caused, I nodded. The damp jacket and frigid air made me shiver.

"Stu, you can pick up a few squares of turf at Skagit Farmers' Supply for the really bad spots. You will need to stake it for a couple of weeks until it gets a good toehold. Now, let's go have some breakfast. This fresh air has given me an appetite."

As Virgil walked back to the house, I climbed down from the tractor to unhitch the Bull. Stu met me by the trailer hitch.

"Doesn't sound like I'll be running out of work anytime soon..." I began. I saw the punch coming and managed to turn my head just enough to take it on the ear instead of the eye. It still managed to stagger me and stung like a bitch.

"Listen up," Stu said. "I can promise that you will never, for one little second, run out of work as long as I'm around. From now on, you better watch what you are doing because I am not taking any more heat for your screw-ups. Give me half a reason and I will fire your ass. Are we clear?"

Still holding one hand to my ear, I nodded.

Following breakfast, I finished mowing in less than an hour with the liberated John Deere. As I drove, I watched Stu working around the three ponds where he appeared to be taking water samples. Then he tossed scoops of feed from sacks he had loaded onto the back of the Bull. The water churned where the meal landed.

My ear still throbbed where Stu had sucker punched me. But the greater injury was to my pride. New job, new rules, I told myself. If I was going to get along successfully with Stu, I needed to keep my ego under wraps and do my homework. Otherwise, I would be a constant target for abuse. But as I watched Stu feeding the trout, a seed of resentment took root—leftover from Heide's betrayal. Every time I thought of Heide's fateful miscalculation, I felt like smashing something. I had a hard time accepting that she had planned the heist over glasses of pinot noir with Jeff, that greedy peacock in a Panama hat.

"Fuck!" I shouted at the sky. There better not be any more punches thrown. My punch card for being victimized was now filled.

When I finished mowing, I returned to the barn to hose off the tractor and hammerknifer. Stu showed up as I was giving the blades a spin to dry them. I turned the key off and climbed down from the tractor. Stu sat on the little riding mower's seat and watched silently as I used an old towel to wipe the tractor dry.

"Looks real nice," he observed. "You planning on taking your date to a drive-in movie? Oh, sorry. You don't have a date." He smiled.

I did not say anything.

"Let's take your truck to go get that turf and get it set in place this morning. If we hurry, you should still have time to do some mowing with the Bull before lunch or before it decides to rain again."

Stu gave directions as I drove the battered Toyota pickup down the hill toward civilization. "Where did you find this piece of crap?"

"It was a good deal."

"I bet," Stu said. He opened the glove compartment and sorted through the handful of papers. "Looks like you forgot to change the title or update your insurance." He studied the registration card. "I imagine Luis Ramirez probably doesn't care one way or the other." He put the card back in the glove box. "Just don't be calling me if you get pulled over by a cop."

How long it would take the cartel to find me, I wondered, if they found the previous owner and managed to trace the Toyota's license. A shiver raced down my spine as I gripped the steering wheel so hard that my knuckles turned white.

Two hours later, the sod was laid in place, encircled by several stakes to which bright yellow nylon rope had been attached. The sun had managed to warm the air by at least ten degrees and the ground was now dry except where it remained in deep shadows from the trees. With the grass already cut to a reasonable length by the hammerknifer, mowing with the Bull turned out to be a relatively swift and simple process. The three gangs of blades cut a wider swath than the other mower and the Bull was faster. A governor prevented the speed from going much over twenty miles an hour, but you could cover a lot of ground at even half that speed, the grass clippings flying up behind like three rooster tails.

The only drawback as I discovered was the lack of a seat belt for the bench seat. It did not take long to find out why the orange machine was called the Bull. Riding it was like riding one of the Brahma bulls in a rodeo. I was mowing at close to full speed when I hit an unseen drainage ditch and was flung from the seat. If I had not been holding onto the steering wheel with both hands, I might have been run over by the spinning blades. As it was, I managed to strike my ribs painfully on the steering wheel. Fortunately, there was no one to see as I stopped the machine, wrapped my arms around my side, and shut my eyes against the pain.

With the Bull's motor turned off, I heard the faint strains of music. Deeper and more mellow than a violin, it swooped and soared over the greensward of the farm like a barn swallow. For several minutes, I forgot about my ribs and everything else as I listened, captivated by the sound coming from the Van de Zilver residence. It sounded like a Placido Domingo album I had sometimes played on Sunday mornings while Heide and I read the newspaper, but without the words. Initially, I assumed it was a recording, but then I heard a bow drawn sharply over the strings as if in frustration and the music abruptly ended.

Shortly after noon, Valerie descended the hill, following a grinning Patsy and carrying a brown paper bag. I stopped the Bull and climbed down to meet her halfway. Lunch was a sandwich with bacon, peanut butter, sweet pickle, and mayonnaise.

"How do you like it?" she asked after I had taken a few bites. She was dressed in her customary overalls and long-sleeved top. Unlike Heide, her hair was long, brown, and naturally curly. Beneath her unflattering, baggy clothes, she was tiny and small-breasted with narrow hips. She was not just petite-sized—even the timbre of her voice was childlike.

"Mmmm," I mumbled between sticky chews. "Very strange. But wonderful."

She grinned. "On the radio, they said it was Elvis' favorite."

"I enjoyed your playing."

She blushed. "Really? You're not just saying that?"

"I thought it was a recording."

"You're lying."

"I never lie," I lied.

"Did you know Mozart played the viola?" she asked, then frowned. "Of course, you didn't. That was stupid of me."

Her face, which had brightened for a moment, darkened again as if one of the clouds that fleeced the sky had passed between it and the sun. "How are you getting along with Stu?"

I sighed.

She stuck the tip of her tongue out. "In case you haven't noticed yet, he's the world's greatest asshole."

"I'm not going to argue."

She cocked her head as if to hear better. "I bet that's the worst thing you ever said about anybody. You are nice, Gray. Too nice. Don't let him push you around."

"Don't worry."

Valerie studied me with that curious manner she had as if hearing much more than what I was saying.

"What are you thinking?" she asked. "Tell me."

As I stared into her half-hidden yet amazing violet eyes, I found myself wanting to confide in her—tell her that Stu was the least of my problems. That being hunted by killers put a whole new perspective on life and its daily ups and downs. But there was no way to mention my troubles without confessing that she could be in mortal danger if the cartel discovered my location. And that could easily result in her saying something to her father, which would mean the end of my stay.

"Nothing," I said. "Thanks for the sandwich. And the concert."

Valerie smiled, her unseeing eyes now closed.

"After a while, crocodile," she said. Then she set off toward the house with Patsy leading her.

After mowing, I parked the Bull in the barn. I was dead tired and sore, but found my spirits renewed. A day that begun so badly had been redeemed by Valerie and her music.

I felt extremely fortunate to have found the trout farm. When I was in dire need of a job and a place to stay, the Van de Zilvers had taken me in and, except for Stu, treated me well. With no friends or family that I could now communicate without putting them in danger and myself at risk, I was deeply grateful. I determined that I would do whatever necessary to assure Virgil and Stu, if possible, that I could handle the job even if it meant researching subjects like farm maintenance and trout rearing.

After living in crowded Orange County, there was something healing in the basic, nearly primitive life at the farm that appealed to me. I liked the smell of evergreens, cut grass, and clean mountain air. I liked seeing my breath in the morning. The rugged beauty of the trout farm was night-and-day different from the postage-stamp-sized, manicured lawns and gardens of Southern California.

As I approached the large pond that fronted my cabin, motion in the dark water near the island caught my attention. Whatever it was, it had not broken the surface. It seemed far too large for a trout, and I wondered for the second time if a muskrat or beaver had made the pond its home.

CHAPTER FOURTEEN

I showered for dinner, letting the hot water run until there was no more. While drying off, I observed myself in the mirror. The red-black bruises on my arm and rib area were turning blue and yellow. The nicks in my face from the speedboat's bullet-shattered windshield were mostly gone. I could use a haircut, but it would have to wait a few more days. The beard that Heide had encouraged me to grow now seemed like a silly affectation and another link to the past. I searched in my bag for a shaving kit.

Vonda was the last to arrive at the dinner table after stopping to pour a glass of wine.

"My goodness, Gray," she said. "Who would have guessed there was a cute man hiding under all that facial hair. Too bad you cannot see him, Val."

Virgil and Stu studied me as if seeing me for the first time.

"You shaved?" Valerie asked.

"Got tired of seeing myself in the mirror. Not to mention dealing with the itch." I brushed my hair back with my hands and hoped they would not notice the lack of socks and untied shoes or, if they did, would attribute my fashion sense—or lack of it—to being from Southern California. Putting on socks and tying the laces on my shoes was still too painful due to my damaged ribs.

The dinner conversation revolved around Saturday's lotto which, according to Vonda, had reached over two hundred eighty million dollars.

"It's all anyone could talk about at the office today," she said. "I swear, everyone at the bank was withdrawing their life savings to buy lotto tickets."

"You're kidding," Virgil said. "Why would they do such a foolish thing?"

"Same reason I would," Vonda said. "First thing tomorrow, I'm going to buy forty tickets."

Virgil laid down his knife and fork and frowned.

"Waste of money," Stu said. "You've got better odds of being struck by lightning than winning the lotto."

"It's my money," she said. "I'll waste it if I want to."

"What would you do with all that money if you won?" Valerie asked.

"What would I do?" Vonda's face lit up. "First thing I'd do is take a little trip to Mexico, stay in the best hotels, see all the places Momma talked about." She clutched her wine glass like it was a bird that might fly away. The *rosé* glittered blood-red in the light of the overhead lamp. "Then I'd pick out a Mercedes Benz. A big silver convertible with red leather seats."

"What else?" Valerie said.

"And then, my dear, I would buy a whole new wardrobe: dresses, shoes, silky pajamas and underwear. Maybe the entire Victoria's Secret catalogue."

As she shimmied her shoulders beneath her t-shirt, I was struck by the differences in the sisters' demeanor. My mother had loved dragging me to horticultural events when I was a kid. The knowledge had come in handy later while working for the landscaping firm, where matching the pots of flowers to the names of plants indicated on a rendering was a requirement. Whereas Valerie reminded me of a shy cornflower, Vonda was like a bold, sensuous calla lily.

"You'd be out of money in less than two weeks," Stu said.

"With what you earn maybe, but not with that much money," Vonda said.

"Couldn't you shop on the interest?" Valerie asked. "Keep the rest in the bank?"

"Now there's a smart girl," Vonda said. "You can be my money manager."

Valerie stared unseeing at the bowl of leftover mashed potatoes sitting in the middle of the table.

"Could you buy me some tickets, too?" she asked.

"You kids are crazy," Virgil said.

I agreed with him but said nothing. I wondered what they would say if they knew there was a hundred million up for grabs sitting in a bank in the Cayman Islands. I recalled what Catania had said about the problem of locating the money. How many banks could there be— twenty, fifty, a hundred? And how difficult would it be to find the correct bank, discover the account name, and password for where the money was hidden? On the other hand, I thought the odds had to be at least as good or better than winning the lotto.

"C'mon, Daddy," Vonda coaxed. "We're just having fun. Doesn't cost anything to dream. What would you buy?"

"Guess maybe if I had that kind of money to throw around, I'd get a new Cadillac." He nodded absently and stroked his chin. "You know, when your mom was still alive, I had this idea of getting one of those big motor homes—the kind you see going down the road with a satellite dish on top and towing a small car or boat. But that was a long time ago."

"Yea, Daddy! He's my traveling man." Vonda raised her glass in a toast. "Forget about the lottery. Why don't we buy that motorhome and all travel to Mexico at the end of the season? Call it a reward for all our hard work?"

Virgil pursed his lips in a way that looked like he was giving the idea some thought.

I remained silent, remembering Heide's face as she died and all that needless bloodshed for an insane dream of money.

Boom. Flash. "I fucked up."

"How about you, honeybunch," Vonda said, running her fingers playfully through the hair on the back of Stu's neck. "What would you do if you won all that money?"

"Knowing Stu, he'd probably buy a six-pack and some beef jerky," Valerie said.

Vonda threw back her head and laughed. Stu cocked his hand like a gun, squinted, and fired at Valerie, a gesture she was unable to see, but likely anticipated.

"I'd find four hundred acres someplace in Montana or Idaho," Stu said, "where they don't even have roads. Then I would build a big log cabin with a view of the mountains and pull up the draw bridge. Any strangers showed up, they'd be shot on sight."

"Ugh." Vonda grimaced. "Remind me again, why exactly did I marry you?"

She turned toward Valerie. "How about you, little sister?"

Everyone turned to look at her. For the first time since I had met her, she was wearing lipstick and her hair was parted. I wondered if she had managed this herself, or if Vonda had helped her.

"Music," Valerie said. "Lots of classical music. Some new pots and pans and a greenhouse so I could grow my own herb garden."

"Why Valerie," Vonda said. "What a spendthrift you are."

Stu chuckled. "We're all talking about what to do with more than two hundred million and Sis here can't come up with stuff that costs more than a few hundred bucks."

"Buy me forty tickets, too, Vonda," Valerie said. "I'll get the money after I clean up the dishes."

"Damn right, girl," Vonda said.

"Wouldn't that just take the cake?" Stu said. "It would be blind luck if you won, pardon my pun."

"I'd also find a nice place to live," Valerie announced.

Silence settled uncomfortably around the table. Vonda

sipped from her wine. I noticed Virgil was frowning.

"Doesn't anybody want to stay here beside me?" he asked.

"What's to stay for?" Vonda asked. "Mildew? Senility?"

"Someplace in a city," Valerie continued, her eyes closed. "An apartment over a bakery so I could wake up every day and smell bread and cinnamon rolls baking. It would have lots of big windows to let the sun in and a cage full of canaries to sing for me. Patsy and I would take long walks every day."

Vonda looked confused. "But who'd watch out for you?"

Valerie frowned. "Why Patsy, of course."

"She means who'd take care of you, Sis?" Stu repeated.

"What's that supposed to mean?" Anger flashed in Valerie's voice. "Who does the cooking and cleaning around here? I'm the one taking care of you guys and getting no respect for it." She smacked her open palms on the table. A spoon flipped onto the ground. I could see it glittering beneath the table, but resisted reaching for it, having learned the hard way not to help unless asked.

"You can't even write a check," Stu added.

"For your information, I can write digital checks with my computer. And if I had all that money, I would not need a damn checkbook, would I? And one more thing." She stood up quickly, her face flushed. "I won't be going on any family trips to Mexico. C'mon, Patsy."

She grabbed the dog's halter, and they left the room.

Right then and there I decided if I ever did find that hundred million, I would give some of it to Valerie. Maybe even buy her an apartment in Paris.

Virgil picked his napkin off his lap and laid it on the table. "I saw this coming. All this talk about money—money you do not even have. Remember what the Bible says, 'You cannot serve both God and money.' All it does is cause trouble."

He pushed his chair back with a screech, stood, and headed for the living room.

"Think I'll join Virgil," Stu said.

"Wait a minute, hon." Vonda looked at me. "We haven't heard from Gray yet."

During the conversation, I had silently continued eating and watching the others. Table warfare made me as uncomfortable as a jackrabbit in a pack of coyotes. My father had frequently used dinnertime as a boxing match. Meanwhile, my mother just sat there, drinking straight shots of vodka, and not saying a word.

"Yeah," Stu said, amused. "Let's hear what fuck-up would do with all that money."

"I don't know," I said. "I guess I'd be happy with what you already have."

Vonda leaned back, a look of surprise upon her face. "Sounds like he wants our trout farm."

In the silence that followed, you could hear the television in the living room. It was evidently a good time to buy a Toyota. "Our dealers won't be outsold," a voice enthused.

"I'm sorry." I felt my newly naked face grow warm. "That came out sounding all wrong. I meant I would like to have a family someday. A quiet home in the country. A fireplace and a yard with a picnic table. Maybe even a horse or pony for the kids to ride."

Vonda was not the only one who was surprised. This was news to me as well. Obviously, there was not a chance in hell of this happening. Not now. Not with a cartel hunting for me and eager to kill not only me, but anyone harboring me. But, as I was discovering, dreams do not die easy. Even unrealistic ones. Uproot one and another was sure to spring up to take its place.

"Not me," Vonda said. "I've got to get out of here before I get old and moldy. As far as I am concerned, Gray, you can have the farm." She stood and headed to the refrigerator. "All you have to do is win the lotto and it's yours."

The speculation finally at an end, she and Stu disappeared into the living room.

I had not noticed Valerie's return until she spoke. "Are you going to help me, or not?"

I began gathering dishes and carrying them to the sink. "Want me to load the dishwasher this time?"

"Okay."

She returned a minute later from the table with another load. Evidently, no one picked up after themselves at the Van de Zilver residence.

"I liked what you said," Valerie said when we were alone.

"About what?"

"About having a family and a picnic table and a pony and stuff." She rinsed the empty bowl in the sink. "It sounded nice."

"I thought your idea of living over a bakery sounded good, too. That's where the writers and artists lived in Paris back in the early 1900s. People like Ezra Pound, Fitzgerald, Gertrude Stein, James Joyce, Hemingway. They called them garrets."

Valerie smiled. Heide's large, bleached teeth had illuminated an entire room when she smiled or laughed. Valerie's smile on the other hand displayed small, even teeth that transformed her face into the first note of a quiet melody.

I looked out the window to the backyard. The light from the distant cabin glimmered, a lonely beacon in the dark cosmos. How long if ever, I wondered, until Heide's death did not seize my heart in its frozen embrace?

"Would your kids be able to take music lessons?" Valerie's voice interrupted my despair.

"My kids?" It took me a second to understand that she was referring to the conversation at the dinner table. "Oh, sure. Music, dance, art, whatever they wanted."

Valerie was silent as she washed pans. "You don't act like someone who lost a person they loved very much."

"What?" I stared at her in surprise. "What do you mean?"

"I didn't eat for more than a week after my mother died."

"You're kidding."

She blushed, something she did frequently. "They took me to the hospital and stuck a tube down my throat."

She rinsed the pan and placed it carefully on the plastic drain board with the others. "Didn't you ever wish you were dead or want to hurt yourself? Or maybe hurt someone else?"

I thought it was a strange question coming from Valerie. On the other hand, I could now better understand wanting to hurt someone. Catania said they found a fair amount of blood in the smaller speedboat which I had plowed into. I remembered little of the collision, other than being tossed into the air, hearing an eerie scream as a body sailed overhead, and then waking in the hospital following a crash landing that knocked me out. I hoped the woman who had shot me and killed Heide was still lying at the bottom of Newport Harbor. The last thing I needed was for the crazy bitch to track me down for a little payback.

When I did not answer, Valerie hurried to fill the awkward silence that followed. "I'm sorry. It's not something I should talk about. Forget it."

Vonda showed up to pour herself another glass of wine. "Aren't you guys done yet?"

"Just finishing," I said, still disconcerted by the painful memory Valerie's question had raised.

Vonda leaned in close to rinse her glass. She smelled of alcohol and Angel perfume. It had been Heide's favorite fragrance. "Why don't you come out and join us, Gray? Be a part of our big, happy family?"

"What about me?" Valerie said. "Aren't I invited?"

"That depends." Vonda hugged her sister with her free arm. "Don't go screwing up this Mexico trip. I've waited too long for a vacation like this to have you do your PMS number and blow the whole thing."

The news was still on the television when I entered the living room. Vonda was curled up next to her father in his La-Z-Boy, a fresh glass of wine in her hand. Stu was alone on the couch reading a car magazine. Valerie sat in an overstuffed chair in a floral pattern at least two decades old that echoed the couch. That left sharing the couch with Stu or a vacant rocking chair. I chose the chair.

Since Heide's death, I had not had the opportunity or the urge to watch television. As I watched the local news, I found it depressing to learn that the drugs, gangs, and violence that plagued Southern California had likewise infected Sedro-Woolley and its surrounding neighbors. You would think that people who lived in such a breathtaking natural environment would be more in tune with health and exercise than needing to shoot up to get high.

Vonda made a derogatory comment about a television commercial. I did not say anything. Since sitting in a front-row seat to personal tragedy, I now found my former career ambition as an art director too unattainable to defend.

The news program ended a few minutes later. Virgil clicked off the television with the remote control. "Let's hear some music. How about playing the Theme?"

Vonda stood and stretched. "Must be time for a bath."

Valerie slid a CD into the multimedia player. Virgil shut his eyes as the first movements of a familiar piano concerto began to play.

"What is that?" I asked.

"Rachmaninov's Rhapsody on a Theme by Paganini," Valerie whispered. "It was Momma's favorite."

The music was gorgeous. It took me a few minutes to identify where I had heard it. Then I remembered it from an old Marilyn Monroe movie I had downloaded from Netflix.

When at last the music ended, Virgil sighed, and I thought he saw him wipe his eyes with a handkerchief. "Now you, darlin'," he said. "You play."

"Oh, Daddy," she protested. "I can't really play this. It's not meant for viola."

"Yes, you can," he said. "Please play for me, sweetheart."

Valerie brought a case out of the bedroom. She removed a viola whose wood gleamed with a rich, golden patina. She plucked each of the strings to tune them and then, without fanfare, began to play the melody we had listened to just a few moments earlier. As she drew the bow across the strings, the sound was richer, fuller, and huskier than a violin. Valerie played with such passion that I found the hairs tingling on the back of my neck. A frown line etched her forehead and her violet eyes stared into a world I could not see or imagine.

"Encore," I said when she had finished.

"That was lovely, darlin,'" Virgil said.

"Beautiful," I added.

"Oh, she can play all right."

I looked up to see Vonda leaning against the doorway in a bathrobe, her hair wrapped in a towel. She held her blood-red wine glass as if to study it in the light.

"My little sister can play like nobody's business. Too bad she can't see."

Valerie flushed.

"Can't play in an orchestra if you can't see the conductor." She smiled. "Ain't that right, Val?"

Valerie laid the viola carefully in its case, latched it, and disappeared into her bedroom.

CHAPTER FIFTEEN

The next day following dinner, I was washing pans, grateful that the day was nearly done when Vonda entered the kitchen. Valerie had excused herself to take a shower, leaving me to finish the dishes and tidy up. Suddenly, Vonda was there watching me over the top of her ever-present wine glass.

"Can I get you something?" I asked.

She wore a cotton t-shirt and a pair of faded jeans. Her feet were bare, and I noted that her toenails were now brown. Her blond hair, worn in a tight bun when she had left for her job at the insurance agency that morning, now hung down around her slender shoulders.

"Maybe," she said. "What did you have in mind?" She studied the remaining wine in the light as if judging its worth, before finishing it in one large swig. "Not bad for a box wine."

I smiled and went back to washing the pan.

"Mind washing this?" Vonda asked as she placed her now empty glass in the dishwater. She ran a soapy hand down my arm. Her fingers slid over mine.

"I like watching a man work with his hands."

I stared at her in surprise. Was she flirting with me while her husband watched the news in the next room? It was obviously a joke, except Vonda was not laughing. She scooped up a handful of suds and dribbled them along my arm from just above my elbow to my wrist. Then she traced her fingers up along the ridge of my arm until the rolled-up sleeve of my shirt stopped her. Sweat broke out on my forehead, and I suddenly felt like a kid in junior high dance class.

"I swear, you are so talkative," she whispered. "I know you're alive 'cause I can hear your heart beating."

"Vonda," Stu's voice called from the other room.

"Yes, sweetie?"

She pressed her breast against my arm, her pelvis against my hip, and I backed away. Since Heide had died, a Novocain-like numbness had suffused my brain. It was as if Heide had taken a part of me with her, leaving behind a refugee incapable of thinking beyond the most basic and immediate needs for survival. Now, the smell of Vonda's perfume and her sexual teasing brought back the horror of watching my wife die while choking on her own blood.

"Where the hell did you disappear to?" Stu called.

"Just getting a refill," she called back. "Can I get you anything? Another beer?" She dried her hands on the front of my shirt. "What's the matter, Gray?" she whispered, "No desire?"

"You're drunk."

"Being drunk doesn't even begin to acknowledge my problems." She retrieved another glass from a cabinet and poured wine from a box in the fridge.

Stu appeared in the doorway. "What is taking you so long?" His eyes swung from Vonda to me.

"I was just asking Gray why he bothers to wash dishes. I don't recall it being part of his job description."

"I don't care what extra chores he does," Stu replied. "As long as he gets his maintenance work done, it's fine by me."

"Then so be it," Vonda said. "We got ourselves a Jack-of-all-trades. Goodnight, Gray." She took Stu's arm with her free hand and they disappeared into the living room.

The next thing I knew, Valerie was standing beside me

dressed in a shabby chenille robe, her hair still wet and uncombed.

"What was Vonda doing here?"

"Just getting more wine. Are she and Stu not getting along?"

"Not since he graduated from being a part-time prick to full-time." Her eyes were closed, but she was facing me as if watching my mouth and listening to every syllable. "Did she say anything about me?"

"Why would she?"

"She likes to make snide comments about me like the one last night about not being able to see the conductor. I can hear the conductor tapping the baton before starting. That is all that matters. I know the music as well or better than he does."

"I don't doubt it."

She reached out and touched my face with her fingers. Her fingers traced my cheek, then lingered on my lips. "Thank you."

"For what?"

"For being here. For letting me 'see' you."

On the way down to the cabin, I considered the obvious competitiveness between the sisters. I also thought about Vonda's question. There wasn't a simple answer why I appreciated helping Valerie with the dishes at night. How could I explain my gratitude for hiring me and giving me a place to stay without giving up my identity and the danger I was putting them in? Or, how a simple, mindless task like washing dishes could help prevent the howling of my heart from drowning me in despair.

***

Any idiot can make a sandwich. Even someone who is blind. It is just about the most stupid, simple, boring thing there is. I always try to add something different—maybe even unique—for Gray. I want him to know he is special to me, more than Stu, Vonda, or even Daddy. I can only do so much since Vonda buys the groceries. Even if I print out a list from my computer with its Braille keyboard, she often does not pay attention to it. Consequently, we are always running out of things like coffee or toilet paper. Then I need to have the missing supplies delivered which is costly, seeing as how far out we live.

Going from cooking for Gray to doing his laundry was the most natural thing in the world. I enjoy making his things clean for him. Before I wash them, I like to breathe in the smell of his clothes. I already feel like he is my mate. He just does not know it yet. But he will soon if I have my way. And if Vonda doesn't manage to fuck it up somehow.

"Whose clothes are those?" she asked when I was folding his laundry to take to him.

"They're Gray's. I washed them for him."

"Jesus, Valerie," she said. "Stu and Daddy know about this? Gray has not even been here a week and you are already making his lunches and washing his clothes. What's next? Making his bed? Or was you thinking of maybe sleeping in it, too?"

"Don't be silly." I felt the heat spreading on my face and neck. "I'm just helping him out while he's getting settled."

"Well, a word of advice, dear sister. Don't be counting your chickens before they hatch."

"What's that supposed to mean?"

She did not answer. I heard her footsteps as she left.

It was only later when I went to carry Gray's clean clothes down to him that I realized she had taken them. "You fucking bitch!"

***

I woke to a clamor, a noise so raucous that further sleep

was impossible. It sounded as if the cabin were surrounded by an army of frogs. How on earth had I missed this racket before? Then I recalled how quickly I had dropped off to sleep on my first few nights in the cabin, too exhausted to notice the late-night cacophony.

I got up and reached for a pair of jeans, wincing from the lingering pain in my ribs as I tugged them on and pulled the wool blanket over my shoulders. An abrupt silence fell over the amphibious assemblage as I stepped out onto the porch. There was a brief interlude and then the concert resumed, fortissimo.

A solitary star flickered among the clouds in the moonless sky before it winked out. I turned my attention to the hill where indistinct black shapes marked the house, barn, and trees. I touched my arm beneath the blanket where Vonda's breast had rested earlier. I could still smell the Angel perfume and feel the heat of her breath against my throat. I wondered if her husband, Stu, was among the "problems" that she referred to. Vonda was just drunk and playing around, I decided, and I would do well to avoid her. The last thing I needed at this precarious time in my life was to get mixed up with a married woman, especially a woman married to Stu.

I wondered what the cartel killers were doing. Had they forgotten all about me? Or were they even now somehow piecing together where I had gone? I recalled the camera chip with the photo of whatever it was that Heide had not wanted me to see. Valerie had washed my jeans. Nervously, I reached a finger into the change pocket and determined that the chip was still there. I looked again at the starless night sky, then let out a long sigh.

Back under the covers, I shivered uncontrollably while waiting for the bedding to warm up and sleep to return. Bone-tired as I was, it was not a long wait.

At breakfast the next morning, I mentioned the frogs.

"Frogs?" Virgil halted a waffle-loaded fork midway to his

mouth. "What frogs?"

I waited for a moment to make sure I was not being made sport of. "You haven't heard them?"

"Not me. You hear 'em, Val?"

"Sure."

"Really? What about you, Stu?"

"I can barely hear anything what with Vonda's snoring," Stu said.

"Very many?" Virgil asked.

"You've got your own amphibian choir."

Vonda walked in, dressed for work in a blouse, jacket, and short skirt, her high heels clicking on the linoleum floor. Stu turned in his chair as he made an obvious point of noticing her legs.

"What was that about a choir?" she asked.

"Dude says he heard a few frogs last night," Stu said.

"Couple of glasses of wine in the evening and I wouldn't know if there were a hundred yodelers and clog dancers next to the bed." She smiled at me. "You ought to try it."

"Couple of glasses?" Stu said. "More like a quart, I'd say. While you are passed out, I cannot sleep, thanks to all the thrashing around and snoring. Where did you get the skirt?"

"It's an old one. Like it?" She made a pose that displayed her legs. They were nice legs.

"Kind of short for work, ain't it?"

Vonda sat down and straightened her skirt with her hands. "This ain't nothing. You should see what the other girls wear."

"I don't care what the other girls wear," Stu said. "I didn't marry them."

"Oh, don't be so picky." She nudged him playfully.

Stu kept his head down as he continued to eat.

"I'll change if it really bothers you."

"What do you want to eat, Miss Universe? We ran out of caviar," Valerie said.

I looked up from my scrambled eggs, but Vonda appeared

either not to notice her sister's sarcasm, or not to care. "Just toast and coffee, thanks."

"In case you haven't noticed," Valerie said, "I've been up since five making breakfast while you slept in."

"You're lucky you don't have to work for a living," Vonda said.

"Yeah, lucky me," Valerie replied.

"Have you tried the blueberry preserves, Gray?" Vonda stuck her finger in the jar and licked it. "Positively yummy."

"In case nobody noticed, we got a weekend coming up," Virgil announced. "Opening Day is just six weeks away."

Virgil's revelation rechanneled my attention. Since Heide's death, without a computer or cell phone to refer to, I could never remember what day it was. The truth was when you finally stripped life down to its most basic ingredients, coping became as simple—or as complicated—as surviving the next twenty-four hours.

"That means we need to gather up all the grass clippings, so they don't lie there too long and kill the grass," Virgil continued. "Stu will show you where we dump the sweeper. After we open, weekends will be our two busiest days, so Mondays and Tuesdays will be your days off, unless there is a holiday. Then it'll be Tuesday and Wednesday."

He turned his attention to Stu. "Monday, if the weather holds up, we ought to see about getting some fertilizer on the grass."

Stu nodded. "I was planning to use a little ammonium nitrate on it as soon as we get all the grass clippings picked up."

Virgil pointed a finger at me. "Remember to stay away from the uphill side of the ponds, Gray. If it rains and that stuff gets into the water, we could lose all our fish. Fertilizer is deadly."

"Don't you go killing off our fish, Gray," Vonda said with a wink. "Save them for our guests."

Virgil started to say something but was cut off by a scream. All heads including Patsy's turned toward the kitchen. There was a sob followed by a gasp of pain. Chairs scraped against the floor as everyone rose from the table. Valerie appeared at the entrance to the kitchen, her face even more pale than normal.

"My hand." She held up her right hand with her left. The slender blade of a fillet knife protruded from both sides. Blood ran in a rivulet down her arm.

"Lord have mercy," Virgil said.

"I'm going to puke," Vonda said.

Stu reached her first. "Hold still," he ordered. He gripped her hand with one of his own and pulled the knife free. Blood filled her palm and dripped onto the floor.

I caught Valerie as her knees buckled and she slid to the floor. Blood darkened the front of her overalls where she clutched her wounded hand in her good one.

Flash. Boom.

I recalled Heide's face as the blood sprayed from her mouth. I shook my head to prevent the horrific memory from overwhelming it.

"Here's a towel for the blood," Vonda said. She tried putting her arm around her sister, but Valerie shrunk from her touch as if scalded.

"I'll get the car," Virgil said. "Someone get her bandaged up so she don't bleed on everything, and we'll make a quick run to the ER."

I squatted by Valerie with a dish towel and began to wrap her hand. "What happened?"

Valerie's eyelids fluttered. "I was in a hurry," she said. "Damn that hurts," she added, a note of surprise in her voice. "I was reaching for a spoon and jammed the blade of the knife into my hand. Someone must have put it in the dishwasher the wrong way."

Stu looked at me. "You loaded it. I saw you."

His accusing tone stung me to the quick. "I didn't put that knife in there."

"Like hell you didn't," Stu said.

"Ease up," Vonda said. "You don't know for sure it was Gray,"

We heard the Cadillac come up the drive, engine roaring.

"Let's get her in the car," Stu said.

I scooped Valerie up, ignoring the stabbing pain in my ribs, and carried her out the door. Although she weighed less than Heide had by at least thirty or forty pounds, I was breathing hard by the time I reached the car. Virgil held the rear passenger door open and I set her carefully on the seat.

"I'm sorry," I said, my voice ragged from exertion and pain. "I swear I don't remember putting that knife in there."

Her upper lip trembled as a single large tear plummeted down her cheek.

"Stay here," Virgil said. "We'll talk about this later."

As I watched them drive away, the last thing I saw was Valerie's pale face in the rear passenger window.

CHAPTER SIXTEEN

It did not take long to figure out how to hook up the large sweeper behind the Bull. Once it was full, however, I did not have a clue where to empty the grass clippings. I tried to ignore the tumult in my brain from Virgil's parting words, Valerie's accident, and Heide's death to focus on where the obvious location for a compost heap would be. I remembered the pile of gravel Virgil had mentioned. It seemed like a good place to begin looking.

To the rear of the barn was a much smaller metal building with a double-wide garage door as well as a regular door. Both were locked. Around back, I found the gravel and a couple of old tires, also a small window with security bars. Curiosity aroused, I tried peeking inside, but plywood had been nailed over the inside of the glass.

A brief search turned up a neglected driveway overgrown with what I recognized from my previous landscaping job as thistle, timothy, and bromegrass, which quickly disappeared into a tangle of trees and dense, shrubby undergrowth. Lacking better options, I followed it.

The further I progressed into the damp and shady forest, the less promising the trail became. A pair of chickadees called back and forth and then fell silent as I approached. Ancient tire tracks were littered with fallen tree branches and the rotting trunk of a downed tree whose bark had long since fallen off, exposing the inner wood now infested with grubs. I was about to retrace my route back the way I had come when I spotted a large shape stored beneath a blue canvas tarpaulin.

On closer inspection, I learned that it was a wooden cabin cruiser. It appeared to have once been a well-made boat with attractive lines and a roomy cabin. Now, green mold discolored the peeling white paint and blackberry brambles had overgrown the stern on one side of the land-locked derelict. The tarpaulin cover was bleached almost white and the seams were splitting. I pulled a thorny cane back carefully from the stern until I was able to read the name printed in faded red script: *Lucky Lady, Anacortes.*

I rested a hand on the boat as I pondered my current prospect. Above the canopy of tree branches, multi-storied clouds floated among a pale blue sky. I was no closer to finding the compost pile, not that it really mattered anymore. I was not looking forward to the meeting with Virgil.

Under normal conditions, I knew I was not stupid enough to put a carving knife in the dishwasher blade up. But my mind was still operating at half-power and subject to brownouts when overloaded so that I could not be sure that I had not done it.

"Neither of us appears to be very lucky right now," I said to the abandoned cruiser.

Stu was waiting for me back at his desk in the barn.

"Where you been?" he asked. "Taking a nap?"

"I was looking for the compost pile to dump the clippings. How's Valerie?"

"A couple of stitches and a fair amount of pain but missed the tendon. Won't be able to use that hand for a month though, so we will get a little break from the viola playing. Can't say as I mind."

He shook his head, smiling to himself. "I knew you were a fuck-up from the first day I saw you, but that upside-down knife in the dishwasher took the cake. That was a nasty thing to do."

Same old Stu.

"Where's Virgil?" I figured I might as well get this over.

Virgil chose that moment to appear at the door to the barn.

"What's going on here?" he asked. "You show Gray where to dump the grass yet?"

"Not yet," Stu said.

"Then maybe I better. I expect you have got more important things to do. C'mon son. Let's take a walk."

We walked in silence past the large pond and the cabin toward the northeast corner of the property.

"You and Stu getting along?" Virgil asked.

I shrugged. "We disagree about a few things."

"The accident being one of them, I suppose," Virgil said. "I'll be honest, young man. When I left home this morning, I was going to fire you. Not a doubt in my mind. Sitting in the hospital waiting room, I had time to calm down and think a little."

He looked over at me. "Doesn't mean I ain't going to fire you. Just means I am willing to talk, maybe ask a few questions. That sound fair enough?"

I nodded. I thought it sounded more than fair, even if I had not consciously put the knife in the dishwasher blade up.

"I like the work you've done so far. No one can say you don't put in a full eight hours and then some. Other than that mess with the John Deere getting caught in the soup, you've shown yourself to be a hard worker, someone who doesn't spend half their time complaining.

"Now I know you didn't mean to mire that tractor or hurt Valerie, but you can't be making mistakes like that around here without seriously injuring somebody sooner or later, maybe even yourself." He paused. "Tell me something. Did you have anything to do with your wife getting killed? Was you driving the car she was in?"

Virgil's suspicion—no matter how misplaced—mortified me so that my ears burned, and the roots of my hair twitched.

"No!"

"I didn't think so, but with everything that's going on, I had to ask," Virgil said.

"Jesus, Virgil," I said, but Virgil put up a hand to cut me off. We entered the tree line and stood at the edge of a large, musty-smelling mound of compost.

"You'll get your chance to speak in a moment, after you hear the rest of what I've got to say. I'll make it short and sweet. You can leave today. Come up to the house and I'll write you a check for the entire month, even though you only worked a few days. Or you can choose to stay. But if you do, you got to promise me there ain't going to be any more mistakes. Because anything more goes wrong and, so help me, I will not ask questions, I will just fire you. Understood?"

I stared at the ground.

"So, which is it?" Virgil asked.

Humiliated by Virgil's reprimand, I was tempted to throw my few things into the back of the Toyota and drive off. But, as I had determined just a few days earlier, I did not have anywhere else to go. And besides, failure made a lousy traveling companion.

"I'm staying."

"Then let me give you one more additional piece of advice. You might be smarter than Stu. You might even be a faster, better fighter, though I would bet against it. But he is my son-in-law and, for better or worse, as long as my daughter is married to him, he calls the shots. So, to the best of your ability, stay out of his way. Don't go stirring up trouble or you won't be doing either of us any favors. I have to cut him a little slack because he's family. I don't have any reason to do the same for you. You get my meaning?"

"Sure."

"Good." Virgil surprised me by clapping me on the back.

"Then you best get back to sweeping if you aim to get done before the weekend."

"Thanks," I said. We began walking back up the hill. "Valerie is going to be okay?"

"She'll get by. Going to slow down her viola-playing for a while though. And dinners might be frozen food for a few days."

"I can cook."

Virgil looked over his shoulder at me. "You're just full of surprises, ain't you?"

CHAPTER SEVENTEEN

As crime boss Whitey Bulger and his wife had proved, with its agglomeration of immigrants, indigenes, and transients, one could abide in relative anonymity in Southern California. People drove in and out of their garages without ever seeing or knowing their neighbors. Unless you belonged to the same gym, shopped in the same grocery store, or exercised your pooch in the same park, you might never see the same person twice in a decade—or maybe even a lifetime. Conversely, I had forgotten what it was like to live in a small town where everybody knew everybody else's business, the more sordid, the better. Once you got the hang of it, knew who to go to, and—most important—how to ask a question without appearing to want to know the answer, there was almost nothing you could not find out.

Saturday morning at the Van de Zilver household was a culinary disaster. Nauseous from pain medication, Valerie retired to her room with Patsy, leaving Vonda bleary-eyed and grouchy in the kitchen.

"Why are you still here?" she shouted at me from the smoke-encircled stove where bacon was being cremated. "Haven't you caused enough trouble for this family? Who is your next target?"

"Careful, Von," Stu said. "He has probably booby-trapped

the garbage disposal."

After offering to help make breakfast and being turned down, I excused myself and drove down the hill to Sedro-Woolley. In addition to wanting to review the photos stored on the camera chip, I hoped to find information at the local library on raising trout and, if I was lucky, something about Cayman Islands' banks. I was due for a haircut and I had a list of items to buy for dinner. But first, I needed to find a place to eat and salvage what crumbs were left of my peace of mind.

Annie's Homestyle Country Cooking was humming with customers. Whenever the door opened, an enticing smell of vanilla and cinnamon would escape. I had to hover on the sidewalk for over ten minutes before hearing my name called and getting a table. The wait gave me an opportunity to observe the entire eight blocks of Metcalf Street, which constituted the center of downtown and was bustling with cars, trucks, and people. Several vehicles sported Canadian license plates with their prominent maple leaf. In addition to the freeway, the street was linked to the North Cascade Highway which meant the frequent traffic of visitors seeking gas and a rest stop mingled with the occasional diesel chatter of logging trucks. Finding a parking place took speed, courage, and no small amount of luck.

Once I was seated, it was another ten minutes before the server arrived to pour coffee and take my order. Her hair was magenta and black, she wore a black top and pants that matched her nails, and her ears bore enough earrings, plus one safety pin, to launch a kiosk jewelry business. Her slippered feet were tattooed with opposing Asian cats and cherry blossoms. Her name badge identified the woman as the owner, Annie.

"What's going on today in town?" I asked after ordering.

"First day of our tulip festival. Where you from, Jupiter?" With that, she disappeared.

"Seriously, where are you from?" she asked when she

appeared several minutes later with a plate-sized stack of Swedish pancakes. Annie's obviously had not yet heard about portion control. "You don't sound like you're from the provinces. Please don't say you're from California."

"What's wrong with people from California?" I whispered. It was highly unlikely that a member of the Sinaloa Cartel was having breakfast at Annie's in Sedro-Woolley this morning, but I saw no reason to test the odds.

"Number one: they're rude; think they're so smart with their Porches, pinot noir, and skinny-assed girlfriends." She blew the hair that had fallen into her eyes. "Second, they spend too much money on homes around here which makes it impossible for us locals to ever hope to own anything."

With a flick of her fingers, she disappeared into the kitchen. While heads at a few surrounding tables turned to see who the latest carpetbagger was, I focused on breakfast.

The pancakes were incredibly thin and the lingonberries that covered them tasted both sweet and tart and I decided I would be eating here Saturday mornings for the rest of my life, or until the Surgeon General shut the place down as a health hazard. Then I recalled how much Heide enjoyed finding such places and how she even fantasized about starting her own café. A carved "Heide's Cafe" sign had hung above our kitchen window, a fact I had forgotten until now.

"What's the matter?" Annie asked. "Something wrong with the food?"

I realized I had been staring at the food without eating. "No, it's great. I just zoned out for a minute. Sorry."

She refilled my coffee cup. "Don't mind me being so nosy. Being curious helps relieve the boredom," she said. "Besides, it's obvious you're not from California.

For a half-second, I thought she was talking about my race. But then she added, "Your boots are dirty."

I decided to ease her mind. Besides, I was enjoying her opinionated commentary. "I work up at the Van de Zilver place. Know it?"

"Course I do. You can't grow up here and run a restaurant without knowing everybody in the Skagit Valley. How's Vonda doing? She still married to that asshole, Stu? Tell her Annie said 'Hi. We should go have fun some night. That's if I can ever find a babysitter old enough to look after my boys and young enough not to be smokin' weed or shooting up.'"

Later, as another young woman approached with a coffee pot, Annie intercepted her. "I got this one."

I noted the hand-drawn smiley face and "Come again" on the bill she left behind.

After paying and leaving a modest tip from the small amount of cash that remained from my impromptu retreat north, I darted through the traffic to the Cascade Mountain Loans and Pawn Shop to have a look around. There were the usual guitars, stereos, a few guns in a glass display case, and a battered sword of undetermined age. A gun might be a good thing to have, I considered, if the cartel showed up someday. Unfortunately, it would be impossible for me to buy one without legitimate identification.

There was also a bookcase filled with cameras, nearly all of them old and coated with dust. I spotted a Speed Graflex, the kind every reporter carried over fifty years ago when life was black and white and slow enough to use a tripod. On a whim, I asked how much it was.

"Let you have it for thirty-five," the proprietor said. He was a large man, over six-feet tall and at least three hundred pounds, which explained the wide aisles in the small store. "You a collector?"

"Nah. Thought I might take up photography."

"You won't have much luck taking photos with that. Even if the bellows weren't cracked and the lens scratched, I don't think you'll find film for it anywhere."

"That's okay. I'll take it." Preserving precious memories was not likely to be high on my priority list anytime soon.

"What about a tripod? Got anything that will work?"

"Let me get this straight: you want a tripod for a camera that doesn't work?" The big man studied me for a moment as if deciding whether I was crazy, dangerous, or both. Then he held up a finger. "Give me a minute."

He disappeared for a few minutes into the back of the shop. When he reappeared, he was breathing hard and carrying a telescoping tripod with one of the thumbscrews missing. "You could tape it," he said.

"How much?"

I could almost hear the wheels turning as the other man considered this. "Tell you what," he said. "I'll give you both the camera and the tripod for forty-five."

"All right."

The other man stared at me. "Ain't you even going to try to chisel me down none?"

"Forgot my chisel."

The man let out something between a chuckle and a wheeze. "Let me clean it up for you." He pulled a handkerchief out of his rear pocket and used it to wipe the camera off. "That looks a little better." Then he did the same with the tripod.

"Where you from?" he asked.

"I work up at the Van de Zilver place."

"You work with Stu Follett?"

"You know Stu?"

"See him down at the Schooner now-and-then having lunch with that real estate fellow who has his picture posted all over town. Sometimes he brings stuff in here. Other times, he buys. Mostly, he looks. Stu's quite a collector."

"What's he collect?" I felt a little embarrassed like I was snooping through somebody's closet, but I was curious, too. And the way I looked at it, living in a small town was like having free access to a marketing research department.

"Yessir." He made it sound like one word. "Got quite a baseball card collection. Guess maybe you seen it?"

"I just started working there."

He nodded. "Are you sure I can't interest you in something else—a TV that don't work, maybe?" He wheezed.

"This ought to do it. By the way, know where I can find a pet store?"

Beads of sweat had formed on his massive brow and he wiped it with the dirty handkerchief, leaving a muddy streak. "Nothing' like that in town. You might try the Skagit Valley Mall in Burlington."

"How about a library?"

"Head six or seven blocks east on Metcalf and turn right. You can't miss it."

A few hours later, I had accomplished most of what I had set out to do, including learning that there were 269 banks in the Cayman Islands. A young male librarian helped me print out a list.

Finding the photo that I searched for on the tiny camera memory card took only seconds. As I scanned the thumbnails on one of the library's computers, I quickly located the snapshot taken the moment before Heide saw me and closed her laptop. It was the last photo I had taken before removing the chip. Even though I had worked with photographic images nearly every day in college when I was studying to be an art director, I was still amazed by the amount of data the Canon digital camera had captured in a thousandth of a second. There in the kitchen shadows were Heide's lovely back with its smooth, pale skin and the rear of her head with its red mane. There too was her glowing laptop screen, still open, with the bank logo, username, and an eight-digit password disguised by asterisks.

I felt a cord tighten around my heart as I stared at the photo, remembering our last few days and hours together. I did not hear the librarian approach until he was standing right behind me.

"What's that a photo of?" he asked.

"Oh, hi," I said, wiping a tear away before he noticed. "Just an outtake from a camera I used to have."

"What happened to the camera?"

"Stolen," I said.

"Well, at least you still have the memory card."

Before heading back to the trout farm, I decided there was time to check out the tulip festival that Annie had mentioned. After driving a few miles north on the freeway, I exited Highway 20, crossed under the freeway, and stopped for fuel using some of the last of my cash at a combination gas-station-convenience-sporting-goods store where a sign in the window advertised "Fresh Bait, Ammo, Espresso."

When I had driven up from Seattle earlier in the week, I had been too preoccupied with pain, grief, and the urgency of finding the Van de Zilver farm to spend time observing the countryside. Now, I had traveled only a few miles across the flat, alluvial valley when the housing developments and strip malls suddenly faded away and the land unwound into sprawling farms, one enormous grid after another, each anchored by a two-story, Victorian farmhouse, surrounded by a few poplar trees and a much-weathered barn, sometimes leaning, or slowly collapsing in upon itself, wooden ships tacking in a sea of furrowed soil.

I turned onto one two-lane country road after another, seeking tulip fields. I had already noted two or three promising locations where cars lined the roads and clumps of people wandered among the rows for picture-taking when I rounded a corner and came upon hundreds of acres of flowers in dazzling rows of purple, lavender, scarlet, white, yellow, gold and orange set against the backdrop of a tall, snow-covered peak. I removed the camera from the truck and carried it and the tripod to the edge of the field where I set it up. Then I stood there, admiring the orderly banquet of color spread before me and, without consciously thinking about it, knowing where I would crop, where I would add fill lights, and what would need retouching if I were directing a film crew.

Observing life through the viewfinder of an old black and white camera was a lot like advertising, I reflected. The consumer sees only what has been carefully edited for them to see: a staged set under artificial lights, a couple of good-looking models, the ad or commercial later retouched on the computer so that there is nothing to remind you of the ugliness of real life. No dents, blemishes, or bruises. No graffiti, gangs, or homeless people. No pedophiles, serial killers, or suicide bombers. One hundred percent artificial.

Occasionally, another car would pull over and a couple would get out and snap a photo or stand for a minute or two. Once, an entire busload of Japanese tourists, older folks mostly, unloaded nearby, the men wearing cameras around their necks, the women carrying cell phones or cameras, and all of them dressed alike. They waded like children, chatting, and laughing noisily, posing for each other among the rows of flowers.

I grew tired and hungry as the day progressed but could not find the will to leave. An emotion I could not describe rooted me to the place long after my fellow admirers had dwindled and finally ceased coming. A breeze arrived, blowing the blossoms, row upon row, like waves.

I kicked at a dirt clod. "Wish you could see this, Heide." I smiled cheerlessly. A knot had found its way into my throat.

The sun began to sink in the sky behind me, burnishing the fields, hills, and mountains with amber light.

"You lied to me. You said you were working late to get a promotion, not to steal a fortune." I glanced up at the snow-covered mountain, now a dome of fire. "Damn you," I whispered. Then louder, "Damn you!"

I did not hear the couple with their little girl chased by a black and white dog until the woman spoke, "Pretty, ain't it?"

I saw that the man's right arm and hand were prosthetic. "Magnificent," I replied, my voice husky.

"We saw you taking pictures from the house. You from a magazine or newspaper?"

I shook my head. The dog spotted a seagull that had landed some distance ahead and he raced after it, the girl following on his heels.

"What kind of film is that you're using?" the man asked. He had a beard that wrapped around his jawline, leaving his cheeks and upper lip hairless. I was reminded of a young Captain Ahab.

"Film? Why, black and white. Silly isn't it? All this unbelievable color and here I am shooting black and white film. Is all of this your handiwork?"

The woman smiled. "We just tend the fields, but the flowers, those are His grace."

"Doesn't it ever trouble you," I said, "the fact that they're so temporary?"

"Not at all," she said. "That's what makes them so beautiful. I'm not saying a mountain lake isn't beautiful in its own way. But there is something special about tulips. If you were to drive by here just a few weeks ago, there was nothing here but plant stalks. Today, there's this bountiful display of color." She waved her arm in the direction of the splendor. "You want a photo of heaven, I believe this is what it looks like. Up here, the Rapture comes every spring."

I did not respond. One man's rapture, after all, was another man's wake.

The man put out his left hand. "Name's Harold. This is my wife, Caroline."

"Gray. You folks been doing this long?"

Harold looked where his daughter and dog were playing. "Since I could straddle a furrow and follow my daddy around. This was his farm before me. You do this picture-taking for a living?"

"Just a hobby."

"Thought so. Your camera's missing the back that holds

the film."

I shrugged. "The film is in my head."

"Where you going, Katelyn?" Caroline called after her daughter who was now some 40 yards away.

"I better go after her," she said, yet lingered, a smile playing upon her ruddy cheeks.

Harold took off his glasses with his robotic hand, blew on them, and brushed them against the front of his shirt.

"I used to go hunting before I lost my arm," he said. "Until one time Caroline noticed I hadn't taken any ammunition. All those years, she thought I was just a bad shot."

"I used to tell my friends," Caroline said, "My poor Harold couldn't hit the side of a barn if he was to walk right up next to it."

Harold laughed. I had to smile.

Darkness had fallen before I made it back to the house. Valerie answered the door. Patsy, at least, looked happy to see me. She pressed her nose into my crotch, her customary greeting.

***

It was getting late and I was beginning to worry that Gray was not coming back when I finally heard his truck in the driveway. From the way she whined, I could tell Patsy was as glad to see him as I was.

"How's the hand?" he asked when I opened the door.

Embarrassed, I touched the sling where my arm with its bandaged hand rested. "Daddy's playing cards in town with his friends. Stu and Vonda went drinking and dancing. If you want dinner, you'll have to make it yourself."

"That's okay."

"Where'd you go?" It had hurt to learn that he had left without telling me, but, by now, the loneliness was like a comforting blanket I wrapped myself in, a protection against

further injury to my soul.

"I had pancakes for breakfast at Annie's Café; you might like to go with me some Saturday morning. Then I managed to get a haircut, check out a book at the library and buy some food for tomorrow. I told your dad I'd be happy to make dinner, though he didn't seem thrilled by my offer."

"Oh, and I visited a couple of tulip farms," he added. "You should have seen it."

In the awkward silence that followed, I heard him sigh. "I'm sorry. That was stupid."

"My mother took me once. The smell of the flowers and the dirt was amazing. I've never forgotten." I started to leave, the pain in my hand now throbbing from clenching my fist.

"Hey, before you go," he said. "I've got something for you." He touched my good hand and placed a small bag in it.

I set the bag on the kitchen counter, then reached in tentatively, found a box and shook it. I felt myself flush as my suspicion grew that he was making fun of me. "What is it?"

"Bird seed."

I turned my head slightly to listen harder. There was something I was missing. "What's it for?"

"Your birds, of course, unless you've got a taste for suet."

"I don't have...." The words caught in my throat.

"That's because they're still in my truck. Wait here."

I waited by the door, confused, my heart hammering so loud I figured he could hear it. His words had let a sliver of joy sneak in like light under a door and it made me shudder in fear and desperate hope.

"This bird cage needs to sit somewhere away from heating vents or drafts," he said when he returned. I heard tiny peeps among the rustlings of paper.

"What did you do?"

"Here. Let me show you." He set the cage down. Then he guided my hand as he opened the cage door and put it inside. His hand was gentle, and I stored the memory of his touch for *later. The birds twittered and fluttered at having their space invaded.*

"They're canaries—a boy and a girl, or at least that's what the lady at the pet store claimed. I'll be damned if I know how anyone could tell. Hold up a finger," he said. "See if one comes to you."

One of the birds landed for an instant on my finger before fluttering away.

"She said they'll be singing up a storm as soon as they get used to their new home."

"How do you close it?"

As he showed me the latch on the cage, I briefly explored the mystery of his fingers. I could smell the birds and his smell, and it made me dizzy.

"What will Daddy say?"

"It might take a few days, but I think he'll get used to them. He didn't know about the frogs, right?"

I felt a smile break across my face for the first time in several days as I stroked the side of the cage and poked my fingers inside. The birds avoided me. "I shouldn't do that. They could have a heart attack and croak."

"Give them a few days to get used to you," Gray said. "Do you like them?" *He sounded nervous.*

"Yes. Thank you."

"I thought about getting you a classical music CD, but then I thought why not get you your own little orchestra? I'm sorry about yesterday," *he added.*

I felt myself stiffen and turned my face away, embarrassed. It was remarkable that he had bought me a gift to apologize.

"Like I said before, I don't remember sticking the knife in the dishwasher."

"I'm sorry, too." *The hurt from the past several years without Momma tore painfully at the slender threads that held my heart together.* "Seems like every time I trust someone, they let me down. C'mon Patsy."

I started toward the bedroom, so he would not see the tears that were tumbling down my cheeks.

"Maybe your expectations are too high," he said.

I ached with wanting, desperate for his arms to wrap around and hold me but could not answer.

"Guess I'd better go," he said.

I heard the screen door hinge as he opened it.

"After a while, crocodile," he called.

"Not so soon, baboon," I whispered.

CHAPTER EIGHTEEN

As preparations for opening day accelerated, I fell each night into exhausted sleep, oblivious to the nightly frog concerts. The bruising and pain from my smashed rib had dissipated. Patsy had taken to showing up at the cabin first thing in the morning when Valerie let her out. She would lie on the floor near the small heater, nose between her paws, and watch as I showered and got dressed for work. Later, she would run circles around me as I climbed the hill to the Van de Zilver house for breakfast.

Valerie seemed untroubled by her seeing-eye dog's behavior. "Without her harness, she's just another dog who needs exercise and affection." Patsy smiled in agreement as Valerie scratched behind her ears. "You should be flattered. She does not care much for Daddy or Stu. Or even Vonda for that matter."

Following breakfast on Friday, Stu ordered me to meet him at the metal building with the barred window. When I arrived, the bull was already parked outside, and Stu had unlocked the garage door and entered. Inside, a large chest freezer and an old upright Frigidaire stood in a corner. There was also a wooden desk which, judging from the many scratches and grooves on its surface, was used mostly for setting things on, and a gray metal filing cabinet. Nearly hidden in its shadow, I noted a closed door with a heavy padlock.

"Here's where we keep the fish food," Stu said. "It's time you learn how to handle this part of the operation. I'll be in Seattle this weekend attending a conference for building inspectors."

From the refrigerator, he removed two opened bags of Oregon Pellets, one with a number five on it and the other with a number three.

"Soon as the bags in the refer run low, grab another one out of the freezer, but don't wait too long. Takes a day to defrost, so plan ahead. Throw these two on the back of the Bull."

I watched as Stu closed and locked the garage door.

"Seems like a lot of security for fish food," I said when Stu joined me on the double-wide seat of the Bull.

Stu's smile held no mirth. He started the Bull and headed toward the barn.

"A child or animal happened to get into the chemicals we store in there, they could come to a lot of grief," he said. "That goes for you, too. I will be giving you one key to open the garage door. Don't be messing with the other door. It's off limits." He turned to face me. "Understand?"

"Why did you say you saw me put the knife in the dishwasher?"

"Because," Stu replied evenly, "you don't belong here. Something about you smells bad. The longer you are here, the worse the stink gets. It ain't a matter of 'if,' but 'when' you're going to cause another accident, leaving me to clean up your mess."

Another time zone, another place, I might have said I was sorry for the trouble I had caused. But for Stu, I said nothing.

"In my opinion, Virgil hiring you was a mistake." Stu poked me in the chest with a finger. "Don't make me regret it any more than I already do."

We continued down the hill. "We'll start with pond three."

The three ponds were laid out in a line stretching from the west to the east, each one roughly one hundred and fifty feet apart from its neighbor. The smallest of the three ponds was rectangular-shaped and located furthest from the barn. It was still early in the morning, too early for a breeze. The water reflected the nearby alder, fir, and cedar trees. Beneath the placid surface, flashes of silver flickered among the dark, mysterious green of the water.

"These are fingerlings," Stu said. "They get the number three pellets. Three stands for the size—three-thirty-seconds."

He withdrew a large plastic spoon full of pellets from the bag. They smelled of fish. "Pay attention to how much I feed them. All the fish need to be fed twice a day. The trick is not to over or under feed them. Too much and the food sinks to the bottom and becomes plant fertilizer. Too little and the fish don't grow fast enough, or they starve."

He cast a ladle full of pellets across the surface of the pond and a horde of silver blades knifed thorough the reflected trees toward the food.

Pond two was twice as large as the first, centrally located, and had the best view of the surrounding hills and mountains duplicated on its surface.

"These fish are larger, what are called 'sub-catchables,'" Stu said. "They average between six and sixteen fish per pound."

Each time Stu tossed a scoop of food out across the pond, the surface would churn for the next several seconds as the fish ate.

"Hungry little bastards, aren't they? Got to keep them reasonably well-fed and separated by size or they'll eat each other."

Stu climbed back on the Bull's bench seat where I waited. "You can't keep six-inch trout and their three-inch cousins together and expect to have very many of your smaller fish survive. It's survival of the fittest."

Unbidden, the memory of the woman shooting at me caused a wave of nausea to wash over me. "Nature can be pretty cruel," I managed to mumble.

"Depends on your perspective. If you're a big fish, it ain't so bad. If you're a little fish," he smiled, "then you best watch your ass."

"What about the test tubes I've seen you filling with water?" I asked, anxious to move on to another subject other than survival, especially with mine being no sure thing. "What's that all about?"

"Spying on me, huh?" Stu said. "I don't think you need to worry about the alkalinity of the ponds going haywire. At least, not this weekend. This is natural, spring-fed water. It has been the same for thousands of years. No reason for it to change anytime soon. At least, none that I can think of. Unless, of course, you let lawn fertilizer run-off into the ponds, in which case it will kill all the fish."

We visited the large, natural pond where the cabin was located last. Its ellipsoidal shape lacked the symmetry of the man-made ponds, but I had cherished its rustic beauty from the first moment I had seen it. Its surface mirrored the tall cedar trees of the island and the cabin. A wooden park bench sat along the eastern edge.

"Your neighbors here are the 'catchables,'" Stu said. "They get the larger, size five pellets. You want to see something impressive, watch this."

He cast the food out over the pond and, as the pellets began to rain down upon the surface, the water erupted violently as rainbow trout leapt and slapped the water with their tails in a feeding frenzy.

A particularly loud splash near the island attracted my attention. "What is that? A muskrat?"

"That was Moses, the Jew trout."

I watched for another sign of the fish, but without success.

"I've never heard of a Jew trout."

"That's just what Virgil calls him because he's so smart," Stu said. "Ol' Moses has been here forever. We think he is a Lake trout because of his size, but nobody knows for sure. He's the main reason why people have been coming up here to fish for the last fifteen or twenty years."

"I'm surprised no one has hooked him."

"Oh, he's been hooked plenty. But he is so big and smart that he always gets away. I have seen him yank an entire rod and reel into the lake more than once. Then the poor sap who hooked him goes down to the bar and tells all his friends and, for the next week, people are lined up around the pond, shoulder to shoulder and three deep, waiting to take their turn trying to catch Moses. He's our star attraction."

Stu turned to face me. "Think you can handle this?"

"I think so."

"You forget something, or need help when I'm not here, you can ask Virgil if he's around. No sense bothering Valerie or my wife. Vonda used to help her dad as a kid, but she claims she does not remember anything. Personally, I think she does not want to remember. Feeding fish isn't exactly her style, know what I mean?"

Given the nasty smell of the food, I could understand why feeding fish was not likely to be very high on most women's priority list. As for myself, however, I was looking forward to getting to know my "neighbors," as Stu called them, especially the one called Moses.

"One more thing." Stu jabbed me in the chest with a finger. "I ever hear about you touching my wife—even in a friendly sort of way—and I'll chop you up with the hammerknifer and feed you to the fish one bite-size bit at a time. Understand?"

I sighed in frustration. Stu's poking my chest was wearing on me. "My wife just died. You really think I'm interested in Vonda, or any other woman for that matter?"

"Like I said, keep any stupid ideas you might have and your hands to yourself."

Tell that to your wife, I thought.

CHAPTER NINETEEN

Sometime during the night, it began to rain, a hard-driving, wanton downpour that drummed on the cabin's shingled roof and reverberated in its wood-paneled interior. I pulled the blanket up around my shoulders and hoped the roof would not leak.

The rain was still falling when I got up and, by the look of it, did not intend to quit anytime soon. The trees stooped like old women, the wind whipped the surface of the pond into retreating ripples and the clouds massed together into a solid, dark plain that obliterated any memory of sun.

After feeding the fish, I retreated to the house for a cup of coffee and asked Valerie if she would like to join me for breakfast at Annie's. Vonda was still sleeping, and Virgil had left earlier to attend an auction. Valerie declined, however, and I drove to Sedro Woolley alone.

After returning to my cabin, I began to read about trout rearing. A little after half-past three, there was a knock on the door. I opened it to find Vonda, an umbrella in one hand and a bottle of chardonnay with a couple of plastic cups riding its top in the other.

"Mind if I join you?"

I stood there, blocking the doorway for a moment as I recalled Stu's latest threat.

"Going to let me drown out here?"

She brushed past me. I took her umbrella and stood it inside the door, then hung her coat on a hook on the back of the door with mine.

"The rain drives me nuts," she said. "I need somebody to drink with."

She removed a wool scarf and tossed it on the floor. She wore a pair of tight-fitting blue jeans and a green V-necked sweater that matched her eyes and displayed a hint of cleavage. Her nose had a slight bump, and her light blond hair was probably chemically enhanced, but I thought she was sexy-looking and more than capable of holding her own in any roomful of women. I was suddenly aware of how small the cabin seemed with one more body in it—especially Vonda's body.

"I don't drink," I replied.

"A shame," she said and shrugged. "On the other hand, perhaps it's just as well. I generally drink enough for two people."

I placed the only chair beside her. "Have a seat."

"Thanks, but I prefer this." She sat down on the cot and started to take off her cowboy boots. "How about turning up the toaster?" She nodded toward the tiny space heater.

"So, tell me," she said a moment later, after I had adjusted the plastic heater to full power. "What's your problem with drinking—addiction or religion?"

"More like a lack of control." In constant pain and anxiety in the days spent fleeing Southern California, I had found temporary relief in a bottle of Jack Daniels.

"Oh, goody." She poured wine into a cup, then set the bottle down. "I like a man with a lack of control, remote or otherwise." She crossed one leg over the other and raised her glass in a toast. "Here's to losing control." She winked and took a sip.

I sat down cowboy style, facing the back of the chair.

"What were you doing? Hope I did not interrupt anything important. I didn't see a sign listing your visitor's hours."

"I don't get a lot of company."

"You just wait until all the local girls find out we got a single man hidden up here in a cabin." She smiled knowingly. "You won't get a moment's peace. What did you pay for that haircut—fifty cents?"

"In answer to your first question, I was reading."

"Yeah? Dostoevsky, Hemingway, Nabokov? I go in for D.H. Lawrence, myself."

I tossed the book onto the bed.

Vonda turned up her nose. "Trout and Salmon Culture? I thought you looked like a more interesting man than someone who studies fish." She tossed the book back. "Go ahead and read. Don't mind me. I'll just make myself comfortable."

She propped the pillow up against the wall and used it as a backrest.

I could not help watching as she inspected the room. Unlike her sister whose demeanor was shy and reserved, Vonda had the confidence of someone who not only assumed, but aggressively demanded her place at life's table. As I had learned, this was often an act, designed to hide an insecure disposition. There were millions of actors and actresses in Southern California. Very few, however, were in the movies.

"I must say, you're about the neatest man I ever saw."

"I don't do well with clutter. I need a certain amount of order to think."

"Really?" She studied me over the top of her cup. "Myself, I could do with less order and more spontaneity. Nothing interesting ever happens around here. Boring as hell, if you ask me. Val and I even know where we are going to be buried. Daddy bought us all cemetery plots, side by side, so we can all be by Momma someday. It gives me the creeps knowing where I am going to end up. When I tried talking about it to Stu, he said I'm crazy. Do you think I'm crazy?"

"You sound pretty normal. So far."

"Normal." She tried rolling it around on her tongue. "I don't think I care for that word." After refilling her plastic cup, she poured a second. "We've established you're not a Mormon or an alcoholic, so have a drink with me." She held out the cup. "The only thing worse than being lonely is being lonely when you're with someone."

I took the cup from her hand and tried a taste. It was not bad.

"To not being lonely," she said, raising her cup in another toast. I raised my cup and took another sip. The rain continued drumming on the roof.

"Those birds must have set you back a few bucks," Vonda said. "I swear I don't know how anyone could live on as little as Daddy pays, or—more importantly—why anyone with brains would want to."

Easy to say if there are not people wanting to hunt you down and kill you.

"C'mon, Gray," she said. "What's your secret? You can trust me." She studied me over her glass. "I bet you stole some money and are hiding out until the heat dies down, am I right?"

I found the conversation steering too close to the truth for comfort, especially the hiding out part. All I needed was for Vonda to dig around on the internet or post something on social media and there could be a hit squad pulling up in the parking lot a few days later.

"I needed a job and wanted to close the door on a painful past."

Vonda got up from the bed and walked to the rain-streaked window. "You disappoint me, Gray," she said to the window. It was growing dark outside. The 60-watt bulb did little to prevent the room from retreating into shadows. Vonda flicked the light switch off. Rivulets of silver streamed down the window. "I can hardly wait to explore the world. To feel like I know it and it knows me."

The silhouette of her body against the window in the dim light was attractive, sensual. I could not help noticing how well her jeans sculpted her legs and ass and I wished I still had the Canon camera. Her profile would have made a great stock photo to be downloaded by ad agencies and design firms as a source of income for many years to come.

"I used to feel that way, too," I said.

She moved closer until she stood over me. I could smell the Angel. It permeated the room.

"Poor Gray. All alone in the big, bad world." She put a hand in my hair, teasing it with her fingers. "You remind me of a little boy who's lost his balloon."

I brushed her hand away.

"I think my sister has got the hots for you."

"What are you talking about?" I looked up to find her smiling. "She thinks I ruined her hand—which I didn't for what it's worth."

"Whether you did, or didn't, she still thinks you're about the best thing to happen around here in a long time. I had to help her with makeup before dinner last week. I have not had to do that since we were little girls going to a birthday party together. Too bad she can't see what you look like." She traced a line from my ear down along my jaw with a finger. My heart began beating in quick time.

I pulled away and then stood. "I need to feed the fish before it's too dark to see."

"Now there's an excuse I haven't heard before." She took another sip of wine. "Sit back down. I won't bite. Not hard anyway."

When I remained standing, she sighed. "Time to get ready for dinner, I suppose." She sat on the bed to pull on her boots.

As I helped her with her coat, I remembered what she had said a couple of nights before. "What did you mean the other day about 'problems'?"

"What?"

"You said, 'Drinking doesn't begin to acknowledge my problems.'"

"Oh, that." She smiled, but it was a false smile. "Thanks for letting me visit. I loved seeing what you've done with the place." I handed her the nearly empty wine bottle and the umbrella and opened the door for her.

She started out the door, then paused. "No need to say anything to Stu about my little visit. The word "understanding" is not in his dictionary. Oh, and now that we've warmed up the room, you can turn down the toaster."

***

Although there was still an hour left before sundown, I fed the fish in near total darkness, the rain slanting down in sheets of cold steel. Visibility was so poor that I almost missed seeing the dead trout floating belly up, pale as a ghost, in the second pond.

"You save him?" Virgil asked.

"He's in a baggy in the refrigerator," I said, still in my rain gear.

"We'll look at him tomorrow after church. Meantime, do not be too alarmed about one rainbow. Fish die, like anything else. Sit down and have some supper."

CHAPTER TWENTY

The rain continued to fall all night, relentlessly hammering the wooden deck and roof of the tiny cabin and heedless of the anxiety that had been building steadily since finding the dead trout. In my sleepless tossing and turning, the downpour sounded like the marching feet of an approaching firing squad.

Finding the dead trout felt like an ominous omen. After getting the tractor stuck in the mud and then being blamed for Valerie's hand being pierced by a kitchen knife, I knew I could expect no more clemency if the trout were dying because of something I had done. Virgil had warned me not to fertilize too closely to the uphill side of the ponds to prevent poisoning the fish and I had carefully left a barrier of at least ten feet. But with all the rain, it was not impossible to think that chemicals had leached from the lawn into the water. With the way my life had gone lately, it seemed a foretold certainty.

When the clock finally read three, I got up to check on the trout in Pond Two. It was a moonless night so dark that I could not see anything until I had approached to less than twenty feet away. Then I looked on in horror over the rain-cratered surface of the pond where a hundred or more milk-white bellies of trout now floated. For several minutes, I stood shivering in the cold downpour and contemplating my fate as my worst nightmare played out. It would be several hours before Stu returned from Seattle. By then, all the fish might be dead. I decided it was up to me to do whatever I could to save them.

I opened the garage door with the key and hit the light switch. After retrieving the dead fish from the night before from the refrigerator, I laid it and two new fish from Pond Two on top of the cooler. I studied them for clues to their demise as the metal roof rang with the rain's tattoo. I needed the PH testing kit Stu had used but had no idea where he kept it.

A two-drawer metal file cabinet seemed like a good choice, but a search of its drawers turned up only receipts, state and county permits and other paperwork. I turned to the locked door. Stu had warned me against entering, but it was now the only alternative.

I returned from the barn with a claw hammer. The lock was impervious to my blows, but the wooden door and its casing were not. Inside the closet, I spotted a shotgun leaning against the corner with a roll of blueprints. There was also a second file cabinet. In its top drawer, I found a glass flask with stopper and a packet of chemically treated testing strips.

Valerie heard my knocking and came to the door wearing the threadbare robe I had previously seen her wearing. "What's wrong?"

"The fish are dying. I need your dad."

"He isn't going to be happy when I wake him."

"At this point, it doesn't really matter. Tell him to meet me by Pond Two. I need his help if we're going to save his fish."

"What if the fertilizer killed them?"

"Then it's been nice knowing you."

She started to leave, then lingered by the doorway, her fingers inspecting the door jamb. "In case I don't have the chance to say it later, I'm sorry," she said.

"Sorry for what? The fish?"

"I don't give a damn about the fish!" She plucked at the sleeve of her sling. "I'm sorry about what happened to your wife and about everything that's happened to you. Mostly, though, I'm sorry for me."

I was looking at the top of her head. I raised her face gently with the fingers of one wet hand. "It's going to be okay. Go get your dad."

I shivered as I waited in the darkness by the pond. The rain made two kinds of sounds: the hard, intermittent plops of the heavier drops falling from the trees and the softer, rushing din of millions of silver-black butterflies.

Virgil showed up fifteen minutes later dressed in heavy rubber boots and rain gear. I had parked the Toyota pickup by the pond with the high beams on so I could see what I was doing as I knelt in the sodden earth. Beyond me, the lights reflected off the bodies of the floating fish.

"What's going on here?" Virgil asked.

I nodded toward the pond. "We've got a serious problem. I need your help figuring out what's causing it so we can correct it before we lose any more trout."

Virgil whistled when he saw the dead rainbows. "Must be over a hundred. I warned you, young man. If fertilizer has seeped into the water, there ain't nothing we can do about it except stand here and watch 'em die."

"I don't think it's the fertilizer."

"Like you didn't think it was you who put the knife in the dishwasher the wrong way?"

We stared at one another. I fought the urge to walk away and never look back. But there was more at stake than finding a new place to hide. "I swear I didn't spread fertilizer within ten feet of the high side of the ponds – just like you told me. So, you tell me: you think the fertilizer killed them?"

"What else would it be? You see any signs of disease?"

"None," I admitted.

"Then I got bad news for you: it sounds to me like ammonium poisoning from the fertilizer."

I wiped my forehead. "I admit, it sounds like a reasonable

hypothesis. Let's check it out." I held out a test strip and a flask full of water.

Virgil took the flask. He shook it, then dipped the strip into its contents. Valerie approached with Patsy. "What's going on, Daddy?"

"Fish are dying, sweetheart, and we are hoping to find out why."

Vonda arrived a moment later wearing jeans, cowboy boots and a rain slicker. "What is it?" she asked.

"Don't know yet," Virgil answered. "But something ain't right." He tried another strip, then threw it away. "You happen to bring the drops?"

I held up the small bottle of Universal Indicator. "This?"

Virgil nodded. He used the eyedropper to add drops to the flask. Immediately, the color of the water began to change. "Don't that beat it?"

Three faces clustered around the flask. Valerie stood back with Patsy. "What is it?" she asked.

"C'mon, Daddy," Vonda said. "Don't torture us. Is it the fertilizer, or isn't it?"

"Darned if I can say." He lifted his hat and scratched his scalp with one hand while he held the flask with another. "We've got a high acidity reaction. If ammonium poisoning were responsible, I would have thought it would be the opposite, meaning high alkalinity. Something's fishy, no pun intended."

"What are you going to do?" Valerie asked.

Virgil poured out the water sample. "First thing when it's daylight, I'll run the test one more time. If it still shows high acidity, all we can do is call upon the experts at Fish and Game. Probably be Monday before they can get out here which means we're going to lose all these fish."

"I'm sorry, Daddy," Vonda said.

Virgil stared at the pond where the dead fish floated. He looked older, his face deeply lined, in the harsh shadows of the

Toyota's high beams. "I'm sorry, too." He put his arms around his daughters. "Sorry it turned out this way."

I watched as the three shadows of their bodies merged into one dark shape in the bright headlights and I thought that a family forced to share their sorrow was still better than no family at all. They had started to walk back to the house when I called out. I could not see their faces clearly in the backlit glare of the lights, but I felt as if I were standing before a judge and jury.

"Look, I don't know that much about fish, and I wouldn't presume for a moment to be an expert, but I did some reading this past week. I seem to remember seeing something about low carbon dioxide being as fatal as too little oxygen, is that right?"

Virgil shrugged. "It makes some sense, though I've never seen or heard of it."

"Give me two minutes. If it turns out I am responsible for the deaths of these fish, I'll clear out tomorrow and you won't owe me for the work I did."

No one moved or said a word. "Just two minutes," I repeated.

"Okay," Virgil said. "Two minutes."

I waded into the pond. The water was ice cold and I had to step gingerly to keep from falling. It did not take long to find what I was looking for. I reached beneath the surface and pulled out a long, leafy water plant. "Look." During the past two weeks, my body had continued to heal. Some days I almost forget I had been shot. Then I would reach for something or bend over to pick something up and it was like I had been kicked. I grunted as I pulled out another plant. "The pond is thick with them."

"So?" Vonda said. "Even I know that plants are responsible for producing oxygen."

"That's right. But, according to the book I checked out, water plants need carbon dioxide to make oxygen. When the sky's overcast and there's not enough sun, plants and fish are forced to compete for oxygen. And if there are too many plants, due to a mild winter or an early spring, then there's none left over for the fish."

Virgil chewed the inside of his lip as he pondered this for a minute. "Sounds like you might have something. Only trouble is we haven't got any herbicide and, even if we did, we would have to get a permit to use it. In other words, we're still up a creek without a paddle."

"Got a rake?" I asked.

CHAPTER TWENTY-ONE

"A lawn rake?" Virgil said. "What are you planning to do, clean out this entire pond by hand?"

I shrugged. The rain pelted my face. "Figured I'd give it a try."

"I'll help," Valerie said. And before anyone could stop her, she had waded out into the water. Patsy whined and danced nervously on shore for a few seconds before plunging in after her.

"Brrr. It's cold," Valerie said. "Whoops!" She stumbled and nearly fell. "And slippery." She reached beneath the surface of the pond, found a plant and uprooted it with her good hand. "Hey," she said, "this is kinda fun."

Vonda watched as we continued to pull up plants and throw them on the shore. "I can't believe I am standing out here in the freezing damn rain even considering getting into a slimy old pond with those slimy old fish to pull up weeds." She shivered. "Oh, hell." Then she, too, waded in.

"I'll be back in a few minutes with a rake and garbage sacks," Virgil said.

Some four hours later, when the rain had finally ceased, and the sky had lightened, I finished throwing the last plastic garbage bag onto the back of the Bull to be emptied on the compost pile. Vonda had gone to bed two hours earlier, complaining of the cold and exhaustion, but not until after putting in two very tough hours of work—something no city girl I knew would have done. With only one hand to pull weeds, Valerie had nevertheless stuck it out for the entire four hours, with a break in the middle to make hot chocolate and coffee for everyone. Standing in his hip waders, Virgil had held the bags to throw their weeds in. He had finally announced he was going back to bed a few minutes earlier. Six more trout had died, making the final total ninety-three dead.

"What about the other ponds?" Valerie asked.

"They'll need to be checked and maybe sprayed," I said. "But they're probably not in as critical condition. This pond gets the most sunlight which is probably why it grew such an abundance of plants."

"Are you ready for some breakfast? I imagine you worked up an appetite."

"How about if I take a shower and change first?"

"We'll wait for you," Valerie said.

Valerie and Patsy followed me to the cabin. Once I crossed the threshold and saw the cot, however, my thoughts turned from food to sleep. I kicked off my shoes. Then, realizing that Valerie could not see me, proceeded to undress. When I was naked, I sank down onto the cot. The pain from my damaged ribs had spread to every inch of my body and I began to shiver uncontrollably.

"What are you doing?" Valerie asked.

"You know, if it's alright with you, I might crash for a couple of hours until I have to feed the fish."

"I understand. You sound exhausted. That was something," she said. "We would have lost all the fish if you hadn't figured out what was wrong and how to save them. No way Stu would have done what you did."

Patsy began to whine at something she had found. She pawed at whatever it was that lay underneath the cot.

"What are you doing, girl?" Valerie reached to pet the dog.

When she stood, she was holding Vonda's scarf. "What's this?"

"Looks like Vonda's scarf," I said.

Valerie dropped it on the floor as if it were crawling with bugs. "When was she here?" she demanded. Her pale cheeks had blossomed red.

"Yesterday. She stopped by while I was reading."

"I see," she said. "C'mon, Patsy." She opened the door. As she shut it behind her, I had only a brief second to observe the look of anguish that etched her face.

***

I was feeding the fish their noon meal in a cold, blustery wind that whipped the surface of the ponds and scourged my exposed cheeks and ears when I saw Virgil walking toward me. He still wore the suit he had worn earlier to church.

"Anymore dead rainbows?" he asked.

"None." I cast another scoop of pellets over the pond and we watched as the fish rose.

Virgil continued looking out over the pond. "You know, something like those trout dying happened to most guys, I wouldn't expect to see 'em again. That was a real test of faith. It took guts. Brains, too."

I shrugged, embarrassed by Virgil's praise, and threw a second ladle of pellets.

"Nobody asked you to learn about trout rearing," Virgil continued. "If you had not studied up on it, we might have lost another hundred fish or more before we figured out what was killing them. Make a long story short, I think you're ready to take over the feeding and care of the trout in addition to your regular duties."

"What about Stu?"

"Stu's got a full-time job with the county. I don't think he will have a problem with it. Besides, as soon as we open, he'll have plenty to do in his other job."

"What's that?"

"Customer service," Virgil said. He turned to leave. "Oh, one more thing. My daughters said I better give you a raise. From now on, you can expect another hundred dollars a month on top of what you're already making."

"Thanks," I said, smiling briefly. "Thanks a lot."

The saddest part of being alone, I reflected as I watched Virgil trudge up to the house, was having no one to share the good times, or bad times. I cast another scoop of pellets across the pond's placid surface and watched as the trout fought over the food, their sleek bodies flashing silver in the cold sunlight.

***

Momma said good knives are worth their weight in gold. They do not require sharpening very often because they keep their edge. They cut quick and clean. The handle and blade are balanced so that they feel like they were made especially for your hand. I keep them all in their holder arranged by size. Except the special one. That one I keep in my secret place.

I like how the pain stings. Instant. Intense. Like an E^7 note on a violin. Wiping away all the darkness and troubles from my mind. I am here. Now. Alive. If no one is around, sometimes I scream.

Vonda probably wonders why I ask her to buy so many paper towels and bandages. I tell her it is because I am clumsy and cannot see what I am doing when I prepare meals. The truth is I can slice a tomato, carrots, or potatoes faster and better than people who can see.

Oh, there is a lot about me that nobody knows.

"Valerie V-de-de," Momma would sing to me when I was little, making a sound like the chickadees. "Who knows my Valerie V better than me?"

Nobody. Nobody but you, Momma.

Nobody.

PART II
OPENING DAY

No man can lose what he never had.

-Isaac Walton, *The Compleat Angler*

CHAPTER TWENTY-TWO

Following the attack on the speedboat, I had lived through unrelenting hell, forced to flee for my life after leaving my identity and everything I owned behind. I had been close to being fired for getting the tractor stuck in the quagmire, then blamed for injuring Valerie's hand, and nearly fired again for the death of the trout.

That Sunday, the skies finally parted—figuratively at least—and I was finally able to go about my work without worrying about what disaster the next day would bring. All I had to do to stay afloat was to avoid Stu and remain invisible to the rest of the world. How hard could it be?

The gift of the canaries was accepted, if not entirely appreciated. And, after one too many complaints about her cooking, Vonda welcomed my renewed offer of help.

Sunday dinner was my turn to cook. I found an Indian market in Mount Vernon where I shopped for spices and condiments.

"We don't get many Indian men in here," the storeowner said as she rang me up. She wore a traditional sari.

"I'm not surprised," I said. "I don't think my father knew how to boil water."

Questions followed about where I was from, where were my parents were from originally, and so forth. Several lies later, I was able to make my escape with the goods.

"Holy smokes. What did you do to the chicken?" Vonda asked.

"I mixed in some ginger root, a little garlic, some tomato sauce, coconut milk, cloves, cardamom, cinnamon and, of course, curry powder. I hope it is not too hot. I tried to keep it mild." An exotic bouquet of scents suffused the entire house.

"What did you do to the rice?" she asked. "It's delicious."

"Onions with more cardamom, cinnamon, and cloves, plus almonds and raisins for garnish."

"It's like eating in a restaurant," Vonda said. "Gray can cook anytime he wants as far as I'm concerned."

"Now he's going to cook, too?" Stu asked. "What's next, paying our bills?"

Stu had arrived home late Sunday afternoon only to learn that the trout had been saved from oxygen depletion and that I had broken into his locked closet. His irritation with me was palpable; he was now on his third vodka and Squirt.

"I still say we should have fired his ass when he messed up the lawn with the tractor—which I had to pay for by the way. Then he injures Valerie, so she can't cook."

"There's no proof he did it," Vonda said.

"Yes, there is," Stu said. "I saw him."

I felt myself flush. I started to object, but Valerie found my arm with her hand as if to quiet me.

"If you saw him put the knife in the dishwasher wrong, why didn't you make it right?" Vonda said.

Stu glared at me but said nothing.

Valerie remained silent as she sampled the food in tiny bites. She hesitated when she came to the artichoke. "What is this?"

"It's an artichoke," I said. "You peel off the leaves and dip the fat part into lemon yogurt sauce, then drag it between your teeth."

The artichoke had been my idea based on a simple recipe

Heide once tried. I thought she would approve.

It took Valerie a couple of tries, but there was no doubt from her expression that she was warming up to the experience.

"It's like velvet. Smooth. Sensual."

"I'm surprised you know that word," Vonda said.

"Heard it on TV once or twice," Valerie said innocently.

"Where did you learn to cook like this?" Vonda asked.

"My mother. I am not anywhere near as good as she is. Was," I added. Always better to cover my tracks, I realized. She would no doubt have offered numerous suggestions for improvement, but I thought she would have been pleased to see that her Indian culinary education efforts had not gone completely to waste.

Virgil had pushed up his glasses and was studying the artichoke as if it were an artifact from another planet. "Don't it make you wonder who it was first thought to try eating one of these?"

"More than likely someone who was starving to death and didn't have any real food to eat," Stu said.

"Speaking of starving to death," Virgil said, "it's a miracle we didn't lose a lot of our fish this weekend while you were enjoying yourself down in Seattle. If Gray had not done some reading up on trout—something he was not asked to do—those fish would have starved from not enough oxygen. When was the last time you checked the water chemistry, Stu?"

"Yeah, Stu," Valerie jumped in. "It's almost like you wanted the fish to die so you could blame it on Gray."

"Well?" Vonda asked.

Stu had been studiously avoiding looking at everyone. Now he glared at each of us like a wounded animal.

"For your information, I wasn't in Seattle enjoying myself," he growled. "I was attending an important conference for my job. Also, those chemicals and strips degrade over time, which is why I was storing them in a closet. If you..."

Virgil cut him off. "Frankly, Stu, I don't want to hear any more excuses. As of this minute, I am putting Gray in charge of the trout, including feeding them and maintaining the chemical balance of the water. You got a problem with that?"

Stu stood, tossed his napkin on the table, and left without saying anything.

***

The weather stayed stubbornly cold and wet the following week. Herds of slow-moving nimbostratus beasts filled the sky from horizon to horizon, day after day, offering no relief from their dreary monotony. From my meager wages, I bought a new hat and jacket at Walmart. Stu seemed unperturbed that I had taken over feeding the fish but expressed outrage that I had broken into his storage closet.

"I specifically told you to stay away from my stuff." We were standing in the small building where the fish food was kept. Stu had nailed the closet door shut as soon as he arrived home and saw the damage.

I shrugged. "I needed to save the trout."

"What else did you see?" he asked.

"I wasn't taking inventory."

Stu studied me.

"I guess I saw a shotgun. Other than that, I was in too much of a hurry to worry about what else you might be hiding. Locking up the testing kit like that almost makes me think Valerie was right; you wanted those fish to die so you could blame it on me."

"Don't mess with my stuff again," Stu poked me in the chest with his finger, "or there will be consequences."

Being poked by Stu was becoming tiresome and I knocked his hand away. "Keep your hands off me, Stu."

Stu stared at me, rolling the toothpick in his mouth, then grinned before leaving.

Nearly as worrisome as Stu's paranoia was Valerie's moodiness. Since finding Vonda's scarf in my cabin, she had withdrawn into her own private world. For several days, she did not appear for breakfast. While she still prepared dinner, she did not speak unless spoken to and then retreated to her room as soon as she finished eating, leaving cleaning up to me, with the occasional visit from Vonda. An uncomfortable silence, as gloomy as the weather cloaked the dining table whenever she was present.

I did not see myself as a meddler in other peoples' affairs. Because of my own troubles and loneliness, however, I was perhaps more attuned to Valerie's mood swings than the rest of the family. From what I had observed, she had no friends and no activities outside the farm other than occasional walks with her seeing-eye dog. While it seemed obvious to me that she was unhappy, the other family members appeared not to notice, or, if they did, not to care.

I missed her midday visits with Patsy when she would appear carrying a brown bag containing a sandwich that was often a strange combination of ingredients, always intriguing to the taste buds but sometimes barely edible. Blackberry jam and fried egg was surprisingly tasty, but catsup and cucumber were a failure. More than the food, however, I missed her comradery. She had been the first of the family to welcome me and my biggest defender. As petite and unappreciated as she was, I could not help but feel protective. And those rare times when she smiled, well that was something special.

I spent much of the time mowing the damp, heavy grass with the hammerknifer. While Vonda grumbled about the rain, I took satisfaction in a well-ordered routine and a simple, almost monastic lifestyle. After being credited with saving the trout, Stu left me alone to tend the fish and look after the grounds. The work was hard but undemanding mentally. Four weeks after arriving at the Van de Zilver home, my injured ribs were mostly healed, and my strength was back.

For the first time since Heide had died, I began to think less about surviving from moment to moment and more about the future. The intrusion of the past upon the present, while still disruptive, was no longer the constant mental barrage it had once been. My loneliness, however, was growing. Little by little, I could feel it spreading like a cancer within. Once, while washing dishes and overhearing a love song on the radio, I had to squeeze my eyes shut to hide my grief and prevent the tears from spilling down my cheeks.

Even the Graflex camera offered no escape. On a brilliant Saturday morning, I drove to Anacortes and parked on a hill overlooking the ferry terminal. There, I could listen to the deep bass rumble of the ferries' engines and observe the swirling eddies in the blue-green salt water of Puget Sound, which was caused by the tide change and the churning of the enormous propellers as the huge ferries arrived. Cars, trucks, and people were disgorged and then reloaded before the huge ships departed once again. Through the scratched lens of the Speed Grafic, the bustling seascape was reduced to a 4x5 postcard with the San Juan Islands and the Strait of Juan de Fuca posing in the background. The scene was breathtaking, but I could not enjoy the beauty. It might have been the solitary young woman with short red hair pushing a bicycle onto the ferry. Or the dozen black cormorants perched expectantly on the pilings like funeral attendants that caused the scene to blur before my eyes so that I packed up the camera and departed soon after.

Ironically, it was a question from Stu that pulled me back from the precipice of suicidal thoughts. At the Van de Zilver Sunday dinner, conversation turned to the upcoming fishing season, which was due to open on the last weekend in April.

"Guess you might have figured out already," he said, "that fishing season opens in three weeks?"

"Why do you wait until then to open?" I asked out of curiosity. "Isn't that giving away your single most important advantage to your competitors, the state fisheries? I thought the whole idea of a trout fishing farm was that you didn't need a license."

As if in accord, one of the canaries let out a peep from the family room. Virgil put down his fork, heavy with mashed potatoes.

"Why not open a week early?" I asked.

Stu eyed me over a bottle of Bud Light. "It's simple. Partly it is the weather conditions, but mostly it is because people do not think about trout fishing until the television news and the sports section in the newspaper mention it, which is always two, maybe three days before the season opens."

"People need the media to tell them what to do?" Valerie asked. Several faces turned at once, as if surprised she could still speak after such a lengthy spell of self-imposed silence.

"Stupid as it may sound to you, Sis, that's pretty much the way it is," Stu said. "We could open early, and no one would know. We'd be sitting around with nothing to do but twiddle our thumbs."

"What about advertising?" I asked.

Stu chuckled. "You must be smoking the fish food."

Vonda snorted.

"Who's got that kind of money?" Stu asked. "We're not exactly McDonald's, in case you haven't noticed."

Virgil had not said a word. Now he spoke up. "Wait a minute, Stu. Let's hear what Gray has to say."

"Doesn't cost anything to listen, right?" Vonda said.

Stu rolled his eyes in disgust.

"Got some paper and a pen or pencil?"

Valerie hurried to the kitchen and brought back a small pad of paper and a pen, no doubt from a carefully organized drawer. I quickly sketched a small space ad with a smiling fish and filled it in with a headline. "What about something like this?"

Vonda read the copy, "Get a jump on the fishing season. Our rainbows can't wait."

I added a line of copy at the bottom before handing the notepad back to Vonda.

"You catch 'em, we clean 'em," she said.

"I like it," Valerie said.

"What's something like that cost?" Virgil asked.

"I don't know. Maybe a hundred bucks or so."

Virgil's eyebrows rose.

"I'd suggest running it more than once. Probably at least two weeks in the *Skagit Valley Herald.*"

"How do you expect to make any money throwing it away like that?" Stu asked.

"That's not all," I said. "We'll need some signs. I can paint them, but materials are probably another hundred."

In the silence that followed, I shrugged. "I'm guessing we won't make any money the first weekend, or maybe even the next. But we'll make some happy new customers, and they'll tell their friends."

"Can I see that?" Virgil asked. He pushed up his glasses as he studied it.

"What do you think, Daddy?" Vonda asked.

"I can have an ad ready by Wednesday—Thursday latest— for running in next week's paper."

"What's your investment?" Stu asked. "I don't hear you offering any skin in the game."

"Tell you what," I said. "I'll put up the money to run the ads and make the signs. You can pay me back later. If it doesn't work, it's my loss."

"Go for it, Daddy," Vonda said. "What have you got to lose?"

Stu crossed his arms over his chest.

"I don't really see how we can go wrong," Virgil said. "I say, let's give her a go."

"Have you considered how are we going to be ready in time?" Stu said. "We've got fishing rods to be repaired and strung with line and fences to be painted. And one more thing:

you cannot put up signs without a permit and, slow as the county bureaucracy is, I guarantee you are not going to get a permit in the next three months, let alone the next couple of weeks. Have you forgotten all the hassle we went through just to put that little, bitty trout farm sign in the front yard?"

Virgil sighed. "You've got a point, Stu."

Having faced off with my father, a man who would not begin to say "maybe" until he had taken a pound of flesh, I was not ready to give in. "Haven't you heard of bootleg signs? Real estate people would be out of business if it weren't for temporary signs on weekends."

I looked at the faces around the table. "The fish are ready. The only thing I can't vouch for is the weather."

"Bootleg signs," Vonda mused. "I kinda like the sound of it."

The next two weeks flew by in a rush of mowing, feeding the trout and preparing for the early opening. I found a FedEx office where I used a computer to design the ad and a flyer that Annie consented to post in her restaurant by the cash register.

The ad broke ten days before the opening with a brief news story I wrote in the *Herald*. The phone began to ring the same day the ad appeared with people calling from as far away as Seattle and Bellingham to ask for directions. As it continued to ring throughout the next several days, the Van de Zilver household seemed to waken from a deep slumber.

I was encouraged to see Valerie's mood improve and the return of her peculiar midday sandwiches. One day it was roast beef, cheese, and apple slices. Another day, it was peanut butter, celery, and raisins. I never knew what to expect. Quite often, I would remove the bread and eat the ingredients individually.

Even Virgil seemed to quicken his step. He showed up one night after dinner when I was painting signs in the barn. "What can I do to help?"

"Can you paint?"

"I used to be pretty fair with a brush."

I handed him the brush and paint. While he painted, I continued to sketch the letters onto boards with a carpenter's pencil.

"You've managed to get this place stirred up these past few days," Virgil said while carefully filling in with color the letters I had drawn. "I've got to admit, you've added another dimension to the trout business."

I smiled, grateful that life was finally on the upswing, my mental health on the mend and my work, however menial, had value once again.

"One thing I don't understand," Virgil said a little later, "what's in this for you? Why risk your own money? It's not like I pay you a great deal."

"Just putting my money where my mouth is. Besides, I'm fairly confident what a little promotion can do."

For a few brief seconds, I allowed myself to remember my iMac computer with retina display and the ease of designing something as simple as an ad or a sign. My fellow students at Otis would laugh if they saw my working conditions now as I sat cross-legged on the barn's cold concrete floor, the only light coming from fluorescent tubes high overhead and the sound of crickets chirping from just outside the open door.

Virgil took his time. I noticed he liked to stop and admire his work.

"I expect you miss your father," he said after a while.

"I never really had a father," I said. "I had a foreman."

"What did he do, you don't mind me asking?"

"He is—was—a physician. The kind who believed there was only one way to tie a suture or earn a living. Going to art school didn't fit within his frame of reference."

Virgil nodded. "My dad was about the same. Summers, he made me hoe weeds in our vegetable garden from sun-up to sun-down with never a break except a half-hour for lunch. Never paid me one red-cent of allowance either. Said he did not believe in it. Had a Chevy he kept garaged. I had to keep it spotless, inside and out. Miss a speck of dirt and he would let me know about it. Sometimes I think he cared more about that car than for me."

I continued to sketch letters, warmed by our conversation.

"I always wished I had a son," Virgil said. "Someone to carry on the family name." He waved his paint brush in the air, and I began to wish I had spread a few more newspapers on the concrete. "Don't get me wrong. I would not trade my daughters for anything. I am sure they were both easier to raise than a son would have been. Even when Val needed a special tutor to teach her Braille, she was really no trouble. As sweet a girl as you could imagine most of the time, but now and then with a temper. Just like her mom."

Then Virgil said something remarkable. "I think my daughter has taken a shine to you."

For a half second that felt much longer, I was afraid Virgil meant Vonda.

"Valerie may not be as pretty as some girls," Virgil said.

Truthfully, I thought her delicate natural beauty to be more attractive than many of the young women in Southern California who spent hundreds—even thousands—of dollars on hair, nail, and skin care, not to mention teeth whitening, breast augmentation, and other enhancements.

"But she's a hard worker," he continued. "Always looking to please me and her sister. Not a big fan of Stu, as you probably noticed. They can be as cantankerous as a couple of wildcats. Best to keep 'em separate if you don't want to see the fur fly."

"Anyway," he continued a few minutes later. "If you and my daughter were to hit it off, might be you could take charge of this operation someday. Maybe even run it once I'm gone."

I was too startled to respond.

"Just thinking out loud," Virgil added after a period of silence. "Not going to change my will tomorrow."

"I have to ask: you wouldn't have a problem with my Indian heritage?"

He looked up at me. "Listen here, son. There are some up here who may have a problem, but I ain't one of them, and Valerie for damn sure is not one of them either. If everyone were as blind to color as she is, I believe the world would be a much happier place."

It took me a minute to digest Virgil's declaration. In a few seconds, he had just destroyed most of my preconceived beliefs about older, rural white males.

"What about Stu and Vonda?"

Virgil snorted. "I don't think Vonda would hang around one second if she had someplace better to call home. You've heard her. She thinks fishing and living in the country are for hicks and people down on their luck. As for Stu," he looked at me, "he could be planning to keep this farm running after I am gone, but I don't think so. Just between you and me, I am not sure he didn't have something to do with those fish dying. Plus, I don't think he is cut out for cleaning fish and waiting on people. Got an attitude like God made him better than the rest of us poor folks."

I was temporarily too overwhelmed to speak. Virgil obviously was not aware of the Sinaloa Cartel and its sicarios who were probably hunting for me right now and eager to kill not only me, but anyone foolish enough to hide me. Fortunately, I did not have to respond.

"Where do you intend to put these signs?" Virgil asked.

"I thought I'd drive down the road and post a sign wherever I came to an intersection that looked busy."

Virgil nodded. "Unless you are looking to burn a lot of fuel and time, ask Stu or Vonda to ride along. They can show you the best places." He stood. One of his knees made a popping noise, and he rubbed it.

"I believe I'll let you clean up," Virgil said. "Think about what I said. Might be a future here for a hardworking, smart young man like you."

I watched in silence as Virgil walked out of the barn and into the cool, dark night. I finished painting the last sign and laid it aside to dry. After giving up hope of ever having anything resembling a normal life again, I found Virgil's offer mind-boggling. I felt like Lazarus must have two thousand years ago. Back from the dead.

CHAPTER TWENTY-THREE

"Would either of you be willing to be my guide setting up directional signs tomorrow morning?" I asked. It was the day before we were to open, and I had just finished helping Valerie clean up the Friday evening dinner dishes. As usual, Vonda and Stu were sitting in the living room, watching television.

Stu ignored me.

"I'll help," Vonda offered.

Stu stared at her like she had lost her mind.

"He doesn't have a clue about local traffic patterns and the best sign locations," she said. "We'll be lucky if folks don't end up in Wenatchee."

"He made his bed," Stu said. "Let him lie in it."

"Why not help out?" she asked. "Seems to me, he's working for the benefit of us all, even you." She turned to me. "What time were you planning to leave?"

"Six."

She made a face. "You sure you couldn't go later? Lord knows I need my beauty sleep."

Stu laughed. "Be a cold day in hell before you see this woman out of bed that early on a weekend. There would have to be a going-out-of-business sale at Nordstrom."

"Then why don't you go?" Valerie said from the doorway. No one had seen her enter. "He's only trying to bring us some business."

"I've got better things to do getting us ready for fishing," Stu said. "And they don't include setting up illegal signs."

Mindful of his threat to cut me up into fish food if I so much as looked at his wife, I did my best to put the matter to rest. "I appreciate your offer of help, but I'll make do on my own."

And so it was with more than a little surprise as I drove past the house early the next morning with a light drizzle falling and a chilly mist swaddling the hills, that I saw Vonda poke her head out the back door, her hair still unbrushed, and wave.

Two minutes later, she exited the door dressed in blue jeans, rain hat and parka.

"Good morning," I said when she had climbed into the Toyota's passenger seat.

"No, it ain't," she said. "It's colder than a loan officer's heart at Christmas, it's wet, and I want to be back in bed, so get a move on before I change my mind. Here," she said, and handed me a commuter mug of coffee as we exited the driveway. "Valerie made it."

"That was kind of her."

"I don't think she was too keen on my coming," she said.

"And why would that be?"

"Because she's a jealous little bitch."

I drove in silence for few minutes as I enjoyed the coffee and pondered Vonda's reply. "As a married woman, don't you find her jealousy a little odd?"

"Not really." She pulled a pint bottle of caramel-colored liquid from her coat pocket, unscrewed the cap, and took a pull. "Matter of fact, I find it kind of amusing."

"What's that you're drinking?"

"Nectar of the gods. Want some?" She held up a bottle that smelled of over-ripe fruit. The label read, "Apricot Brandy."

"Thanks, but I'm the designated driver this morning. Did you run out of wine?"

"Wine's too cold in the morning." She took another pull on the bottle. "Besides, wine is a sad, fire-in-the-fireplace kind of drink for when the day's winding down, but you're still hoping something might come of it. Wine helps hide the truth as long as possible. By the time you realize the evening has turned out to be shit, just like all the others, you are past caring. This stuff, on the other hand," she held up the bottle, "is full of surprises. Kinda perky. Like me." She winked.

We drove down narrow, unlined ribbons of asphalt that wound between tall evergreens and alder trees so dense with new leaves that it was impossible to see what lay beyond. Thick and unruly from the never-ending rain, the grass that hugged the shoulder was over a foot tall and so green it shone nearly black. Tiny birds—chickadees, juncos, nuthatches, and the occasional goldfinch—swooped and flitted from shrub to shrub. We passed the Mountain View Estates—"Models Open"—and a small market where a faded sign proclaimed, "Food Stamps Accepted." A rust-scabbed Cadillac, missing a door, was decomposing in the weeds out back.

"Tell me about your wife," Vonda asked.

"What do you want to know? She was tall, red-haired, and liked to laugh. She could also punch hard enough to give you a black eye." Which she had accomplished once when I criticized her checkbook balancing. Or lack thereof.

"Did she want kids?"

I frowned. "She wanted to travel, live in a big house on the waterfront, drive a fast car—all stuff we couldn't afford."

"Sounds a little like me," she said, her words beginning to slur. "Stu is a world-class skinflint. For our anniversary, he used to send me a box of flowers, but no vase. If I were lucky, he'd take me to the buffet line at the Indian casino." Vonda took another swig. "Now, he doesn't bother. I doubt he remembers the day at all."

"Not exactly a romantic, is he?" Even at this early hour with no makeup, her hair tucked under a watch cap, and wearing a bulky parka, Vonda was more than pretty enough to turn men's heads.

Forty-five minutes after starting out, we put up the last of the signs, each of which featured a smiling trout pointing in the direction of the Van de Zilver farm. We stood in bracken fern and ankle-tall grass near the edge of a two-lane county road where another road dead-ended, forming a "T." Water gurgled nearby as it coursed through a drainage ditch. A stand of alder and Douglas fir trees rose behind us. The countryside remained muffled by the heavy mist that dampened sound and limited visibility to a few hundred feet. Ours was the only vehicle we had seen.

I hammered the signpost into the rocky soil, so that the sign would be seen by cars traveling from any of three directions. I glanced over at Vonda and caught her scrutinizing me.

"We'd better get back," I said. "Our first customers are apt to show up soon."

"Don't worry," Vonda said thickly. She had by now consumed well over half the pint of brandy. "Stu will take care of 'em. Sure you don't want a taste?" She held the bottle up. "Guaranteed to warm you up."

"Let's go." I started back to the truck.

"Hey," she called out. "You with the frown. You're a party-pooper, know that?"

On most days, you could see the line where sky and land met. Today, however, was not one of those days. Clouds, hillside, trees, shrubs, and asphalt had merged to become a soft, green-gray smudge.

Vonda stuck her arm through mine. I turned again toward the truck, but she pulled me to her.

"Stop for a damn second." She stared into my eyes. "You really know how to bolster a lady's confidence. Am I that unappealing to you?"

I started to say, "It's not—" and then her lips were on mine.

The bottle fell with a thud and her hand grasped the hair on the back of my head. Her tongue searched my mouth and I tasted rain and brandy and teeth.

We heard the car approaching at the same time and I pulled away. "Time to go."

The mood in the truck for most of the way back to the farm was quiet as Vonda stared out the window. "What was that about?" I asked.

"A girl just needs to have fun now and then," she replied. "I swear, you are without a doubt the world's greatest killjoy."

Remembering Stu's threat, I said nothing.

"Tell me something, Gray," Vonda said. "Did you come here thinking you were going to save us all from ourselves?" She took another swig of brandy. "I guess now that you saved a few trout, you think you can walk on water, too."

CHAPTER TWENTY-FOUR

While I had done my best not to show it, I had spent the past week anxiously watching the sky, my ears attuned to the television for clues about the weather. My fear was that it would rain on the Saturday we opened, and all my hard work and bravado would come to naught when no one showed up. Then Stu would make sure I ate crow for at least the rest of my life.

And then I remembered that other Saturday when my wife and my life had been taken from me by a fucking, red-lipped bitch and it was like something woke the beast.

By the time Vonda and I arrived back at the trout farm, the mist had evaporated, and a diamond-shaped field of blue had nudged its way through the clouds. The gravel parking lot displayed a motley assemblage of sedans, SUVs, pickup trucks, and one Harley-Davidson motorcycle. Virgil was waving to the driver of a recreational vehicle, directing him to park on the grass alongside the driveway. Someone, probably Valerie, had set up a large stainless-steel percolator on a card table near the back door with a bag of Styrofoam cups. A half-dozen balloons lined the fence surrounding the kids' playground. Beautiful. I made a mental note to commend her.

No sooner had we rolled to a stop by the barn than Stu was storming toward us, exuding anger with every step.

"What took you so long?" he demanded. "Can't you see we've got customers?"

"They wouldn't be here if we hadn't put out signs," Vonda said. She brushed by Stu without saying anything more.

Hands on his hips, Stu watched her as she made her way to the house. He swiveled to face me. He looked like he wanted to poke me in the chest again but thought better of it. "You remember what I said about fish food?"

The taste of rain and brandy were still on my tongue, the warmth of Vonda's lips and the press of her body still imprinted in my mind. "Nah, I forget. Want to remind me?"

"Let's get to work," Stu said. "I'll show you how to clean fish. Meanwhile, it is your job to make sure everyone has got a line in the water. Give 'em one of our bamboo poles if they need one. If they do not catch fish, we don't make any money."

Two men, both well over sixty-five, climbed out of the front seat of an immaculate, vintage Oldsmobile. It exhibited the original two-tone, brown and cream paint and upholstery, its chrome glistening in the early morning sunlight. They grabbed rods and a tackle box from the trunk and, without a word, headed down the hill toward the large pond. The women who had ridden with them were left with unloading lawn chairs, a picnic basket, and a coffee thermos.

"Can I help you with that?"

"Well, ain't you the gentleman?" said one. Neither was much above five feet tall and both had that shapeless, nearly sexless quality that some older women get. Their hair was dyed different colors—one platinum, the other chestnut—but they had a matched set quality about them, like salt and pepper shakers. Sisters, no doubt. I carried their chairs and picnic basket, walking slowly to keep from outdistancing them as they traversed the uneven ground in their matching white tennis shoes and white socks with the fuzzy balls in the back.

"Ain't it pretty, Doris?" the one with chestnut hair remarked.

"Like a postcard of Ireland that I once saw," Doris replied.

I looked up from watching their feet and saw the truth of what they said. A swallow performed acrobatics over the emerald lawn as it searched for moths. A jagged row of snow-flocked mountains, like the parapets of an enormous, ancient castle, rose above the clouds. The patch of brilliant blue sky I had noted earlier was reflected in all three ponds. The statue of a cherub on the island held his hands in the air as if in praise. An air of peace and tranquility infused the farm, so that you almost expected to hear a Gregorian chant or Celtic harp playing in the background. The quality I most appreciated about the broken camera sitting on the desk in my cabin was its ability to slow, if not halt the flow of dissonant human activity down to a quiet scene like this that almost resembled an Impressionist painting.

Heide had not enjoyed fishing. We tried once, driving several miles to a local lake at 6 a.m., but she complained of being bored and cold and we were back home within an hour. I thought she would have loved the beauty of the trout farm, however. She said it was just such places like this where one could most clearly see God's influence. And, menial as it was, I was proud of my work preparing the trout farm for these visitors.

The big pond that fronted my cabin (I had taken to calling it "mine" since Virgil had given me a raise) was circumscribed by several anglers, and one of the men from the Oldsmobile already had a fish on. The tip of his lightweight fiberglass pole bowed and bobbed as a flash of mercury flung itself across the pond's surface, slashing the water with its tail to throw the hook. I admired the rainbow's refusal to succumb to the likely inevitable end.

"Fight like hell, brother," I said to myself.

I set the chairs down near where the women's husbands were fishing. Across the water, someone else played a fish until the arc of the pole suddenly relaxed as the fish escaped and a curse resounded clearly across the water.

"Anything else I can get you?" I asked the women.

"Can you come to my home later and wash my windows?" Doris asked. The two women chuckled as she pulled a dollar from her purse. "This is for helping."

"Oh." I stared at the money, embarrassed. No doubt I probably looked like I needed it. "That's okay. I was just doing my job."

Doris seized my wrist and stuffed the bill into my hand. "C'mon, take it. Don't be stubborn."

Behind the lenses of her glasses, her green eyes were small and bright. I wanted to hug her, but figured it might embarrass us both.

"Thanks. I'll check back later to see how you're doing."

Nearby, a young father with a shaved head picked at a large nest of fishing line, while a toddler sat on her heels nearby and played with the strange, colorful objects in the tackle box.

"Problems?"

"Maybe your fingers are nimbler than mine." He held out one of those cheap plastic fishing poles they sell in toy stores.

"Tell you what: let me get you one of our bamboo rods so you can continue fishing while I work on this."

The bamboo poles were nine to ten feet long with a similar length of leader upon which was strung a bobber and a hook. A good, arm-extended cast would carry the bait out a more than adequate distance from shore. The action of the crude homemade poles might not be as good as those of more limber fiberglass, but their simplicity was unbeatable, and the fish could not care less.

After several minutes of failing to untangle the line, I gave up and moved on. I dug worms in the compost pile for a young family, their towheaded son barely old enough to walk, but alarmingly mobile. He was followed everywhere by his mother, her ponytail bouncing as she tried to stay between him and the water's edge.

While keeping one eye on the towhead, I spoke to a couple from Vancouver B.C. The man was dressed in a tweed jacket and wool pants, casting a dry fly with studied care, while his female companion, equally tall and slender, sat nearby in a folding chair and read a book. I passed a woman in curlers who was wearing sunglasses, a black leather jacket, and a miniskirt that displayed thighs the envy of a fullback. She carried a small white poodle in one arm and appeared to be wading through a minefield as she stepped delicately in her high heels through the wet grass.

A large black woman and her two daughters had taken up residence on the metal park bench at the east end of the pond. The girls played cards, drawing from a deck between them, while their mother read the newspaper. A fishing pole stood braced against the back of the bench. Another was propped up on a forked stick that had been stuck into the ground.

"Check your bait, Donelle," the mother said.

"Already did," one of the girls answered with a tiny lisp while displaying a mouth full of braces.

"Check it again. I thought I saw the rod give a little twitch a while back."

The girl rolled her eyes. "That was on account of you sitting down." Nevertheless, she began to reel in.

I continued making my rounds as more anglers arrived. The fishing action was going strong; I saw several fish being pulled from the pond or added to stringers. By eleven, both sides of the long driveway had become parking lots, and there were more cars and trucks and a couple of RVs parked up along the road. The size of the crowd threatened to overwhelm Stu, whose job was to measure the trout, clean them, and collect the money. The line of people waiting with their catches had grown steadily. Stu worked at a specially built table near the foot of the driveway. A yardstick for measuring the trout was nailed to the back splash and a short length of hose ran water into a trough along one end.

Between the way the morning had started out and the success of the early opening, I was feeling good. "Need some help?" I asked.

"Watch me gut this one," Stu said without looking up. He slit the trout's belly with a slender filleting knife from the vent to the throat, reached in and tore out gills, pectoral fins, and innards in one quick move, tossed the offal in a garbage can lined with a plastic bag, and then rinsed the body cavity with water from the hose. With their heads and tails intact, the trout were then placed in a clear plastic bag, sides gleaming as if they were still alive and might swim away even now if given the chance.

"Think you can handle this without stabbing yourself or an innocent bystander?" he asked.

"I'll manage."

For the next two hours, we worked side by side. I chatted with the customers while cleaning and bagging their fish. Stu measured, totaled up the fees, and collected the money. He also grumbled. He grumbled about where Vonda was and why hadn't someone brought food, didn't they know it was lunch time, when were the damn people going to stop coming, why did I think I was so fucking smart, and so forth.

"If you hate this so much," I asked, "how come you married the daughter of a trout farm owner?"

"Wasn't my intention to live here."

That made two of us.

Stu straightened up and rolled his shoulders. "Arizona Diamondbacks offered me a big bonus to sign right out of high school. I was assigned to their Reno Aces Triple A farm team. Vonda and I got married and rented a nice apartment. Everything was looking good and then I blew out my arm pitching. Game over."

The Canadian couple showed up with a nice stringer of fish. Slit, tear, toss, rinse. I quickly found a rhythm for cleaning the dead trout. The garbage can contained a growing mound of blood and guts that proved fascinating to children.

"That why you ended up here?" I asked after the couple left.

"Not immediately," Stu said. "After two years at Skagit Valley Community College, the county hired me as a building inspector. We were living in Burlington while Vonda attended Western Washington University. Then the girls' mother got sick, and Virgil needed help running the place." He rinsed blood and fish slime from the table. "Not exactly the career path I would have chosen."

The large black woman appeared with the two girls and held up a large trout with a couple of smaller ones. "Got a whale here and a couple of his little brothers."

"Congratulations," I said. "That's probably the biggest fish so far."

"Told you, Donelle," the mother said. "First time fishing and you caught Moby Dick."

Donelle rolled her eyes while her sister checked out the guts in the garbage can.

"What are you going to do with that mess?" the mother asked. "Compost it?"

"Feed it to the fish," Stu said. "Can't compost it or we'd have every bear, weasel, and raccoon in the North Cascades paying us a visit. A week from now there wouldn't be any trout left to catch."

Valerie showed up a few minutes later with Patsy and sodas to ask when we were planning to stop for lunch.

"Where the hell is Vonda?" Stu asked. "Doesn't she know she's supposed to swap places with us so we can take turns eating?"

"I'm not in charge of her," Valerie said. "You're her husband."

Soon after Valerie returned to the house, Vonda appeared and replaced Stu. She wore a pair of yellow plastic kitchen gloves and a pink apron over blue jeans and a sweatshirt. She was slower than Stu, but no one seemed to mind.

"How's that nectar of the gods working?"

She frowned. "Now I remember why I dislike drinking in the morning. It just sucks the spit out of you for the rest of the day."

Stu did not make it back until over an hour later. "You can grab lunch now," he said. "Just make sure you're back in thirty minutes."

I wiped my bloody hands on a towel before hurrying up to the house. The smell of fried bacon permeated the kitchen. Valerie had made my new favorite sandwich: bacon, peanut butter, mayonnaise, and sweet pickles.

"What took you guys so long this morning?" she asked.

"Thanks to your sister's help, I thought it went pretty fast. I didn't get lost, and the signs appear to be working."

"Did she make any snide comments about me?"

"Not a one," I said.

"Daddy said we're already had more people in a single day than we usually get on a weekend. He left to buy more bags for the fish, but said he'd be back to take us all out to dinner tonight."

Personally, I thought going to bed early was a better idea. A lack of sleep plus the amount of work getting ready for the past week was finally taking a toll. My shoulders and back ached from bending over the cleaning table.

"Would you mind if I sat in your father's La-Z-Boy, put my feet up and closed my eyes for a few minutes?"

I felt like I had barely sat down when Valerie began shaking my shoulder. "Wake up, Gray. I think something's wrong."

According to my watch, fifteen minutes had passed. I groaned. "Stu's probably ready to kill me."

"We may have a bigger problem."

Then, over the sound of Patsy pawing at the door and whining, I heard a woman's screams.

CHAPTER TWENTY-FIVE

Valerie grabbed Patsy's collar to restrain her, and I bolted from the house, a lump in my throat and my heart beating too fast. There was no one at the cleaning station. Fishing had stopped. People moved in ones and twos toward the screaming, which was coming from one of the smaller ponds. I burst past Vonda. Stu was climbing out of the pond. In his arms, he held the limp body of the towheaded boy I had seen earlier. His pale arm was flung out to the side and one of his tiny, red tennis shoes was missing.

"My baby," the mother shrieked as she fought Stu for her son's body. Her husband pulled her away, lifting her high as she continued to struggle, her legs kicking in the air as she clawed at his arms. "Let me go, goddammit! Let me go!"

I made my way anxiously through the crowd.

"Fire department is on their way," one of the guys from the Oldsmobile said, holding up his cell phone in confirmation.

Stu laid the boy carefully on the ground and, after checking his pulse, began CPR. I dropped to my knees beside him.

"What can I do?" I asked.

Stu's brown hair hung in front of his eyes and he tossed it aside without missing a beat. "I got this. Go up to the road and wait for the paramedics. Get 'em down here fast. One minute delay and he'll die."

Stu continued pumping the toddler's tiny chest, while his mother wept and his father struggled to restrain her as the circle of onlookers continued to grow.

The fire truck arrived. I directed the men down the hill toward the pond where Stu and the boy were. A sheriff's car arrived soon after. It was followed within seconds by two more. The ambulance was less than a minute behind. Filled with dread, I pursued it down the hill. The boy was now wearing an oxygen mask and strapped to a stretcher. After sliding him into the ambulance, a paramedic helped the mother climb aboard to ride with them.

The clouds had disappeared, and the sky had become a brilliant blue, but the serenity from earlier had fled. My mouth felt dry as an ashtray, and I desperately wanted a beer or something stronger. Before returning to the fish cleaning station, I stopped by the house where Valerie stood in the doorway with Patsy.

"It's bad," I told her. "Someone spotted a small boy floating in Pond Two. Stu gave him CPR until the paramedics arrived. The ambulance is taking him to Skagit Valley Hospital. The fire department is packing up their stuff, but the police are still here interviewing everyone."

"You'd think people would do a better job of watching their kids," she said. "Do you think he'll make it?"

"Don't know." My earlier enthusiasm had been replaced by dread.

Valerie, who I believe could hear thoughts as well as most people hear spoken words, said, "It's like Momma told me. 'You can't run from your fate.'"

I stared at her for a few seconds before putting it together. How else for a mother to explain to her young daughter why the cancer that was growing within her was not going to stop. Not until you were dead?

"Sorry. I have to go."

***

I heard the fear in his voice and I knew right then, though I did not want to believe it, that everything was ruined. Momma was right about fate, just like she was right about everything else. It listens and waits. Like a cat waiting to pounce.

When the man came to the door, I was dusting the knickknacks on the piano, even though I had just cleaned them the day before.

"You live here?" he asked.

"Excuse me, officer," I heard Vonda call out from just behind him. "Can I help you? I'm Vonda and this is my sister, Valerie."

"Like your names. What do they call that? It ain't rhyming."

"Alliteration," Vonda said.

"Alliteration," he repeated. "That's it. Tell me, Vonda, where were you and your sister when that boy drowned? Did either of you see what happened?"

"My sister's blind and can't see nothin', but I saw it. I was cleaning fish and had just packaged up some trout for people who were leaving when I heard the screams. I ran down the hill to see what was happening. I saw my husband, Stu, doing CPR, trying to save that poor little boy's life. So tragic. No idea what his parents were thinking, letting a little tyke roam around like that. No supervision."

"Okay. That sounds about right based on what I already know," the police officer said. "By the way, you happen to know who owns that pickup truck parked down by the barn with the California plates?"

"Sure," Vonda said. "That belongs to our maintenance man, Gray Reynolds."

I must have gasped or something because they both quit talking. "You okay, Sis?" Vonda asked.

If I had had my knife, I might have stabbed her right there.

"You know where I might find your maintenance man?" he asked.

"He should be down there helping out, probably at the cleaning table working beside my husband," Vonda said.

"In case I happen to miss him, you tell Mr. Reynolds that he needs to get his vehicle registered with the State of Washington A-S-A-P. If I see it with those plates on the road, I'm going to write him a ticket."

"What was that about?" Vonda said after he had left. *"You went all red and crazy-faced for a moment. Thought you might puke or something."*

"You're a fucking idiot, Vonda."

I could not say how I knew that Gray was hiding from someone or why, but I was afraid my careless sister had just let the cat out of the bag.

***

After burning off the remaining clouds, the sun was slowly sinking beneath the tops of the tall evergreens that bordered the west side of the property as I collected trash in a plastic bag. There were empty beer and soda cans, broken leaders with lead shot weights and hooks still attached, and cellophane wrappers. I spotted a tiny, red tennis shoe floating in Pond Two. Valerie showed up with Patsy as I was using a bamboo fishing rod to retrieve it.

"You didn't come to dinner," she said.

"I didn't feel like eating. Did you hear anything?"

"Not yet. Vonda tried calling the hospital, but they wouldn't tell her anything. Daddy said we all need to pray."

"Pray?" I could think of nothing else to say. It was clear to me that God had moved, changed his email address and phone number without telling anyone.

"Listen to me, Gray." Valerie's face turned fierce. "I only know one thing. It was not your fault. You didn't have nothing to do with that little boy drowning in one of the ponds." Her voice cracked and what came out after sounded a like a sob. "His mother should have been watching him better."

"Yeah." I stooped to pet Patsy and got my face licked in return. "Thanks, Valerie. I think I'll turn in and get some rest."

"Are you sure you wouldn't like me to bring you something to eat?"

"Thanks, but I'm tired."

"Take care, brown bear," she said.

When I did not reply, she added, "Just remember, it wasn't your fault."

As I made my way to the cabin, a swirl in the water caught my attention. I glimpsed a huge tail fin as it curled and then disappeared beneath the nubilous black water. At least one thing had gone right this day. No one had caught Moses.

I entered the tiny cabin, desperately needing a shower to remove the stink of the fish and aspirin to relieve the pounding behind my left eye. I saw the Speed Grafic camera sitting on the small desk and walked over to pick it up. I held it in my hands, examining its fragile, outmoded technology for maybe a minute. Then I slammed it into the desk, smashing the bellows. The glass lens fell onto the floor, and I crushed it beneath my boot.

CHAPTER TWENTY-SIX

As it turned out, the toddler had not drowned, but his close call had generated profound changes to the trout farm operations and, most of all, to my future.

"We dodged a bullet yesterday," Virgil announced at breakfast the next day.

Valerie stopped pouring coffee and sat down as every face turned to focus on Virgil at the head of the table. Patsy was laying down by Valerie's chair, but sat up at attention as if understanding the importance of what was about to be said.

"I just got off the phone with the father," Virgil said. "The boy's okay."

A collective sigh rose from everyone and the canaries twittered excitedly from the other room.

"Woke up at the hospital and asked for ice cream." Virgil nodded. "I told him I'd pay for the hospital and ambulance."

"That's wonderful, Daddy," Vonda said.

"I wouldn't call it 'wonderful,'" he said. "If that boy would have died, our business here could be over. Likely as not, they'd sue us for everything I've got, including the farm."

"Wouldn't the insurance cover it?" Vonda asked.

"Unless they found a loophole like negligence or some other hard-to-define term." Virgil stirred the coffee in his Cadillac mug. "And they'd make darn sure we never got coverage again.

"My point is we can't have any more accidents like this. I have already been on the phone with the Skagit County Health and Safety Inspector. They'll have a team up later this week to do a thorough inspection and could shut us down for good if they don't think we can prevent children from drowning."

He paused to ensure he had everyone's full attention. "Here's what we're going to do to see that doesn't happen. First, we're going to drain Ponds One and Two."

"Wow," Valerie said as she slumped in her chair like someone had let the air out of her. Patsy laid her head in her lap.

"All the fish from Pond Two will be transferred to the big pond. I will try to get a buyer for the fingerlings in Pond One. Gray is going to build us a sign, since he's good at it, with a warning, 'No lifeguard on duty. Call 911 in case of emergency.' Then we're going to hang a life ring and nylon rope attached to a signpost."

"When are we supposed to do all this?" Stu asked.

"We're closed down for the week, so we've got plenty of time."

"Guess we won't be needing those bootleg signs," Stu said.

My face grew warm. My marketing expertise had nearly caused a toddler's death. And now, the farm's livelihood would be curtailed in ways none of us yet understood.

"We'll look to start up again a week from today, after the inspection team has cleared us," Virgil said.

"Daddy?" Everyone turned to look at Vonda.

"Stu and I were talking last night about how it might be a good time to sell the place," she said.

In the stunned silence, I recalled Virgil's recent proposition regarding a permanent position on the farm. The offer and my future suddenly seemed as fleeting as the morning mist.

"I ran some numbers on our sales versus expenses for the last two years," Stu said. "If it wasn't for the business write-offs, we couldn't afford the taxes on this place."

"Don't listen to them!" Valerie said.

"Who said anything about selling?" Virgil said, his voice rising. "Besides, who'd want it? Especially after word about this accident gets out?"

"I might know someone," Stu said.

There it was—revealed at last—the mystery of the roll of blueprints in the locked closet and what Stu had no doubt been planning long before my arrival. I had to hand it to him for waiting patiently until the perfect moment to present his plan.

"To do what exactly?" Virgil asked.

"To develop the land," Stu replied. "Forty acres would be room for a lot of nice homes."

Valerie's face was flushed and her hand trembled as she set down her fork. "Momma said this place would belong to me and Vonda someday."

"This someone got a name?" Virgil asked. He stared hard at Stu.

"Name's Bob Halonen," Stu said. "You might have seen his name on home-for-sale signs around the valley. Bob said when we were ready to sell, he might be interested in developing the place. Put in a cul-de-sac and surround it with big, fancy homes."

Valerie wiped tears from her reddened cheeks and made a snuffling sound. Always sensitive to her master's emotions, Patsy licked her other hand.

"Now, Val," Vonda said. "There's nothing wrong with having the money instead of dealing with the responsibility of keeping up a place like this. Think of all the places you could go, things you could buy."

"What's Gray going to do if you sell the place?"

"He's a smart guy," Stu said. "He'll find another job. Besides, he's just a hired hand."

Stu's words twisted in my stomach. Days earlier, Virgil had invited me to become part of the family and help run the place.

Now, less than three days later, I was back to being a "hired hand." Once more, I could hear the universe chuckling at my misplaced optimism.

Valerie slammed her good hand on the table. "I don't want the money. I vote for keeping it just the way it is."

"Just keep on losing money until we're bankrupt, is that what you want?" Stu asked.

"That's enough!" Virgil said, his neck wattle inflamed. "It's my damn farm and I'll sell it if I want, when I want. Until such day arrives, we got a nice little business going here that we need to attend to."

As everyone stood to leave, I began carrying plates to the kitchen where Valerie was running hot water, tears streaming down her red cheeks. "It will be okay," I lied.

When we were finished cleaning up and I was about to leave, she stopped me. "Don't worry, Gray. If they want to sell this place, they're going to have to do it over my dead body."

I drove back along the route where I had posted the bootleg signs with Vonda the morning before and wished she and her bottle of apricot brandy were riding along with me. Her banter and the alcohol might have helped me forget the image of the towheaded boy, whose carefree frolicsomeness had nearly cost him his life. It served as a grim reminder of that other Saturday and how quickly events can change for the worse. Once again, I had rolled snake eyes. And now I had another worry—that I might need to find another place to hide very soon.

***

The odd-looking truck halted within a few feet of the water's edge and the engine died. A moment later the door to the cab was flung open and the driver dropped to the ground. He was a middle-aged black man, whose hair and beard were already thick with the hoarfrost of age, his broad shoulders beginning to stoop. He looked up from his clipboard as I approached. "You Van de Zilver?"

"Sorry. I'm just the maintenance man."

"Figured as much," he said. "You don't look like a 'Van' something or other. No offense." He smiled.

"Pretty place you got here," he said, his eyes taking it in. Even on a windy, overcast day, the farm was an island of rustic splendor girded by the blue-cragged North Cascades. The air was sweet with the scent of new mown grass.

"Saw something on the television news the other night about that little boy nearly drowning in the newspaper. Shame. Something like that probably will not help business. What is the mortgage payment on a place this size? Got to be thirty, forty thousand at least, am I right?"

For a moment, I thought Nathan might be a covert real estate salesman searching for listings. "Couldn't tell you. I just work here."

As if he understood what I was thinking, Nathan quickly apologized. "Hey, I'm sorry. I did not mean anything by my question. You and me, we're working stiffs, right? I got two kids in college and a third in high school. Lucky if I can make the rent payment each month."

Thus reassured, I offered my hand. "I'm Gray."

"Nathan," the other man said.

"Like a cup of coffee, Nathan?"

"When we get done here, I'll take you up on that." He withdrew gloves from a rear pocket and began pulling them on over large, heavily veined hands.

I looked over at the truck where a stubby tank squatted on the back of a flatbed. Slender cylinders ran along either side.

"Those are compressed oxygen canisters and the refrigeration units," Nathan said, following my eyes. "Rainbows are fussy critters. You have to maintain a cool, consistent temperature to keep their respiration and metabolism down. I am about to fire up the generator, so we do not end up with any dead fish. You can give me a hand hooking up the chute for pumping the trout from your pond into the truck. Then we'll load up your fingerlings and I'll haul them away. Give me a minute to take care of business. Got a few things to sign."

Nathan busied himself about the truck. An engine coughed once as it started up, then chugged away quietly. A robin called to its mate with a full-throated warble.

I helped Nathan twist the sections of aluminum piping together to form a lightweight, but sturdy tube that reached from the truck to beyond the water's edge. "Hold onto the chute with both hands so it doesn't move around," Nathan said. "You might want to support it with your knee. It will be heavy once the water and fish start flowing through it. I'll turn on the pump."

Nathan returned just as water and fish began rushing through the pipe and into the truck.

"They're beautiful."

"That they are," Nathan said. "Beautiful, but doomed eventually, as are we all, humans and fish alike."

Later, as we walked toward the barn for a cup of coffee, I posed a question that suddenly popped into my mind. "Say that you wanted to move a single fish. How would you go about doing it?"

Nathan squinted at me. "What size fish are we talking about?"

"Pretty big."

"How big is 'pretty big'? Twelve, fifteen inches?"

"Bigger." I spread my hands over two feet apart.

"Hooiee!" Nathan looked at me like I had lost my mind. "Like a salmon?"

"Yeah. Like a salmon."

"First of all, I wouldn't do it. It is illegal to haul a live salmon or other game fish unless you have the proper license. The state would throw your ass in jail and fine you. Might even take your vehicle away." We walked in silence for a little ways.

"But if I did," he resumed thoughtfully, "I guess I would get me a big old plastic garbage can with a lid that seals, then fill it up with water and add some ice. Then I'd get me some sodium amytal."

"What's that?"

"Barbiturate. Slows down the fish's metabolism, prevents too much waste from being excreted and fouling up the oxygen supply. Also mellows the fish out. Happy fish travel better, same as people."

We reached the barn and the door to Stu's office where the coffee was. I paused before going in. "How much of this stuff would I need?"

"'Bout a half grain per gallon should do the trick. I believe I just might have some in the truck."

"Listen, Nathan." I put a hand on his arm. "I don't want to cause any trouble for you."

"No trouble." He looked at me with a sad smile. "I do believe we're all just sinners here."

***

Mid-morning the next day, I spotted Valerie working on the roses. Earlier I had seen her feeding the rabbits. I stopped the Bull and joined her. Patsy got up from where she lay and waggled toward me to get her ears scratched.

"Seems like I owe you another 'thank you.'"

"What for?" Valerie cocked her head sideways in that familiar way she had of listening.

"The other day when you worried about what I was going to do if your father sold the farm." I watched the fingers of her left-hand slide delicately over the canes, determining the best location to prune. "You didn't need to that. Stu's right. I'm just a 'hired hand.'"

"Don't be stupid, Gray. You are like family. Except nicer."

Valerie snipped with her shears and a tall stalk fell to the ground. "I can't believe Daddy would sell the farm. He promised Momma he would always keep it in the family. She called it 'an heirloom.'"

During the past few days, whenever I thought about what I would do, or where I would go if the job at the trout farm ended soon, I was forced to punt. Finding another place as remote as this with free room and board and no tax forms filed with the IRS would take a good deal of research, not to mention luck. Nor did I have enough money saved to live longer than a few weeks without working. Without ID, signing up for unemployment was impossible. Joining the growing hordes of homeless people that overwhelmed every city, large or small, with their bags of belongings, shopping carts, and chronic health issues was not high on my list of preferences. As tenuous as my current meager circumstances were, the bottom still looked a long way down.

Valerie selected another stalk and clipped it. "What I can't figure out is, if taxes on this place are so high, how come Daddy never said anything before?"

"Maybe he didn't want to worry his daughters." I switched the subject. "How can you do that without wearing gloves?"

"I can't wear gloves and feel what I'm doing," she said. "Momma taught me how. You have to start by cupping the flower. When it is no longer full, the petals no longer moist and shiny, it is time to go. Then I work my way down carefully, avoiding the hard thorns, and snip just above the first foliage." She demonstrated.

"You try." She handed me the pruning shears. "Close your eyes and allow yourself to feel. Just be careful you don't cut off your finger by mistake."

I planned to cheat by picking out what I thought was a gangly, thorn-free shoot before closing my eyes, but it proved to be a poor choice. "Damn!" I jerked my hand back. Deep red blood welled up from the tip of my thumb which throbbed painfully.

"Give me your hand," Valerie commanded.

"What for?"

"Just do it."

She gripped my hand tightly, running her fingers over mine until she found the blood. "Hold still." With her other hand, she reached out, found a rose cane and tightened her hand around it.

I saw what she was going to do but was too late to stop her. She winced. When she opened her hand, a large thorn protruded from her palm.

"Jesus, Valerie. What are you doing?"

She removed the thorn with her teeth. Blood welled up into the creases of her palm. She squeezed my thumb and held it tight. "There. Now we're blood brothers just like Native Americans."

"That had to hurt," I said.

She frowned, her eyes at half-mast. "Momma said nothing worthwhile comes without pain."

"That may be true for pregnancy and assembling Ikea furniture, but I fail to see her logic. I am pretty sure Native Americans have retired any blood brother ceremonies, if they ever had them, especially since the advent of HIV. What other crazy, dangerous things did your mother teach you?"

Valerie resumed her precise pruning. "She taught me everything I know. She took me to concerts, movies and plays. She even took me to the Nutcracker ballet. The usher let me lay my cheek against the side of the stage, so I could feel the leaps of the dancers while I listened to the music and the squeak of their ballet shoes."

She sighed. For a moment, I almost expected her to cry.

"She was always dragging Vonda and me around exploring, until Vonda decided she didn't want to go anymore. Momma was like a scout leader, travel guide, and mom all rolled into one. I remember going to an antique store when I was just five or six. She placed my hands on all these strange, old, musty-smelling things. I can still feel the velvety texture of a tasseled lamp shade. In the scarred wood of an old, rickety cupboard, Momma said you could feel the stories of the families that once owned it. When she died, I lost not only my mother, but my best friend and teacher."

"She sounds like the world's greatest mom."

"Except for one thing," she said, her voice suddenly brittle. "She left me with THEM."

"Don't your dad or Vonda ever offer to take you anywhere?"

"Nope."

"Then what would you say to doing some exploring with me?"

"Explore where?"

"I was thinking of a picnic at the Skagit River."

For a moment, her face glowed, before immediately darkening again. A frown weighed down her heavy brows. "I don't know."

"Why? What are you afraid of?"

"Don't know what I'll find. Afraid of making a mistake, of being hurt. Or looking foolish. I probably look foolish right now." She brushed the hair out of her face. "Vonda's always picking on me, informing me that something's not right about my appearance. If it isn't my hair, it's my skin, or my clothes. It's always something."

"Did it ever occur to you that she's just jealous? You have a rare, natural beauty she'll never have."

She smiled for a second before frowning again. "What has she got to be jealous of? She can drive, go wherever she wants, get dressed up to meet people, and make friends without worrying what she looks like." She moved sideways to another rose. "You can't imagine how stupid it feels to spend a lovely day at a party, all dressed up, and find out afterwards that everyone was laughing at you the entire time because your dress was stained with blood from your period."

"This happened recently?"

"Well, no," she said.

"When then?"

"Seventh grade. But Vonda still talks about it like it was yesterday."

"Okay. I can see we need some basic rules. As your blood brother, I promise I will always tell you if you look foolish."

She raised her head, her eyes closed. "There's just one thing I need you to promise me."

"What's that," I asked warily.

The frown was now gone from her pale face, replaced by a look of fear. "Promise you won't leave me. At least," she hurried on when I didn't reply immediately, "promise me you won't leave without first telling me that you're going. I couldn't bear being abandoned again."

It seemed like a reasonable request, but, as I was learning, reasonable and predictable rarely ate at the same table. In fact, just that morning, I had been teasing my brain with how to solve the problem of an eight-character password—one that might magically open the door to $100 million.

"Don't worry," I said. After all, what was one more lie at this point?

CHAPTER TWENTY-SEVEN

I was sitting on the concrete floor of the barn adjusting the blades on the Bull when I heard a noise and looked up to find Vonda watching me. She wore a yellow halter top and cut-off jeans. Her feet were bare, and her toes looked freshly painted a mint green.

"Don't mind me. I'm just admiring the view." She studied me over a glass of wine.

It was warm in the barn with no breeze, and I had taken off my shirt. The rich verdure of the trout farm's grounds had turned a green-gold as the days lengthened and the reluctant rain gave way to entire weeks of sunshine.

I used a crescent wrench to make quarter turn adjustments on one side of a gang of blades. Then I fed a sheet of paper into the blades and turned them by hand to see how evenly they cut. Instead of cutting, however, the blades spun freely.

Frustrated, I wiped a drop of sweat from the end of my nose and sat back. I had been at it for twenty minutes and was not any closer to success. My anxiety over the prospect of losing my job was not helping.

Vonda crouched down on her heels less than five feet away. After another series of adjustments, I tried the piece of paper again. This time, the blades would not turn at all. I crumpled up the paper and threw it aside.

"Like some help?" Vonda held out a hand. "I might be available. For a reasonable price."

"Be my guest." I laid the wrench across her palm and she handed me her wine glass.

First, she used the wrench to undo the turns I had just made. Then she walked to the other side of the blades and, crouching again, attempted another adjustment. The fitting was stuck, however, and she strained to turn it.

"Let me," I offered, but she ignored me, and after several grunts, the fitting gave way.

"Now try," she said, wiping the damp hair out of her face with the back of her hand leaving a smear of grease on her forehead.

This time, when I turned the mower blades, they sliced the paper neatly.

"Perfect."

She sipped her wine. "I used to do this for Stu. He ain't the type for making fine adjustments."

"The obvious question is then why did you marry him?"

"It might be hard to you to believe, but he was the pick of the litter. In this neck of the woods, it does not get any better than dating the star baseball player in the county. Stu was going to be my ticket to the big time: New York, Chicago, LA and all the rest. The finest restaurants and hotels. Flying first class. Then he fucked up his arm and, just like that, it was all over. Here I am once again, stuck in the middle of bum-fucking-nowhere."

"What's so funny?" she asked.

"You."

"Why?"

"First of all, you talk like a redneck, but Stu says you've got a degree in literature from a university."

"That ain't nothing. That's just how everybody talks—up here, anyway. Talk to any hick farmer and you'll find out he's got a degree from a university."

"Based on the way you adjusted those blades you could make a living as a mechanic. Yet I've also seen you dressed up in heels and a short dress like you were going out for a night on Sunset Strip."

"That's never going to happen." She frowned.

"The point is, you're not exactly easy to categorize."

"Is that a bad thing?"

I shrugged. "Actually, that's a good thing. I think. Contradictions look good on you."

"Glad you think so." She took another sip of her wine. "Guess you know things will be changing if this place sells. We won't be needing a maintenance man."

"So I've heard. Stu makes sure I am fully aware of my temporary situation. What will you do?"

"Now ain't that the question?" Her gaze turned back toward the barn door. "Probably get a divorce, take my money, and move someplace sunny and warm. Find a man whose idea of a good time ain't drinking beer and shooting squirrels. You know anyone might be interested in the position?"

We smiled at one another. Beads of sweat pearled in the space between her breasts. I forced myself to look away and stood.

"I better get back to work. I've still got to replace a few blades on the hammerknifer."

When I looked over my shoulder, Vonda was bent over to pick up the wrench. With an ass and legs like that, I could see why Stu might feel paranoid. She brought the wrench to me, padding silently in her bare feet on the barn's concrete floor. Some women walk like they just had sex—slow, loose in the hips, and lovely. Instead of depositing the wrench in my outstretched hand, Vonda placed its cold tip against my bare chest.

"Daddy says, 'Never leave a good tool lying around.'"

"What's your husband say?" I reached for the wrench, but she refused to let it go.

"You don't fool me, Gray Reynolds." Vonda smiled. She pressed her pelvis against mine.

"You want everything in life packaged into nice, neat little boxes, but guess what?" she asked softly. "Life doesn't come that way. It's messy as hell. People fighting, divorcing, losing their jobs, getting sick, and dying. And..." Her eyes focused on my lips and her voice sounded ragged, as if she were winded. "As surprising as it may sound to you, more than a few of them having sex."

"You are going to get us both killed. Stu could walk in that door any second."

"Being scared is part of the fun," she purred, her eyes closed now. "Makes it more exciting."

Her hand brushed the front of my jeans where an erection had suddenly made them uncomfortably tight. "I know your secret, Grayson Reynolds."

I gasped as, for a moment, I thought she had discovered my identity.

"You pretend you're not human." She studied me with the slitted eyes of a cat. "But whether you want to or not, it's just a matter of time until you're mine." She turned and padded away silently her bare feet. "Round and round the mulberry bush." She made a popping noise.

I could not sleep that night. I tossed and turned in the narrow cot, listening to the frogs until I finally surrendered and rose to stand at the railing of the porch. Riding the tractor hour after hour with little to think about, I had occasionally remembered the taste of Vonda's drunken kiss, the careful way she painted her toes, and how she threw her head back when she laughed. Knowing these were dangerous thoughts, I had pushed them out of my mind. Now, with the memory of the sweat pearled between her breasts and her lips within an inch of my own still fresh, my mind flitted from place to place like the long-legged water bugs that skittered across the surface of the pond where the full moon was reflected.

I glanced up in the direction of the Van de Zilver house. No lights were on. A fish jumped somewhere nearby. Black, concentric circles fanned out from the sound. Normally, it might have been a comforting sound. But tonight, I felt edgy. Like I was the one being fished for. According to Catania, the cartel was out there somewhere plotting their revenge.

I had read that fish continued to feed all night long on bright, moonlit nights, which explained why fishing was often poor the following day. I thought about Moses. I had begun to think of the huge trout as a fellow prisoner. We were both being hunted by people who wanted us dead.

I sighed. It might be time to begin searching for a new place to live and work. Before Virgil sold the farm or Stu's jealousy erupted. Or before the cartel found me and demanded their pound of flesh. It was also time to focus more energy on solving the mystery of the eight-character password guarding an account in the Cayman Islands that might still hold $100 million in illicit drug money.

CHAPTER TWENTY-EIGHT

I picked Valerie up for the promised picnic on Monday morning of the following week. To my surprise and disappointment, she seemed less than thrilled that she had agreed to come along. Patsy, on the other hand, appeared quite happy as she sat nearest the pickup's passenger door with her head out the window.

"Will we be home in time for dinner?" Valerie asked. "Daddy doesn't like it when I'm away from home."

"Don't worry. We're not going that far."

Because it was a workday for everyone else, traffic on the county road was moderately heavy, and I was forced to follow a slow-moving logging truck. The road was too narrow and winding to pass. While driving, I studied Valerie out of the corner of my eye. Unlike her sister who often wore clothes that displayed her figure to full advantage, Valerie wore mismatched clothes, including a large white sweatshirt, baggy pants, and tennis shoes. Though she wore no makeup, her youthful face glowed in the sunlight like a Rembrandt painting. Her mood, however, was guarded.

"You look nice," I offered.

She shrugged. "You could be lying, and I wouldn't know."

"For what it's worth, Valerie, I think you look lovely." I thought it was sad that she did not know how beautiful she was. "You have about the nicest smile I've ever seen. Of course, I have only seen this phenomenon once or twice. Lunar eclipses are less rare."

She smiled briefly before her frown returned. "I appreciate you asking me along, but leaving the house, even for a few hours, is difficult for me. I am always worried someone will mess things up while I am gone. Whenever they borrow a sweater, put the matches back in the wrong drawer, or leave the rabbit hutch unlocked, it drives me crazy." Her voice hardened. "I used to know where every piece of Momma's jewelry was. Now, I can't find more than half of it. Vonda would lose everything we own in about a week if it weren't for me keeping track of stuff."

"Sounds like a problem you're either going to have to learn to live with or get your own place."

We had driven by several small farms. Now the road opened onto the main highway and I turned east toward the North Cascade Mountains.

"Just out of curiosity, what made you change your mind about coming with me today?"

"Someone tried to discourage me."

I glanced over at her. She looked like she had just bitten into a lemon. "Who would that be?"

"My sister, of course."

"Why would Vonda care?"

"You tell me! She normally doesn't care what I do unless it's something she's interested in."

I winced. On opening day, Vonda had been drunk on her ass, flirting like a horny teenager. More recently, in the barn, she had played the seductress to the hilt, almost as if she had wanted Stu to catch us. Now she was staging a competition with her sister? What would she do next? The question worried me. I did not need Stu looking for any more excuses to get rid of me. Or chop me up into fish food.

"Long ago, Vonda looked out for me," Valerie said. "Once,

when we were kids, she beat up a couple of bigger girls at Lake Cavanaugh who had stolen my towel and were making fun of me. But she always acted jealous if I got something and she didn't. If I got a hat, she had to have one, too. Or if I got invited somewhere, a birthday party or whatever, she would get snippy unless she was invited.

"So, going along with me today was purely the result of sibling rivalry?"

She sighed. "I didn't mean it to sound like that. Vonda's remark maybe helped me overcome my other concerns."

As we neared the mountains, the two-lane road began to climb in winding stretches between tall fir trees, but there was still no sign of our destination, the Skagit River. We continued several miles further east until road and river finally met. My only previous encounter with the river had been when crossing its broad, flat expanse on the freeway overpass in Mt. Vernon. This was another river entirely. Swollen with run-off from the nearby mountains and squeezed within a narrow channel lined by glacier-scribed boulders, it thundered with a cold, white fury. The noise was clearly audible through the pickup's passenger window where Patsy began to whine and then bark.

"Wow. I'd forgotten how thrilling the river sounded," Valerie said.

"When was the last time you were up here?"

"Not since Momma died."

We drove the next few miles while listening to the river and not saying much. I found a place to pull off the highway and drove down a rocky, narrow track that made the Toyota's springs shriek their displeasure.

"This should do it." I grabbed the knapsack with the lunch Valerie had packed. I took her hand, and we followed a well-traveled footpath, Patsy on one side of Valerie and me on the other. Heide's hand had been smooth and cool, even on hot days. While smaller, Valerie's hand was rough and sweaty.

There were few trees on this side of the river, but the rocks, pieces of driftwood washed up by winter storms, and uneven terrain made the walk difficult for Valerie. It would be easy for her to twist an ankle, or fall, so we proceeded slowly.

"I didn't realize how difficult the walk would be," I said.

"My mother once made Vonda take me with her on a double date. The poor guys did not have a clue what to do with me. Vonda and them talked like I wasn't even there."

"I'm sorry. I can't imagine how difficult your life has been."

"How much further?" she asked.

By the time we reached the river, I was hungry and ready to sit down for a rest. I halted before a massive erratic. Its flat top promised a dramatic view of the river and a lovely spot for a picnic. A narrow ledge wound its way to the top. A child with normal eyesight could have scaled it easily, but for Valerie, climbing could prove hazardous.

Patsy barked, eager to continue.

"What's wrong?" Valerie asked over the restless, rushing sound of the river. "Why did you stop?"

"I was looking for a good place to picnic, but I don't think this will work."

She withdrew her hand from mine and took a hesitant step forward, then another. She found the rock with her hand and explored its grainy surface with her fingers. "Were you thinking of climbing this? How high is it?"

"Maybe fifteen feet. Too high," I added.

"I can feel a large groove. I bet we can climb it."

"Forget it. Even if you could make it to the top, what about Patsy?"

"Show Gray how you can climb the rock, okay girl?" Valerie unhooked the dog's harness. Patsy wagged her tail as if she understood her master perfectly, then placed both paws on the rock. She barked once.

"That's right," Valerie coaxed. "Climb the rock."

Patsy started up, using the narrow ledge formed by the

crack. Before I could stop her, Valerie followed, crouching low and using both hands to feel her way.

"Are you sure about this?" I imagined a broken arm or twisted knee, but there was no stopping them. All I could do was watch, grimace when she faltered, and follow with the picnic lunch.

Valerie was not a fast climber. Each step or handhold had to be searched out by touch, inch by hesitating inch. Two-thirds of the way up, she paused, and I saw that she had taken a wrong turn. Instead of following the widest part of the crack, she had taken a smaller fissure that had eventually petered out. I was about to direct her back to the proper route when the lip of rock she was standing on suddenly gave way and she lost her footing. A cry escaped her throat. She clung to the rock only by her fingers.

"Wait!" Having been blamed by the family for injuring her hand, I could well imagine their fury if she fell and broke her ankle or leg. "Don't move until I reach you."

Patsy whined from the top of the rock.

Valerie's right foot found a tiny depression and she continued to cling to the rock face, while with her left foot and hand, she explored the rock's surface.

"Where's the ledge?" she cried.

"Nine o'clock," I yelled. Damn. Did she even know what a clock face looks like?

Evidently, she did. She found the ledge again with the fingers of her left hand and slowly began to pull herself up. By the time I was able to reach her, she had regained her footing and was making slow if steady progress.

Though the distance covered was less than thirty feet, we were both sweating when we reached the top. There was a smear of blood on Valerie's chin where she had scraped it and when she grinned, her teeth were bloody.

"What took you so long?" she said.

"You're amazing. Not very bright, but amazing."

"Patsy's amazing." She patted the dog's head. "I'm just obstinate. Besides, getting up wasn't so bad." For just the second or third time since I had known her, her violet eyes were open wide and gleamed as if lit by an inner light. "Getting down is the hard part."

I groaned. "Now you tell me."

"Want to play a game?" she asked. She unfolded a blanket from the backpack she had made me carry.

"I'd rather eat."

"Tell you what," she said. "We can eat and play the game at the same time."

"What's the game?" I unwrapped a tuna, pickle and olive sandwich from the backpack and handed it to Valerie.

"The game is to describe what you see so the other person can see it. You go first."

"Okay," I said doubtfully. How was she going to tell me what she 'saw?' On the other hand, as she had proven when pruning the roses, she was quite capable of surprises.

I took a bite of sandwich and chewed as I considered how to describe where we were to someone who had no references for color or visual imagery.

"We're in a rocky gorge," I began hesitantly. "The rock we're sitting on happens to be the great-granddaddy of all the other rocks. The river here is probably forty or fifty yards across. Upstream, it's compressed into half that. The noise you hear is water smashing into the boulders that line the riverbed. Beneath this rock is a pool. The water is deep and clear and shot through with sunlight." I paused. How could she possibly know what sunlight or clear water looked like? Hell, I wasn't even sure why I invited her, except I felt sorry for her being stuck on the farm without a friend except for a dog. We were both clearly out of our element here—me challenged verbally and her visually.

"Go on," Valerie urged.

"Hidden within my own shadow, I can see three large

trout, maybe fifteen, eighteen inches long, sitting down there, hugging the bottom, in a holding pattern. A kingfisher— that's a bird with a big bill for catching minnows—just swooped by, twisting, turning, skimming the water's surface, looking for lunch. He didn't find anything this trip. Across from us, there are trees. Cottonwood, I think. Their limbs are covered with new leaves."

"What else?" Valerie asked. Her eyes were closed, and a smile played upon her lips.

"Below us, the river gradually fans out, becoming shallow. There's a riffle followed by more white water." White? This was not getting any easier.

"Anything else?"

"A tree, missing most of its bark, jutting into the river. The water beneath it is shadowed. A good place for another trout to hide maybe."

She was silent for several seconds, listening.

"I guess 'shadow' is a dumb word to be using."

"Actually," she said, "I liked it. I have no idea what one looks like, but I know how it feels. Cool."

"Exactly!" I said, relieved. "Now, it's your turn."

"Shhhh! I'm listening."

I waited patiently as Valerie sat, eyes closed. A line of ants marched in single file across the surface of the rock and a corner of our blanket, attracted by a package of fig bars. I thought about squishing them, but there were too many.

"I see a river," she said. "Wild as a unicorn running free, its long mane flowing behind it in the wind. You can hear the thunder of its hooves flying over the rocks as it gallops by."

"That's beau—" I started to say before she cut me off with a wave.

"We're sitting upon the scarred remainder of one of the great stone battlements of a once mighty fortress from the age of giants," she continued. "A secret cavern runs deep into the base of the mountains. Below us, watching us even now, is an ancient dragon who lies coiled beneath the water at the entrance to the cavern. His scaly skin is woven from the nightmares of children and is magical so that no one can see him except when he wants them to. He waits patiently as he has for thousands of years for people to come sit upon this rock. He overhears them chatting foolishly about their silly dreams while eating their picnic lunches. He opens first one eye, then the other, stretches out a long, razor-sharp talon." She extended one arm. "And plucks them away, never to be seen again!"

I stuck the sandwich in my mouth and clapped.

"Shush!" She grabbed my hands. "You'll wake the dragon."

I removed the sandwich from my mouth. "Think he'd let us go if I gave him a few of my olives?"

"Are you kidding? Olives are his favorite snack, right after tuna fish and pickles." Valerie tossed the rest of her sandwich into the river. "Sorry about that. It sounded better than it tasted."

***

I leaned back on my elbows with Patsy lying beside me, feeling the sun-warmed rock beneath me, and I felt my body begin to change. It was as if the spring that held all the parts of me together was finally letting go, releasing my arms, legs, hands, and feet, even my fingers and toes. My lips tingled and I felt my face flush. For a moment, I thought I might faint. I lay on my back and grabbed a handful of Patsy's fur for reassurance. Her coat felt like velvet, so smooth and soft, I wanted to wrap my face in it, drink in her animal smell. I might have moaned. I heard Gray ask, "Are you okay?" I felt a ridiculous grin break across my face. "I'm more than okay. I'm wonderful."

I reached over with my left hand and sifted his soft, flannel shirt between my fingers. I only wanted one thing in the world and that was for him to make love to me. The only time I had ever been this close to a boy was a high school dance. Then I remembered what Momma said, "If you snooze, you lose." So, I grabbed a handful of his shirt and slowly pulled his face down toward mine. His hair fell against my face as I drank in his smell and the faint odor of tuna fish on his breath. My body was still coming apart, unfolding, like a flower, and I began to shiver though I was warm.

There was a moment when I felt him resist and I was afraid. I so desperately wanted Gray to respond. Then, to my joy, he brought his soft lips to mine. I could not help myself as we mashed our lips together and I forced my tongue between his lips to taste him like the romantic stories I had read. I reached for his jeans and fumbled with his zipper and I could not stop quivering, like there was electricity running through my veins instead of blood. Then he lay down on me and I opened my legs.

I felt the sun on my face and a breeze blew softly across my cheek and I heard every note the river and the trees and the breeze made, like some enormous celestial orchestra, as Gray moved inside me.

Afterwards, I curled my body next to his and lay my head in the crook of his shoulder. We lay like that for a while, nobody saying anything. I heard him drift into sleep and tears ran down my cheeks and it was almost like the forest heard me and wept with the sweet joy and incredible sadness of it.

CHAPTER TWENTY-NINE

I'm sorry, Heide. I do not know what I was thinking. In fact, I am pretty sure I was not thinking at all. Just reacting. Surprised that a young, beautiful woman, blind since birth, wanted to make love with me for the first time, lying on an enormous rock in the sun by a roaring river. With me. On a rock. Can you imagine? We didn't even manage to take off all our clothes.

In her shyness, Valerie had fought to keep my eyes from viewing her nakedness. Or so I believed.

Valerie was still smiling the next morning. Vonda noticed.

"What's with you this morning?" she asked.

"Nothing," Valerie answered before darting away before anyone could ask more questions.

Later, when she brought my lunch out to where I was working, she grasped me by the arm and pulled me to her.

"Is anybody watching?"

"Not that I can see."

"Good."

We made out like teenagers in a dark closet. Her lips missed mine initially by a country mile, but she had tenacity. She also had fervor. They may have heard us in Everett.

"Maybe I can sneak down to see you tonight after everyone's asleep," she said as she was leaving.

"What if you get caught?"
"Yeah." She smiled. "What if?"

***

Later that afternoon, I was cutting grass with the Bull, the clippings flying up behind from the three gangs of spinning blades, when I saw the thin, shark-like figure in the dark suit and white shirt, waiting up by the road. The temperature suddenly seemed to drop thirty degrees. It was late in the day and a breeze had come up that was bowing the limbs on the alder trees and fluttering their leaves. I parked the mower several feet away, shutting the engine off before I approached the other man standing just on the other side of the fence.

"How'd you find me?"

"It looks like you've healed pretty well," Catania said.

I glanced down at the angry, puckered scar that bloomed among the muscles of my side.

"Once again, how'd you find me?"

"Well, there was the money."

I frowned, thinking the FBI agent thought I knew where the $100 million was hidden.

"Took us a while," Catania said. "What was it? A camera you bought at Tom's Antiques?"

"You're kidding." I studied the other man for several seconds, trying to make sense of it. And then I understood. "You did something to the bills in my wallet."

Catania nodded. "In addition to the serial numbers, there was a tiny amount of radioactive ink invisible to the naked eye added to the bills. They finally turned up, and we were able to track them to the bank and then to where you made your purchase. When we showed him your photo, the owner had no problem in remembering you. Frankly, I had given up. I figured you would have spent that cash within a couple of days—not weeks. But computers, bless their little digital hearts, they never give up."

"All that money out there—millions and billions being spent every day—and you were able to spot my three 20s and a 5?"

"When it comes to cash, it's not really millions and billions. You would be surprised how few people handle cash today. Most transactions are handled by debit or credit cards and the rest of it checks."

"Then there was the license plate search by your local sheriff's department," Catania added. "Someone there must not have anything better to do." He smiled and shook his head. "By the way, that was highly illegal, but very clever swapping your truck for a gardener's pickup on your way out of town. Took us almost two days to figure out what you'd done."

"What brings you up here?"

Catania rested a manicured hand on the top rail of the white-washed fence. "I thought it was worth a trip to see what you were up to. Make sure you weren't driving a red Ferrari convertible. Or maybe sipping martinis on a yacht in Anacortes."

"Like I told you before, my wife said the money is in a bank in the Cayman Islands. I don't have a clue which one." Lying, I had discovered, was becoming surprisingly easy. Almost easier than the truth.

"Yeah," Catania said. "I can see that."

"They're not safe, you know," he added, nodding toward the house. "If our people can find you, they can find you."

"You're telling me I can't stay."

"Not if you care about these people."

"Don't they have better things to do than hunt for me?" I protested. "Besides, what happens if I leave and they show up after I'm gone?

"Leave some breadcrumbs somewhere for them to follow," Catania said, "but not too close."

"Breadcrumbs?"

"Like a speeding ticket in Boise."

I snorted. "I couldn't get a speeding ticket in that leaf hauler if I drove it off a cliff."

"You'll figure something out. Just don't wait too long."

I turned away so Catania wouldn't see my anguish.

"Hey," Catania said. "You found this place. Maybe you'll find another."

***

Stu was waiting for me when I drove the Bull into the barn, a toothpick in the corner of his mouth.

"Who was the suit you were talking to?" he asked after I turned off the Bull's engine.

"Real estate agent. I told him to give you a call."

Like I said, lying gets easier the more you do it.

"That right?" Stu nodded, but sounded skeptical. "He's likely a day late and a dollar short. Bob Halonen is coming up this weekend to look the place over, maybe make an offer."

In my despair, I could think of nothing to say. Even my sarcasm had temporarily abandoned me.

"Guess you'll need to think about where you're going to go next," Stu said.

"What makes you so sure Virgil wants to sell? He didn't sound that happy when you and Vonda brought up the idea."

Stu removed the toothpick and flicked it out the barn door. "Tell you the truth, I don't know that he does want to sell. Yet." He smiled. "Once I show him how bad this place has been burning money these past few years, I think he might feel different. Fact is, I am pretty sure of it. You'd be amazed what property taxes are these days."

I pulled a t-shirt on. "That ought to make you and Vonda happy. What about Valerie?"

"Don't be too worried about Valerie. Virgil will likely buy a house with an acre of land somewhere. Unless he has been taking cooking classes that I do not know about, he will need Valerie to take care of things, just as she does now."

"Anyone ever consider what Valerie would like?"

"Not me," Stu said. "But then it doesn't really matter what she wants. She'll get by as long as Virgil is around."

Disgusted, I turned to leave.

"Before you go," Stu said, "it looks like I might need your marketing skills after all. You still have those signs and the artwork for that ad you ran?"

I stared at him. "You've got to be kidding."

"Got an idea for a fishing derby from the owner of the local auto parts store. He's willing to pay for the ad and put up money for the grand prize."

"What's the grand prize?"

"Catch Moses and win a thousand bucks."

CHAPTER THIRTY

Unable to sleep, I tossed and turned as I considered possibilities for an eight-digit password. Each time I shifted to one side or the other of the narrow cot, its springs would protest loudly.

Earlier, I had persuaded a clearly disappointed Valerie that tonight was not going to work for our planned rendezvous. If Catania was right, I might only have a few days before the cartel showed up. Starting a relationship now could be a death sentence. But I could not tell her that without blowing my cover, so I faked having a migraine.

Over the past few weeks, I had already reviewed dozens of password possibilities, but nothing that felt right, or even close. I needed to find another place off the grid to hide before the bad guys and girls arrived. The odds were stacked against me, but if I could crack the bank security, it might make the difference between being homeless in Portland or living on a small vineyard in Portugal.

Sometime during the night, a heavy fog rolled in, enveloping the farm. I lay listening to the intermittent plops of condensation falling from the cabin roof and striking the deck. There were other noises, too. Strange noises like footsteps. At first, I thought it was Valerie. Then my overactive imagination kicked in. As the minutes ticked by, I grew certain I was being surrounded by gunmen from the cartel.

I opened the door to discover that the rest of the world had disappeared. The farm lay hidden beneath a heavy mist on a windless early morning. Other than the drips and those mysterious footsteps, there wasn't a sound.

Patsy arrived a few minutes later. Instead of entering the cabin as was her custom, she remained on the porch, staring off to the east. When I finished dressing, I joined her.

"What is it, girl?" I heard a rumble deep in her throat and the ruff of fur around her neck stood up stiff as a brush. "Stay."

I tiptoed across the deck and walked softly in the direction Patsy's nose was pointing, my hands balled into fists. Visibility was virtually zero. The fog thickened the further I went from the cabin. The air was supersaturated with moisture so that my cheeks were slick and my eyelashes heavy with dew. Even my clothes were becoming water-logged.

Unable to see, I proceeded slowly. Eventually, I would reach the tree line and, with the fog so thick, might easily walk right into a tree. Then I really would have a migraine.

The grunt, coming as it did so near and sounding unlike anything I had ever heard, made me jump. While I waited for the pounding of my heart to subside, I listened for another sound as I strained to peer through the veil of mist. Pawing and heavy breathing sounded off to my right. I crept forward, wondering if a neighbor's horse had jumped a fence and wandered onto the trout farm.

Beneath the shelter of a large cedar tree, the fog thinned, and I spotted five animals, all staring calmly at me. At first, I thought they were deer. Then I saw the male with its immense rack of antlers and massive shoulders. I watched in awe as the huge creatures stripped berries and leaves from huckleberry bushes.

That night, as we were doing dishes, I told Valerie about the elk herd.

"I missed seeing you last night." A smile flitted across her face.

I noticed that she had chewed her fingernails down to the quick. "Momma told us about them. She said they migrate down from the mountains. They are always long gone by hunting season. But, as far as I know, they have never visited our place since she died. Stu said he'd fill the freezer with venison if they did."

CHAPTER THIRTY-ONE

The Gordon's Auto Parts Fishing Derby had been well underway for several hours when the appointed time for my lunch arrived. A breeze had sprung up. It rippled the surface of the water and whispered among the trees. I noticed an empty plastic bottle and soda cans lying in the grass. A paper wrapper tumbled past. I would need to pick up trash before tomorrow morning. I made a note to mention the need for another litter barrel. Judging from the length of the line, we could also use another port-a-potty as well. That was unless someone caught Moses. Then the crowds would likely thin as soon as the word got out.

As I jogged up to the house, I could hear Valerie practicing the viola. I had not heard her play music since hurting her hand. Now, unlike the lyrical quality I remembered from earlier, her playing sounded disjointed and almost angry. She stopped playing when she heard me enter.

"Gray? That you?"

"What's that you're playing?"

"Nothing." She frowned in concentration as she tuned her viola, plucking a string with one hand and turning the tuning peg with the other.

"How's your hand?"

"The pain is good," she said. "It helps keep my mind off

other things."

What were these "other things," I wondered. The possible sale of the trout farm, or simmering jealousy over her sister's teasing were likely candidates. Though I tried, I could think of nothing to say that would cheer her up and I wolfed down a chipped beef, cream cheese, and red pepper sandwich in silence.

"I better get back."

"Hey, there's something you should know." She continued tuning strings. "There were several strange telephone calls today."

I froze. "Strange how?"

Her chin started to tremble. "I may have screwed up."

"What do you mean?"

"The first several times, they just hung up when I didn't answer."

I waited.

"The last time, they left a message. Said they were looking for Devon Mudiyam."

She tapped her fingers on the viola's fretboard. "They said it was important that he call them back as soon as possible. That he owed them some money, but everything would be okay if you—he—called them back."

"I should have picked up the phone. I could have at least lied." She put down the viola. "I looked it up. Mudiyam is an Indian name. It's you they're looking for, isn't it?"

"Don't worry. You did fine," I said.

Following Valerie's disclosure, I was close to panic. Should I leave immediately, or could I risk waiting another day or two?

The derby had attracted a large crowd of predominantly men, many of them wearing camo and bright orange vests, eager to collect the thousand dollars for catching Moses. Unlike the serenity and goodwill of most days at the trout farm, however, people argued and fought over places to stand

and cast their lines. Whenever lines got crossed, I hurried to untangle them before crude language and simmering tempers flared into blows. At one point, I had to use the newly installed life ring to rescue a drunk who had fallen into the pond while trying to retrieve his lure from a shrub on the little island. I had just finished hauling him out of the water when there was a loud bellow followed by swearing.

It took only a moment to locate the source and to see the reason for the outcry. I borrowed a pair of wire cutters to cut the barb off a treble hook that had snagged a large man's ear. I handed him the remainder of the treble hook. "Here. A souvenir."

After noting the large quantity of empty beer cans, I addressed the other two men in their party. "Your friend needs to see a doctor. Might need a tetanus shot in addition to a stitch or two. Can either of you drive?"

"Mind your own business, Tonto."

"Wrong hemisphere," I said.

***

That night, I stood leaning on the railing of the deck to the cabin. I had waited until dark before baiting a large, single hook with a nightcrawler and casting toward the island beneath the fir trees where I suspected Moses might be hiding.

My secret and, according to Nathan, illegal plan was to thwart Stu's derby plans by catching Moses and releasing him into the nearby Skagit River. At least one of us could live free from being hunted. For how long—that was another matter.

Earlier, I had saved a bag of ice from the fish cleaning station which I had emptied into a bag-lined, 50-gallon trashcan hidden behind the barn. In my distraught state, I was not just trying to save a legendary trophy fish, but attempting to foil an army of assassins.

I held one advantage over all the men and women who had

earlier thrashed the water with their lures and baited hooks hoping to catch Moses. As I was returning to the cabin following dinner and doing dishes with Valerie in the cool of an evening, I had often seen the swirl of a large tail fin near the northwest side of the island as Moses fed on insects.

I carefully cast my line out in that direction tonight. While I waited patiently for a strike, I continued to think about passwords. Heide had kept a journal in which she would sometimes stuff photos from magazines and write short, blog-like entries in her large, looping cursive. The fact that she kept a private journal had bugged me. I wondered what secrets may have been hidden there. Once while she was taking a bath, I snuck a peek.

I found references to a weekend date in Ojai as well as our honeymoon in Hawaii interspersed with numerous affirmations and places she hoped to travel. There was Paris, of course, London, Prague, Santorini, and Rome. One place that stood out due to its slightly more exotic location was Turkey—specifically Istanbul, which happened to be the correct character count. Sandwiched between a champagne bottle label, a business card from a restaurant in Laguna Beach and a pressed flower —the white plumeria she had worn behind her ear when we were married—was a photo and caption torn from a travel magazine of the Blue Mosque. Making the challenge of finding the correct password more difficult, was the fact that I would be locked out if I guessed wrong more than three times. And due to her financial industry employment, Heide was clever enough not to use a common word or name without modifying it with numbers or symbols. It was a sad fact of life that we were now living and working in a world populated by armies of cyber criminals.

A twitch in the tip of the fiberglass fishing pole caught my attention. I watched for several seconds until it moved again. Carefully, so as not to spook whatever might be nibbling at the nightcrawler on the other end of the line, I reached for the pole. It nearly leapt into my hand and I barely seized it before it disappeared into the pond. Monofilament line unspooled from the reel with a high-pitched whine. No sooner had I heaved back on the pole to set the hook when it went limp. Whatever it was, it was gone. Then I heard a sold splash somewhere nearby followed by a jerk like a waterskiing tow rope and I knew that this was a very big fish, and it was still hooked.

The fight on my hands tonight was everything that an angler could wish. For more than ten minutes, the huge fish performed all manner of acrobatic flips, runs and changes of direction as it desperately sought to regain its freedom. I refused to fall for its tricks, however, and eventually it lay spent, in the dim shallows. When I first beheld the trout's girth as it rolled, I was certain that it was Moses. I slipped on a pair of latex gloves to avoid infecting the fish with any human bacteria. It was only when I began to lift the fish by the gills that I spotted the telltale red ribbon of a rainbow trout illuminated in the light of the cabin. It was a lovely fish, something over twenty-two inches in length, I guessed, and by far the largest trout I had seen caught—but it was only a second cousin to the great Moses.

I used the needle-nosed pliers to free the hook from the trout's lower jaw, then steadied him upright in the shallows. He had fought with such fury that he might stop breathing and drown now if not supported. When at last he recovered, the trout gave a slap of its tail and disappeared once again into the invisible depths of the pond.

CHAPTER THIRTY-TWO

According to Stu, our resident expert on anything baseball related, the derby's first weekend was "a grand slam."

While several hundred trout had met their maker that day, no one had caught Moses. Consequently, the prize had been raised to $1500 which meant that the crowd of anglers would likely be even greater for the coming weekend. Of course, my intention was to be long gone by then. I was planning a trip to the public library to search for a job and a place to hide. It was also now time to try my luck at breaking into the Cayman Island bank account set up by Heide and her friend, Jeff.

I was mowing with the hammerknifer up along the road, carefully skirting the whitewashed split rail fence that I had earlier repaired, when I heard the engine of a large vehicle approaching. It had rained heavily early that morning, soaking the grass. By noon, however, the last of the clouds had fled across the mountains, replaced by a robust sun in a cerulean sky. Now, heat waves danced among the patched and cratered asphalt road. A yellow school bus wound nearer, changing hues in the deep shade of alder, reappearing a moment later into brilliant light. Crickets hummed and chickadees called from the field just beyond the blackberry-vined, barb-wire fence across the road. The air hung heavy, a hammer of humidity and pollen from thistle and cottonwood.

The bus came to a yellow halt. Unoiled doors complained, then disgorged one small boy dressed in a t-shirt and blue denims. The engine roared as it started up. The bus coasted around the corner, roared again and was gone. The boy stooped to tie one black tennis shoe. Then he slipped down the opposite bank into shade and was gone, too. Another week and school would be over, the yellow bus parked and forgotten until school started again in the fall.

Vonda drove up a few minutes later in her car, a white Honda sedan. She waved as she passed by on her way to the barn to park. I didn't wave back.

Until Catania's visit and the mysterious phone calls, I had found driving the John Deere to be profoundly satisfying as therapy. Now that my life had become a tangled knot of complications, however, I found it annoying. My presence here was putting the Van de Zilver family in danger. There was just one small problem to making my getaway: where to go that afforded the same anonymity and invisibility. Not to mention hospitality.

Then there was the hundred million, which was an entirely different brain twister. Had the cartel or the FBI already found the enormous sum, or was it still sitting there waiting for me to come up with the correct password? Even if I did somehow manage to decode the correct series of eight letters, numbers, and symbols, where could I stash that much money so it could not be found or traced back to me? Would I even live long enough to be able to spend it?

The crack sounded like gunfire. Though I ducked reflexively and brought the tractor to an immediate halt, I was not fast enough. Something sharp struck the back of my head, neck and shoulder and stung my ear. I dove to the ground and crouched behind the John Deere's rear wheel to provide protection from the road in case I was being shot at. Then I removed a triangular chunk of glass from the back of my neck. There were other, smaller pieces of glass still attached to my hair and skin. My fingers were now slick with blood. I touched my ear and discovered I was bleeding there as well. A warm trickle ran down my back.

I found the shattered green beer bottles, nearly invisible in the grass. I might have seen them before running over them if I had been paying better attention. Virgil had warned me about the hammerknifer's tendency to hurl rocks and glass at you. The rear metal shield positioned behind the spinning blades was meant to protect anyone standing behind the mower. Unfortunately, that left the driver exposed.

Vonda opened the screen door following my knock. She had changed into cutoffs and a shirt that she had tied beneath her breasts that showed off her trim belly. "Howdy, stranger. Why didn't you come in?"

I held up the blood-soaked t-shirt I had used as a bandage. "Would you mind driving me to an urgent care facility?"

"What's wrong?" Valerie called from the other side of the room.

"Nothing, sis," Vonda replied. "Let me take a look," she said to me.

I bent down while she examined my injuries. "Looks worse than it is," she said. Over her shoulder, she added, "He's a little dinged up. I need some tweezers, antiseptic and bandages."

"Let's go down to your place and I'll have you fixed up good as new in no time."

Valerie returned with a first aid kit. "I'll go, too."

Vonda snatched the kit from her hand. "I got this, Val. You stay here."

"Vonda!"

"What?"

"You know what," Valerie said.

"What was that about?" I asked as we walked to the cabin. I felt another trickle of blood run down my back and fought off a moment of dizziness from the heat and possibly shock.

"That was nothing. Bitch seems to think I owe her

something."

"Must have been very difficult being born blind and losing her mother as a kid," I offered.

"Yeah, guess what? I lost my mother too," she said. "Not only that, but I went from being an only child, to suddenly being my little sister's nursemaid. Once Valerie was born, it was like I no longer existed."

I opened the cabin door and followed her inside.

"Sit down." She nodded toward the chair. "In my opinion, she's had it easy."

"How can you say that?"

She used the tweezers to lift something from my neck. "Hold out your hand." She laid a sliver of green glass in my palm. "Green, like Heineken. You find the bottles?"

I shook my head. I was contemplating whether the bottles were an accident, or a deliberate act of sabotage planted by Stu. Or worse, a warning from the cartel.

"Ow."

"Sorry. That piece was in deep." She laid another sliver in my palm. "You're bleeding from a couple of places." She wiped several blond hairs from her face, leaving a smear of blood on her cheek.

"Mom was always taking her places, signing her up for private music lessons and what not. Me, I was lucky to get a used clarinet for band practice. While Miss Valerie was attending plays and going to concerts, I got to stay home to clean her room and the rest of the house."

"I'm sure it wasn't easy on either of you." I hesitated. "But..."

"Let me guess: you think she's a touch loony like everyone else up here?"

She ran her fingers through my hair, lifting it from my head and neck as she explored for more glass, then stood so close that when I turned my head, I was looking at her throat from barely an inch away. When she pulled my head forward

227

to examine my neck, my lips rested on her neck. The smell of her soap and shampoo were intoxicating.

"Oh, boy," Vonda said. "This piece is nasty. I'd offer you a bullet to bite on, but I forgot my shooter."

I felt a sharp twinge as she removed a glass splinter.

"Hold out your hand," she said.

I looked down at the wicked, curved green fragment she placed in my hand. I also noticed a pale pink nipple winking at me from beneath her shirt.

"I think I got it all. Let me wash off some of the blood so I can see better."

She returned from the bathroom with a washcloth that she had wetted with warm water. As she began to wipe the back of my neck, she rested her body against mine. Her strokes were slow. Tender. Erotic.

I dropped the glass slivers on the floor, not caring whether my bare feet would find them later and sighed. I remembered the sweet, consuming surrender of making love and how it was with Heide, our spontaneous lovemaking sometimes ending on the floor, the back of a car, the balcony of our apartment and, once, even in the dressing room of a Victoria's Secret as women giggled nearby.

When she finished my neck, she ran the washcloth over my shoulders and down my back. Her breathing grew louder as she moved the now bloody cloth down my chest and then my stomach. Needing an escape, however temporary, from the heartache and anxiety that tormented me, my desire ignited, and I was suddenly weary of trying so fucking hard not to do something I wanted so much to do.

She dropped the washcloth and her hands, smooth as blades of grass, slid up my cheeks and into my hair. My own hands traveled up the pathways of her body and found her breasts irresistible.

"Oh my," she breathed. She bent down and we kissed, long and hungrily. The rest of it came easier and quicker than it should have.

Afterwards, I thought I would feel racked by guilt and anxious about Stu's threatened response. But as we lay together on the tiny cot, sunlight streaming in the gaps between the window and the roller shade, a fly buzzing furiously against the glass, and a thin layer of sweat bathing our bodies, I couldn't prevent my hand from exploring the wonder of Vonda's body. It was no great surprise to either of us when she guided me into her yet again.

***

I began worrying the moment Gray came to the door. He was hurt—I didn't know how badly—and now Vonda was in his cabin. I had been pacing back and forth from the kitchen to the far end of the living room, listening to the ticking of the clock and waiting for her to come back. And the more time that went by, the more my worry turned to hate. I wanted to stab her in the eyes, let her know what it was like being blind and teach her a lesson she would never forget!

Finally, unable to stand the pain a second longer, I buckled Patsy's harness around her and started down the hill.

I felt the tug from Patsy at the same instant I heard the duck as it lifted from the pond. I knew it was a mallard by the way its wings squeaked, just like Momma taught me, and I wished I could fly away, too. Leave behind all this worry and hate and pain. But I had to know the truth.

Near the edge of the pond, I stopped. The noises coming from the cabin told me everything. Vonda could not be quiet if you paid her a million dollars and she was certainly not trying to be quiet now. I stood there, the tears running down my cheeks. I might be blind, but I was not unseeing.

"You won't believe this, Momma," I cried. "This time she's really done it. She's stolen Gray from me."

Unable to resist the strange sounds coming from the cabin,

Patsy jerked her harness from my hand, and I fell face first in the grass. I clawed the grass and the earth beneath it with my fingers as I wept for my loss. First Vonda, then Gray. And now, even my dog had betrayed me.

I lay there, feeling sorry for myself, until rage took over. I needed to go back to the house. It would not be easy without Patsy, but I had done it before.

As I stumbled up the hill, I chanted under my breath, the words like the shrieks of a bow across the strings of my viola.

"I'll kill them. Kill. Kill. Kill."

PART III
MOSES

But the Lord called out to the man, "Where are you?"

-Genesis 3:19

CHAPTER THIRTY-THREE

"Heard you were injured yesterday," Stu said at breakfast. "That why you didn't come to dinner?"

I set the coffee cup down carefully before any sloshed out. "I missed seeing some beer bottles while mowing with the hammerknifer up by the road."

"You see a doctor?"

"Vonda took care of it."

Bandages covered the worst of my injuries, but guilt was tattooed on my face when I had looked in the mirror that morning.

"From what I heard," Valerie said, "that ain't all she took care of."

Vonda's fork stopped halfway to her mouth. I felt like I had been kicked in the walnuts. Valerie was the one person on the planet that I could trust, and I had betrayed her. Was she now about to start a war at the dining table? Although I had tried muffling Vonda's grunts, groans, and profane exclamations during our lovemaking, it now seemed possible that she had overheard us. From habit, I took a quick inventory of all the cutlery and their location on the table. My dad had never actually tried to murder me during our dinnertime brawls, but given his thundering threats and sometimes physical blows, I was never sure of his intent.

Stu stared at Valerie, then me, before turning to Vonda sitting next to him. "What's she saying?"

"I have no idea," Vonda said. "What <u>are</u> you saying, Val?"

"You know," Valerie said.

"No," Vonda said icily. "I don't, actually."

Virgil had heard enough. "You girls going to sit there and squabble all day, or can we get to work? Today's an important day. The prize money for catching Moses has been raised, which means we will see at least as many or more folks today as last Saturday and Sunday. In addition, I got a call from the real estate developer Stu mentioned being interested in our property. He is coming up today and bringing his wife and kid. Said he thought they might do a little fishing and kill two birds with one stone."

"Are you sure you want to do this, Daddy?" Valerie asked. Her voice trembled. "Where would we go? This is the only place I know. It took years for me to figure out where everything is, and that was with Momma helping me."

"Now listen, darlin,'" Virgil said. "Ain't nothing set in stone. Bob's just looking around, talking to the bank, maybe seeing what could be done about developing the trout farm if he bought it. Take a lot of money to pull something like that off. In addition to the cost of the property, you have got infrastructure to worry about, fees, permits, taxes. Be a sizable investment before you could ever sell a lot or reap a penny of profit. I guess Bob must have the thing figured out." He chuckled. "I may be just a farmer, but I'm smart enough to leave the financial details to the accountants."

Neither Stu nor Vonda laughed as Valerie's earlier comment continued to fester. In my guilt-ridden state, I had noted Virgil's use of the word "stone" not just once, but twice. Stoning, as I recalled from my days in Junior High Baptist Bible Camp, was the Biblical punishment for adultery. I sprang from my chair and began carrying dishes to the sink.

Valerie ignored me as I loaded the dishwasher. Once the

others left, I noticed that the house was quiet. Too quiet.

"What's with your birds? Why aren't they chirping this morning?"

"They flew the coop," she said.

I wiped my hands on a dish towel and went to look. The cage door stood empty. A few tiny yellow feathers were all that remained among the scraps of newspaper and seed husks.

"I must have forgotten to close the cage when I fed them," Valerie said from the kitchen.

"Are they somewhere in the house?"

"Nope. They're gone."

I watched Valerie from the doorway. From everything I had observed, being less than careful was not part of her repertoire. Was she so upset about the possible sale that she let the birds out, or was it something else? Something more worrisome? Was letting the tiny birds go a message to me?

Perhaps it was for the best. If Catania was right, the cartel could be knocking on the door any day now. Meanwhile, Stu seemed certain the farm was about to sold. And thanks to Valerie's provocative comments at breakfast, I now had Stu's potential revenge to worry about. Delaying my departure suddenly seemed insanely imprudent. I needed to leave. Now.

"I'm sorry," I said to her.

"Yeah." She ran a finger over the cutting edge of a knife. "I bet you say that a lot."

CHAPTER THIRTY-FOUR

The locals turned out that Saturday in record numbers for the chance to catch Moses and not only collect a check for $1500, but earn bragging rights forever. As Nathan had predicted, the smaller, recently introduced trout were easy to catch. So easy, in fact, that by mid-morning, we had already cleaned more fish than the total for our best day previously. I wished I could say it was a fine thing, all these people communing with nature, but, at some point, it turned into a fishy-smelling slaughter.

The work was steady and wearying. Stu and Vonda cleaned fish while I handed out poles, baited hooks, and knotted leaders and tried to keep everyone from killing each other when their lines got crossed. Though she refused to talk, Valerie brought us sandwiches and sodas at noon.

Meanwhile, I kept shooting glances toward the parking lot where I had seen a couple of burly guys exit a black SUV. My survival instinct was now on high alert and my overwrought brain was screaming "Danger!" I began hastily considering where to go without endangering others if I had to make a run for it. The tiny cabin would not do; I would be trapped. Better to take my chances in the woods.

I also spotted Stu, arms crossed over his chest, watching me from a distance. My stomach flopped around like a fish on land.

As it turned out, the two men I had mistaken for killers were just interested in fishing.

A cry rose like a wave from the other side of the big pond. After jogging to a vantage point where I could see past the tree-covered island, I spotted an older teenage boy opposite me, his fishing pole bowed in half.

"We caught Moses!" his girlfriend shrieked.

Everyone stopped to watch as the fish made a run. Even twenty yards away, I could hear line spooling off the reel in a high-pitched whine. Then there was a loud splash followed quickly by an audible snap as the nylon fishing line parted. A collective groan rose from the crowd of onlookers.

Moses was clearly not going to give up without a fight. I smiled to myself as I climbed the hill to check on how Vonda was doing. She wiped an arm across her brow. Even with dark stains on her apron and a smear of blood on her cheek, she still looked sexy as hell.

"How about if I take over for a bit? You look like you could use a breather."

"I would kill for a hot bath and a glass of wine, but it's going to take the two of us to handle the crowd wanting their fish cleaned."

"Stu say anything more about Valerie's comment this morning?"

"He's acting like a lit stick of dynamite, being rude to customers, throwing fish guts on the lawn." She shook her head. "He's also been asking lots of questions, like what was I doing in the cabin, how long was I gone, and why didn't I let Valerie tag along. I told her she's just pissed that I cleaned up your wounds."

"'Pissed' doesn't begin to cover it. Valerie says her canaries escaped, but I'm worried," I said.

"You think she let them go?"

I shrugged.

"You probably figured out by now she thinks you belong to her. Can't really say that I blame her. There ain't a lot of options up here."

"Is that what attracted you to me? A lack of options?"

Vonda measured one trout carefully before speaking and then only when she was turned toward me so that the customers would not overhear. "Guess I've managed to make a mess out of your life as well as my own."

"For what it's worth, my life was already a mess."

Working together, the line of people quickly evaporated. Another cry from the pond drew our attention so we were both facing downhill. I remembered her scent from the day before and had a suicidal urge to pull her body tight and kiss the place where her neck became her shoulder. With no one looking, I reached out a hand toward her back, like a drowning man reaching for the surface, and knowing I couldn't get there.

"Stu will probably kill us both," I said.

"You might be right, but I ain't sorry. Not one little bit." She reeled around to face me, a look of fury on her face. "What if all we get on earth is this? Just a few minutes of stolen bliss surrounded by acres and acres of neglect and heartache and a few feeble attempts to drown the pain?" She peeled off her rubber gloves and threw them down on the cleaning table.

"And by the way, it would have been nice to share a little sweet talk afterwards, something to make a girl feel like you cared." She took a step toward the house before pausing. "I thought you were different, but you're just the same as Stu. The least you could do is pretend that you cared more about me as a person than an inflatable sex toy."

What the hell? For a woman who had seemed so eager to have sex at the drop of a hat, she now demanded post-coital chitchat? Was it the remote location, lack of neighbors, or something in the water that made everyone crazy? Or was it me? The longer I stayed here, the more I was in over my head, swimming with the trout.

CHAPTER THIRTY-FIVE

I was brushing fish scales from the cleaning table when Virgil arrived.

"I thought I better catch you up on things," he said.

"You sold the farm," I said.

He nodded. "Escrow is in sixty days, which will give us time to sell off the machinery and clear everything out."

So that was that. I was back to Square One. Do Not Pass Go. Do Not Collect $200.

"There's a couple things I should mention," I said.

Virgil looked like I had peed on his Rockports. "Go on," he said warily.

"That time I broke into Stu's closet to look for the chemicals, I saw a roll of blueprints. I think he's been planning the sale of the farm for a long time."

Virgil did not seem surprised. "I wouldn't doubt it. I'm sorry my daughter married him. I never thought he was worth a damn. The two of them can ride off into the sunset if that's their desire."

"One more thing," I said. "You have probably noticed how unhappy Valerie is over the prospect of a sale."

"Oh, that," Virgil said. "That's just women stuff. A guy will get angry or sad, maybe drink it off. Next day, he is back to normal. Women, on the other hand, need to mope around for a few days. That is just the way they deal with things. Nothing to get worked up about. It's just their nature. In some ways, I believe women are tougher than us men. Didn't you have any sisters to learn from when you were growing up?"

"No, I didn't. And you're right. There's a lot I don't understand about women." How my poor Heide would have laughed at that.

"Don't you worry," Virgil said. "I'll find a little place close to town for Valerie, her dog and me. She can cook and clean just like she does now, and everything will be fine."

I doubted Valerie would agree that everything was just fine like her father assumed. "I don't think she's ever gotten over the loss of her mother. The death of the single most important person in her life must have been devastating, especially with Valerie so dependent on her mother for her schooling and social development."

"Uh huh," Virgil said.

I felt the ice beneath me shift. "I guess what I'm suggesting is that she might benefit by seeing a therapist."

"A therapist?" Virgil reacted as if I had suggested locking Valerie in a room with a serial killer. "You must think my Valerie's crazy and that I'm crazy, too. Them shrinks act like they believe everybody is a pervert."

I had been expecting an argument, but not this.

"Homosexuals and atheists, most of 'em," Virgil continued. "I wouldn't trust a therapist for one minute with Valerie. I read a magazine once said they have been known to hypnotize a woman and take advantage of her. And I guarantee this—" Virgil pointed a finger at me like it was a gun. "If you tell one something personal, it would be all over the Valley the next day."

I thought of mentioning the fact that such behavior was illegal, not to mention unethical, and would result in the loss of a license to practice, but I did not think Virgil was interested in another of my opinions.

"You ever visited one of these so-called therapists?" Virgil asked.

"No," I admitted.

Virgil shook his head. "People in California must think different than us simple country folk. We'd never so much as tell a stranger what was going through our heads as we'd take down our pants and relieve ourselves in public."

"You listen to me, young man. If I have told you once, I have told you a dozen times to keep your ideas about me, my family, and this farm to yourself. I explained the rules your first day here. This is my farm, my fish, and my daughters. I will take care of them without any interference from you. You want it different, you can leave now. Got me?"

Virgil did not wait for an answer. I watched as the older man stomped back toward the house in his Rockports.

***

Vonda was notably absent from dinner.

"Where's your wife?" Virgil asked.

"Said she thought she might have a touch of the stomach flu," Stu said.

He had not eaten any of his food and was stirring it around on his plate with his fork.

"By the way, what did you mean this morning, Val?" Stu asked.

She cocked her head. "About what?"

"You said, 'That's not all she took care of.'"

"Why don't you ask her?"

It was so quiet that I could hear the fan blades turning overhead and the faint hum of the refrigerator in the kitchen. I missed the cheeriness of the canaries. Their musical repertoire may have been limited, but never tedious.

"I'm asking you, Sis."

I was preparing to shove my chair away from the table to

fight when Valerie saved us from Armageddon.

"I heard she helped clean up his place. Said it was a 'fucking disaster.'"

"Since when do you use profanity?" Virgil asked.

"Just repeating her words," Valerie said.

CHAPTER THIRTY-SIX

I retreated to the cabin where I leaned against the porch railing. Trout rose to feed upon the water bugs skittering across the pond, sending silent circles rippling across the surface. The first stars of the evening were becoming visible in the evening sky.

I saw my darkened reflection in the pond's water and could not recognize myself. What happened to that young man—the one with big dreams and a respect for proper behavior? I had arrived at the farm without hope, desperate to hide from the cartel. Miraculously, I had discovered a place of incredible beauty and a family who took me in and helped me heal. And how did I repay them? By betraying not only Stu, but Valerie and causing jealousy to turn the family inside out. Now, I needed to disappear again before I caused any more trouble.

Prior to being shot and my wife murdered, a job as a maintenance man for a trout farm would have been my last choice for employment. But the job had turned out to be ideal except for one minor detail: the people living here were the picture of a dysfunctional family. Everyone had an agenda that conflicted with everyone else. Virgil wanted a son. Stu wanted money to buy freedom from people. Vonda wanted someone to take her away from here to a life of fancy homes and clothes and travel. And sex. Valerie desperately wanted a husband, but what I suspected she really needed was a psychologist—someone to heal her from the grief and hurt locked inside since her mother's death.

A large white moth fluttered about the cabin's porch light and I wondered if it was Heide's spirit come to comfort me.

Heide and I had not talked about having kids. We didn't have the chance to get that far along. And I never told her this, but it was the first thing I thought of when I met her. Well, maybe not the first thing, but definitely the second.

It was no matter now. "Water under the bridge" as my mother used to say. Trouble found me once, but I got lucky. Now it had sunk its teeth into me, and I did not think it would ever let go.

Even if I were able to locate the money and move it before anyone else got their hands on it, the odds were slim that I would ever be able to spend it. The cartel or the FBI would likely track me down. Even so, it was worth a try. Other than my miserable life, I did not have much to lose.

By now, I had entertained dozens of password possibilities and had written down a list of ten from which to cull two or three finalists. After analyzing Heide's behavior and habits, I felt I might be getting close to figuring it out. Or maybe not.

I about to turn in when a loud noise in the water startled me. I spotted a wake fanning out against the surface of the pond that seemed far too large for a trout or a duck. Whatever it was disappeared on the other side of the island which remained outside the cabin's light.

I retrieved a flashlight from the cabin. By the time I reached the eastern edge of the pond, however, the wake had disappeared. I waited patiently for a long minute before a swirl in the water caught my attention. I hurried after it, anxious not to lose sight of whatever it was. Then the beam from the flashlight fell upon a sea monster plowing the water in exhausted fury.

"It's a fucking submarine," I said in an awed whisper.

The behemoth was swimming slowly while towing something. As I watched, the fish swung his tail in a wide arc that sent ripples lapping noisily against the shore. Several yards behind him, a tree root surfaced, then sank again.

Valerie opened the door at my knock.

I handed her a large trash bag. "I need some ice cubes. As many as you can spare."

She cocked her head to the side the way she often did. "Are you having a party?"

"Don't ask questions, okay? There isn't time."

She considered for a second before returning to the kitchen. I heard her emptying the entire ice maker tray into the bag.

"Whatcha doing, darlin'?" Virgil called from the living room.

"Just cleaning out the refrigerator," she replied.

She handed me the bag a moment later. "Hold on. I'm coming, too."

I wanted to tell her no but could not risk a disturbance that would attract Stu or Virgil's curiosity.

She reappeared seconds later with Patsy on her harness. "It's Moses isn't it?"

"I think so. He's still hooked."

"What are you going to do?"

I hesitated. "I'm going to try and capture him."

"And then what?"

"And then I'm going to let him loose in the Skagit River where he can be free from everyone trying to kill him."

"I'm going with you," she said. "So is Patsy."

"Listen, Valerie, I don't want to get you in trouble, nor do I have time for arguments or explanations."

"You don't have to worry. We can keep a secret, can't we Patsy?" At the mention of her name, the dog licked her hand.

"You promise not to tell or do anything crazy?"

She held up two fingers. "I promise."

My intuition warned me that I was taking a dangerous risk, but perhaps a Moses rescue mission would help to lift Valerie's spirits. It might also give me an opportunity to tell her I was leaving as I had promised during the so-called "blood-brother ceremony."

After filling a large plastic trashcan halfway with water from a hose, I dumped in the ice cubes and then backed the Toyota up to the eastern edge of the pond. I used an eyedropper to add several drops of the sodium amytal to the water as Nathan had coached me. Forgetting my weariness for the moment, I worked quickly and as silently as possible so as not to alert the rest of the family.

Perhaps Moses knew we were there to help him. More likely, he had used up the last of his strength fighting the tree root that had become snarled in the heavy fishing line. I grabbed the line and pulled him to shore where he lay still except for the machine-like pumping of his gills and the opening and closing of his hooked jaw.

"Jesus, what a monster," I said. Patsy whined in agreement.

"Help me see," Valerie said.

"Here." I handed her a pair of latex gloves. "Put these on. And hurry. We don't have much time."

Once she had the gloves on, I placed one hand on Moses' tail and the other near his nose.

"Wow," she said. "He's really something isn't he?"

"The biggest fish I've ever seen."

I used a pair of needle-nosed pliers to snip the barb of the large hook, then backed the hook out of the corner of Moses' jaw. A second hook hung beneath the first. Someone had used heavy monofilament line and dual hooks of the type used to catch large salmon and halibut. Their efforts had very nearly succeeded.

It took both hands to lift the heavy trout into the garbage can in the pickup truck. Even curled up, Moses took up the entire space. I held him upright for several seconds, but each time I let go, the exhausted fish would immediately roll onto his side. I began to worry that we were too late to save him, and the great fish might die before we could get him to the river.

"What now?" Valerie asked.

"Now we drive him to the river." I tried to sound confident. "If everything goes right, it will be all over in less than an hour." I fastened the top of the garbage can to keep water and fish inside and then roped the handles to the fittings on the truck bed to keep the can from overturning.

"Patsy and I are going, too."

"What I'm about to do isn't exactly legal. We could both end up in jail," I warned.

"If Stu or Daddy finds out you stole Moses, the law will be the least of your problems," Valerie said. She was already climbing into the passenger seat.

"C'mon, girl," she coaxed, and Patsy leapt in to join her.

I drove as fast as I could without overturning the trash can or getting a ticket. The last thing I needed now was to explain to a cop what a lunker trout was doing in the back of my truck.

We had been driving for ten minutes, and I had slowed to turn onto the highway when Valerie and I both heard a hollow thump from the rear of the truck. After stopping, I hurried back to the garbage can to remove the lid. Moses was lying on his side and not moving. "I'm afraid he's dying," I said when I returned to the cab.

"Hang in there, Moses," Valerie coached. I noticed she had clenched both her fists.

A few minutes later, I spotted a turnout near the river and drove down it as far as the truck could go. The walk from the truck to the river carrying a few gallons of water and an enormous fish in an industrial-strength Hefty Bag slung over my shoulder was grueling. Valerie followed with Patsy. Twice, I stumbled over rocks and nearly fell. By the time we reached the river's edge, my arms and back ached and my shirt was soaked with sweat. I untied the knot in the bag and peered in at the huge fish lying on his side.

"Is he okay?" Valerie asked.

"Doesn't look very good," I admitted.

"It's like you said, Gray. At least he'll have a chance instead of no chance at all."

Her words could as well have been for me, I realized.

"My advice," I said to the fish, "is to find a deep pool with some shade and a few big rocks to hide behind. And, if you're lucky, find yourself a Mrs. Moses, too."

"So they can make a bunch of little Moses," Valerie added.

Dark and sinuous, the river coiled among the rocks. I laid the mouth of the bag in the river water, then slowly lifted the other end of the bag. Moses emerged like something dead. He hung suspended in the shallow water. Nothing moved. Not the hooked jaw or the tiny pectoral fins. Not even his gills.

"C'mon, you son-of-a-bitch," I said as I stroked the fish's side with latex-gloved hands. "This is it. Freedom!" The current began carrying the tail of the fish away from me. One glassy eye stared accusingly as he drifted backward.

"No!" I struck the river with my palm. "Don't you dare die on me, you lazy fucking bastard!"

Valerie began to cry.

I scrambled downstream after the lifeless, drifting fish. "No, no, no," I yelled.

Patsy waded into the river barking loudly, as if encouraging Moses. Then, I thought I saw Moses' lower jaw move. Had I imagined it? I had to wipe the sweat from my eyes to be sure. What I saw next took little more than an instant but would remain engraved in my mind forever as with a powerful flick of his tail, Moses righted himself and moved off down the river into a pool beneath a fallen tree.

"Whooie!" I screamed.

Valerie stumbled forward over the river rocks and grabbed

my arm. "Tell me. What happened?"

"He's alive!" I swung her off her feet.

If someone had been watching, they might have seen a man, a woman, and a dog dancing insanely among the smooth boulders and bleached driftwood on the riverbank. Doubtless they would not have heard their whoops of joy and barking over the deafening rush of the cataract or seen their tears in the moonlight.

***

The drive back to the trout farm started out quiet, but celebratory. Or so I thought. I was giddy after setting the big fish free. Tired as I was, an electric current coursed through my muscles and veins, and I found myself smiling like an idiot.

"Damn, that was good," I said.

Then I looked over at Patsy sitting next to the door with her head out the window and noticed Valerie holding her hands to her face, her shoulders shaking as she sobbed silently.

"What's wrong?"

"You," she whispered. "You ruined it. That should have been you and me making love, not Vonda!"

Oops.

Valerie had obviously overheard Vonda's caterwauling during our lovemaking. I could think of nothing now to say that would help matters. I slowed, worried that she might do something foolish, like jump from the truck. When her crying continued unabated, I found a place to pull off the road and turned off the engine. The occasional passing car or truck illuminated us as we sat, shoulders slumped, in the dark cab of the truck. Patsy huddled on the floor.

Valerie's crying gradually subsided to loud sniffles. I restarted the engine and eased back onto the road.

"Why did—? Oh my God, Gray, how could you fuck my sister? She's married!"

"I don't know!" I sounded exasperated because I was out of excuses.

After listening to her renewed weeping, I added, "Listen to me, Valerie. If you are looking for signs of intelligence from me, you are out of luck. I left my brains back in Southern California—though my father would say I never had any to begin with."

"Momma said you would come."

"What?" I stared at her.

"She said I had to be patient, but a man would come to take me away and be my husband." She swiveled to face me. "She meant you, Gray! You're the man who came."

I sighed. "Your momma knew a lot of things, but she didn't know about me."

"She even described you."

In the faint glow from the pickup's dashboard, I could see Valerie's eyes moving behind her eyelids as if seeing something projected there.

"I know your secret, Gray," she said. "You're running from something. But it doesn't matter. We can hide together."

I had gone from giddy to guilty to unmasked in a few short minutes, and my head was about to fall off my shoulders. For someone who could not see, Valerie was amazingly clairvoyant. The only thing I could do was to tell her the truth which she clearly deserved.

"I lied, Valerie. My wife did not die in an accident. She was murdered. Now there are people trying to find me and kill me for what my wife did."

"What did she do?"

"She helped someone where she worked steal a great deal of money from some very bad people. People who would just as soon murder me and you and your family as read the paper or watch TV. Killing means nothing to them."

She seemed to think this over. When she spoke again, her voice was quiet. "You don't know if they'll ever find you. It might never happen, and then you will have ruined not only your life, but mine, too."

"You're forgetting the phone calls," I said. "Plus, someone came to the farm two days ago."

"Who?"

"An FBI agent."

"Why? What does that mean?"

"He said if he could find me, it meant the drug cartel could find me, too."

"The money your wife stole, do you know where it is?"

"Even if I did, I wouldn't know how to retrieve it, or how to hide it."

"Why would they try to find you if you don't know where the money is?"

"They don't care, Valerie." I sighed in frustration. "They're just making a point."

She crossed her arms over her chest. "Killing someone is 'just making a point?'"

"That's what they do." I sighed. "Entire families. Police departments. A busload of school kids. Even entire villages. They're worse than animals."

We hit a bump in the road that jolted us and caused the truck's springs to scream their indignation.

Valerie shivered. "Did you tell Vonda?"

"Nobody knows but you."

"What are you going to do?"

Valerie was no longer crying, and I began to hope the day's trials were finally nearing an end. Exhaustion had crept into my shoulders and back and made its home there. "The only thing I can do is leave. Tomorrow."

"Take me with you." She faced me. "You're everything I ever wanted just like Momma said." Those amazing blind eyes that saw everything were now open wide. "I love you, Gray. Even though I hate what you did."

"You can't love somebody you don't even know! I am a

washout. A fucking failure just like Stu said."

She punched my shoulder. "Don't say that. Did you know your wife when you fell in love with her? Did you know she was going to steal money?"

She had me there. I wondered what dangerous narrative was playing behind her eyelids as she stared at me.

"We'll go on the run together," she said, her voice urgent. "If they show up, we'll fight. Kill 'em if we have to."

"Jesus, Valerie." I was thrilled by her bravery, but appalled, too. "There's too many. Besides, they are trained killers. We wouldn't stand a chance."

"You have no idea what I'm capable of," she said.

"What's that mean?" I stared at her. The intersection for returning to the farm was just ahead. "We're almost home. Promise me you will not say anything to the others until I am gone. And that you'll stop crying over some misplaced fantasy about me."

"Don't worry," she said after a very long pause. "I won't say anything."

I glanced over at her. A moment ago, she had suggested killing people, as if that were a perfectly reasonable alternative. So why would I believe anything she said now? Because I was tired, because I was running out of arguments, and because all I wanted to do was lay my head on my pillow and sleep.

I turned the truck from the highway onto the country road. Later, I would regret not asking Valerie again about what happened to her canaries.

CHAPTER THIRTY-SEVEN

Before going to bed, I parked the truck in its customary location behind the barn and stored the ropes and trashcan, so there would be no telltale evidence of my piscine rescue mission. Either I had forgotten to leave the porch light on, or it had burned out because the cabin was as black as the bottom of a coal shaft on the dark side of the moon.

I smelled Stu—the anger rolling off him like garlic—a half second before the bat landed, or it might have killed me.

At first, I could only wrap my arms around my head as the blows landed against my face, ribs, and shoulders. Then I flicked out a hand and snatched the bat and then used both hands and all my weight to force Stu backwards until I had his neck pinned against the cedar wall. Only after he had stopped breathing and his blue eyes were the size of balloons did I let him go. He slumped to the floor.

"Get the fuck out." I pointed the Louisville Slugger, now smeared with my blood, at his face.

Stu said nothing for several minutes while the two of us regarded each other. One of my eyes was nearly swollen shut and my ribs were on fire, but he did not look ready to test me again. At least not while I held the bat.

"Where have you been the last two hours?" he said at last. "What evil have you been up to?"

I didn't answer.

"I thought about killing you," he said. "The only reason I didn't is because I was afraid your bones might somehow turn up when they dig this place up for water, sewer, and the other infrastructure needed for a housing development. In a funny way, you owe your life to Bob Halonen."

With a grunt I sat down on the cot, my back propped against the wall. My breath came in painful wheezes. I held one hand to my eye. I was afraid it might fall out.

"I told you to get out," I said.

"I'm leaving now," Stu said. "But, in case you have not figured it out, you're done here. I don't want to see your face at breakfast. In fact, I do not want to see your face again. Ever." He stood in the open doorway. "You've got about four or five hours left before daylight. I recommend making good use of them. Next time, I'll be bringing more firepower than the bat."

After he left, I limped to the bathroom. My face was a mess. One eye was swollen shut, the left side of my face now twice the size of the right. My lip was busted, and my teeth felt loose. I turned on the shower in the tiny bathroom and sat on the toilet as the water drenched me in its spray.

***

The pain prevented sleep. As the sun began to rise, I was struggling to put on pants when there was a hard knock on the door. Virgil entered. He stared at me, then looked at the blood speckled floor.

"Stu do this?"

I had pulled a clean, folded shirt from the bookcase over the bed, but could not get it on over my bruised arm and shoulder.

Virgil studied me. "You going to make it?"

I tried moving my jaw before nodding.

"I should probably take you to the nearest hospital or clinic to get cleaned up, but there's something else happened," Virgil said. "I need your help."

I stared at him with one eye in disbelief. He had to be kidding.

"Valerie is gone. Disappeared sometime during the night."

My first thought was maybe Stu had kidnapped her. But why would he unless Valerie confronted him, and Stu had lost his mind?

"She's nowhere to be found," Virgil added. "I don't know where she would have gone. Didn't take Patsy with her. That's a first."

"I know this could be better timing," he continued, "but I need your help finding her, or at least helping me figure out where she might have gone." He sat on the chair. It creaked with his weight and I worried it might break. "You're the only help I have left. I have not seen Vonda in a day and a half. Hasn't come out of the bedroom. Stu left for town early, but I don't think he'd be any help if he'd stayed."

He wiped his face with his handkerchief.

"She's my baby girl," he said, his voice breaking.

Virgil put an arm around my shoulder and helped me stand. When he saw me struggling, he lifted each arm and slipped it into a sleeve, then buttoned my shirt.

"I don't know what happened between you and Stu," Virgil said. "I'm guessing Vonda had something to do with it. Her momma used to say when Vonda got an idea in her head, she was like a train that jumped the track. No telling where she might end up."

He paused, looked around the small cabin. "Valerie was always the one who seemed like she had it all together. Like she could take care of herself and all of us, too."

Virgil was silent for a minute as if thinking. "Maybe you were right, about her needing professional help. She is more complicated than anyone I have ever known. Even more than her mother, Louise." He paused again. "I can't make sense of this, Gray, and it scares me."

Until now, I had worried about Stu returning with the shotgun and how I was going to avoid him. Now finding Valerie was added to the list. At the very least, I had likely contributed to her disappearance when I had disclosed my plans to leave.

"She's gone for walks before," Virgil continued. "And it's obvious she's mighty unhappy about the farm maybe being sold, but that don't add up to her disappearing, especially with what she done."

He sighed. "The rabbits are dead. She butchered them."

CHAPTER THIRTY-EIGHT

I know what I did was evil, but in a way, it was a kindness to them. No one has ever paid them any notice or taken care of them but me. And I am not planning to be staying around here much longer. Good luck handling things when I am gone.

Oh, sure. Vonda fed them lettuce once or twice when I was sick, but all she did for days afterward was complain. Like feeding rabbits was beneath her.

It was late. I had a pillowcase to put them in and I heard them screaming. If you have never heard rabbits scream, you cannot imagine the sound. I had to hold the bag tight as they kicked and fought to be free.

Thelma is the big one. She must weigh twenty pounds. "That's you and me," Vonda said as we were "watching" the Thelma and Louise *movie on television way back when. She was fourteen. I was only eight or nine.* "We're gonna be like that someday. Riding in a big car, just you and me." *Then a few months later, she discovered boys and that was the end of "just you and me."*

I like listening to movies and television shows now and then, especially cooking shows. But it is not always easy to figure out what is happening when you cannot see. I understand they have subtitles for people who cannot hear, but there is almost nothing for blind people. Just a handful of shows produced with audio descriptions. I prefer listening to classical music and reading books in Braille. The Braille Reading Pals Program that Momma subscribed to for me was my salvation when I was a kid.

By the way, it is not that easy killing something that does not want to be killed as I discovered. The birds were easy. I just snapped their necks, the bones so tiny they barely made a crunching noise. But the rabbits were not ready to give up so easy. They kicked and scratched and screamed until the knife did its work. And then they were dead and hot tears were streaming down my face. So, fuck me. Fuck everybody. Sorry, Momma, but using bad words is the least of my sins.

I needed to think carefully about where to bury them. I could not take Patsy with me. She would be upset. I had to find the place by myself. It was not easy, believe me. Even with my cane, I had to step nice and slow to avoid tripping over a tree root or stumbling off in the wrong direction and getting lost. That would not do. No, that would not do at all. I have not asked for help from anyone since Momma died—not that it would have done me any good—and I for damn sure am not going to ask now.

I hate Stu the most. I have laid awake many nights dreaming of dragging my knife across his throat while he sleeps. From what Vonda's told me, he is tall and strong, but I would make sure he never knew what was happening until it was too late.

Vonda drinks a lot and then passes out. I can hear her snoring all the way from my bedroom. I do not think she would even know what was happening. Do not get me wrong. I love my sister. But I hate her, too. For betraying me. For making fun of me. And for stealing Gray. Everything I got, she had to have, too. Even Gray.

I have thought a lot about how it would be. I'd say, "Vonda, wake up. It's your little sister, Valerie." And then I would bury the knife into her chest. Let's hear what kind of grunts and *squeals she makes with the blade of my knife stuck in her fucking heart.*

Daddy is a good man, I think. Never cheated on Momma, as far as I know. Just did not have a clue about how to care for his daughters when she died. He brought this all on himself. He could have saved us a lot of trouble if he had not listened to Stu and Vonda about selling the farm to Bob Halonen. Maybe then Gray and Vonda would not have done what they did.

Then there is Gray. He is the one who hurt me most of all. I have not figured out how to do it yet. I would like him to say he is sorry before I cut him, but it does not really matter. In the end, the only thing that matters is that we both die and then we can finally all be together. The two of us. Forever. That is how it should be. Like you said, Momma.

No, I have not forgotten Patsy. My traitor dog. I just do not think I could kill that dog if I wanted to. She is the only good thing I have ever known, except for you, Momma. And maybe Gray. Maybe.

***

Vonda did not bother to knock. A black eye dominated one side of her face.

"Jesus. Ain't you a pretty sight?" she said. "Daddy said it looked like Stu tried to kill you."

"Are you sure you want to be here? Your high school all-star is apt to show up any minute." I squinted up at her from the bed where I had not moved since Virgil's visit. It hurt to take a deep breath and the swelling in my jaw made it painful to speak. If that was not enough, I now had a lisp.

"Besides, why are you not looking for your sister?" From what Virgil had said, she had been missing for at least a few hours.

"I'll be leaving in a few minutes after Daddy makes some calls. He asked me to look for her while he drives. But I figured you might need this." She handed me an ice pack.

"Got any aspirin?"

"Before I go looking for Valerie, I wanted to say something." She touched my bruised cheek. "This might be the last time I get to see you. While I was locked up in the bedroom the past day and a half, I did some thinking. You and me seem to have a chemistry. Call it sexual attraction, or whatever."

Where was she going with this? Surely, she was not thinking about sex at this moment.

As if hearing my thoughts, she smiled. "Don't worry, Gray. I may be crazy, but I ain't that crazy. Figured this might be my last opportunity to convince you to ride off into the sunset together. Just leave this place and all the problems behind."

"What about Stu and Valerie?"

"Let them sort out their own problems. They can stay, leave, whatever. I don't care. I hate this place. I hate my husband. I hate being stuck here in the National Geo-fucking wilderness with someone whose life was over at age nineteen."

Her voice broke and I thought she might cry. Or laugh. With Vonda, I was never quite sure what to expect.

"I need a new start. I need something new. *Someone* new. I think you are the someone I need, Gray."

The pounding in my forehead grew. "You've got part of the equation solved. Dump Stu." I wiped blood from the corner of my mouth.

"I know I ain't perfect," she continued as if I was on board her misguided train of thought. "I tend to drink too much and could probably stand to exercise some before my ass starts to droop. But I ain't stupid—no matter how I talk." She tried to laugh but failed. "Shit. I think I might love you, Gray."

She touched my forehead and ran her fingers softly through my hair.

I grabbed her wrist. "Look at me, Vonda! I've got nothing. No money. No job. No future. Maybe no teeth." I spat blood on the floor.

"Yesterday, I admit I needed you. In addition to an ill-considered lust bomb fueled by fear and loneliness, I may have felt affection, however misplaced. Today, however, I need forgiveness. And aspirin. And right now, we need to look for your sister," I croaked. "Before something worse happens."

"Why?" She pulled away from my grip and rubbed her wrist. "I fail to see why you are so concerned about her. All she has done is cause trouble. If she had not said something the other day at breakfast, this might not have happened."

"First, she is handicapped. Not just physically but emotionally—something you or I will probably never understand. Second, she spoke up for me when I needed a job and a place to stay." I rubbed my jaw where the bat had connected at least once. "Third, she brought me a blanket and a sandwich on a cold rainy night when I was trying to catch a few hours' sleep in my truck. Your little sister made me some of the most bizarre sandwiches I ever tasted but, for someone who was hungry and had nothing, it was manna."

Vonda frowned as she circled the tiny room. She was not hearing me and likely never would.

"I probably sound like a crazy fool. It started out being just sexual attraction, but somewhere—maybe when I was laid up with a black eye from my asshole of a husband—it changed.

"You don't even have to love me back. At least not right away." She hastened to wipe a tear away. "We could travel, live off my share of the sale of the farm, find an apartment someplace."

I groaned. In some weird, messed up way, her offer made sense. But that was before. Before Heide died. Before I was shot and being hunted by people who wanted to kill me. And before Stu took out his frustrations on me with his Louisville Slugger. Now I realized how stupid and naïve I had been about love, faithfulness and, most of all, trust—a currency you could earn but never spend without losing all its value.

"I am touched by your offer, Vonda. But I have never felt

so ashamed of myself. I deserved your husband's punishment." I struggled to pronounce the final word clearly. Best to stick to one syllable words. "Besides, you don't really love me. You are just looking for someone to take you away from this. You are afraid there is no one out there. That you might have to spend the rest of your life alone. Or worse, with Stu."

I sounded like I was talking about myself, which maybe I was.

"Oh sure." Vonda's voice dripped with sarcasm. "Let's feel sorry for ourselves. That will solve everything."

"If Stu shows up and sees us together, it won't really matter." I managed to wobble to my feet with a grunt. "I'm going to look for your sister," I announced with a lisp.

CHAPTER THIRTY-NINE

Virgil and Vonda assumed Valerie was running away from home to protest the sale of the farm and would be hitchhiking or had called for a cab. Consequently, they were searching the roads and Mt. Vernon bus station for her in Virgil's Cadillac.

I was no psychologist, but I suspected that the disappearance of her birds followed by the slaughter of her pet rabbits was symptomatic of something more profound than a young woman's anger over the sale of the farm. My hunch was that the affair between Vonda and I had pushed her over the edge of whatever level of sanity she had been clinging to and that she might be hiding somewhere near, planning her next move.

Patsy accompanied me to the Lucky Lady. As we drew close to the derelict, I could hear noises inside.

"Valerie, is that you? What are you doing?"

"Don't come near me!" she ordered.

"Why are you hiding?" I stroked Patsy's ears. It was a warm day. The sun peeked through the leafy canopy overhead. The smell of evergreen trees, moss and earth competed with the sour, musty smell of the cabin cruiser resting on its rusted trailer beneath the ruined tarp. Nearby, I could hear birds warbling and crickets chirping like there was nothing out of the ordinary and no need to worry. As I had learned, however, it was all a trick to make you think things would be okay. Another clever ruse from the master con artist in the sky.

"I got a right to do what I want," she said. "I'm tired of people thinking they know what is best for me."

I took a few steps closer. "I heard about the rabbits from your dad. He found them. Their bodies anyway."

"Oh, crap."

During the silence while I waited for her to speak again, a bumble bee found a dandelion and Patsy snapped at it.

"Must be difficult to hide something when you can't see," I offered.

She snorted. "You sound funny. Why are you talking like that?"

"Stu needed some batting practice."

"That asshole." She continued to move about inside. "I heard you coming from a mile away. Is my traitor dog with you?"

"Yeah. She's here. I'm coming in."

The dog would have to stay outside. In my condition, it would be difficult enough just climbing over the transom.

"Stay," I commanded and hoped she would.

I used a fender on the trailer to climb up and peer into the cabin cruiser. The first thing I noticed was the knife waving in front of my face like a cobra.

"I told you to stay away!" She slashed at me.

I yanked my head backward, but the blade tip caught my upper arm, drawing blood. I grabbed her wrist and twisted the knife away. It fell to the floor.

Valerie scuttled toward the galley in the dim interior like a caged feral animal.

The second thing I noticed were the blood stains on her clothing. It ribboned her arms and thighs where it looked like she had tried but failed to cover it up. A blood-soaked towel lay in the corner near an empty package of bandages.

"What the hell, Valerie. What is with all the blood?" I

climbed into the boat with a grunt from the pain stabbing my ribs.

"They're just scratches," she said. She wiped away a tear from a reddened cheek.

"Let me look." I edged closer, not wanting to frighten her, but backing her into the galley's seating area where I was able to corner her. I clutched an arm before she could escape and pulled up one sleeve. A dozen old scars were revealed among the more recent cuts. After recovering from my initial shock, I tried to put an arm around her shoulder, but she jerked away.

"You're cutting yourself?"

"It's the only thing keeping me from killing myself," she snarled.

"I didn't realize how bad things were. Let me drive you to the hospital or somewhere you can get help."

"Too late." She scrabbled away. "Why are you here? Surprised you're not gone yet."

Why was I here? Why had I not just driven off in the banshee Toyota like Stu had ordered? Was I trying to save Valerie? Or myself? Once again, I was in over my head.

"Don't worry," I said in as calm a voice as I could muster. "I am not making you do anything you don't want to do."

Valerie's rarely used cane rested on the table. The knife, meanwhile, lurked in the shadows on the floor.

"Got any painkillers?"

"Sorry, no meds. Wanna drink?" She waved a bottle of brandy, no doubt stolen from her sister. I had never seen her drink before, but there were evidently lots of things I had never seen Valerie do.

I sighed and sat down. "Why the hell not?"

She passed the brandy, then reached a hand tentatively toward my face. "Where did Stu hurt you?"

"There are streaks of blood crisscrossing your arms and legs, and you are worried about me?" The brandy stung my lips, but tasted good, warming as a ray of sunshine in the dim interior. "Jesus, Valerie. How long have you been doing this?"

She started to cry. I waited while she wiped her nose on a blood-stained sleeve. "Since right after Momma died."

"And no one knows?" I found it incredible that a young woman—not to mention a young blind woman—could conceal such pain and self-harm from her family for so long.

She reached a hand for the bottle. The air in the boat smelled of apricots and mold and blood. "Just you."

Watching her, I had a sudden realization. "You did it to yourself, didn't you? The knife in the dishwasher."

She took a pull on the bottle. "I never said it was you."

"Why would you do that to yourself?"

"Why did you fuck my sister?"

"Because." I paused. "Because I wanted to forget."

"Forget what?"

"That I'm a dead man walking." I felt loss and maybe self-pity like Vonda accused me of. But I was angry, too. At my lisp, my pain, and now this latest affront to my dignity and my pathetic notion of how the world ought to be. In addition to being virtually penniless and hunted by sociopaths, here I was sitting in a derelict cabin cruiser with a disturbed young blind woman after being beaten half to death by her brother-in-law. All because my wife thought she could get away with helping a friend steal a hundred million.

I took the bottle back from her and took a big swallow and let it burn the back of my throat. "I lost everything I knew and loved. I don't even have a place to call home anymore."

"It's not that different—me cutting myself," Valerie said quietly. "It stops the pain of remembering. Of missing my mother. Of feeling sorry for myself. Sometimes it is the only way I feel in control of my life and not drowning in loneliness or hate."

I looked around the boat. There was a small sink, a refrigerator, and a two-burner stove. The seat seams were split, and the once-upon-a-happier-time white vinyl had turned green with mold. "What happened here? What is a cabin cruiser doing sitting in the middle of nowhere?"

She tried to smile. "The boat was Momma's idea. We would go fishing, or just motor around Puget Sound, the Strait of Juan de Fuca, or Bellingham Bay. Just Vonda, me, Daddy and Momma. She would bundle me up in a parka and tuck a blanket around my legs and make me a warm mug of hot cocoa. I remember the wind, the spray on my face, the seagulls squawking. It was like heaven."

Her smile faded a few seconds later. "And then she got sick and we never went out again. Daddy didn't have the heart to sell the boat, but it made him too sad to see it, so he hid it back here."

"I'm sorry, Valerie."

"For what?" She passed me the bottle again.

"I failed you." I took another pull. At least my pain was starting to diminish.

"You ain't the only one."

I reached for her hand. "It doesn't have to be this way. Remember the apartment over a bakery?" She turned her face toward mine, her eyes closed. "You can still do that." I must have been already feeling the brandy because I added, "We can do that."

"Don't lie. Tell me the truth. Otherwise, you are no good to me."

In for a penny, in for a pound. "I am not leaving without you."

"Yeah?" She snorted. "What about Stu? What about the guys that are chasing you?"

"What's Stu going to do? Get a bigger bat? Shoot me? He nearly killed me already."

I studied the sunlight illuminating a spider web in the stern. "I don't know about the others. Maybe I will study kung fu. Become a Ninja warrior. I don't know, Valerie."

"My Ninja warrior." She smiled. She put down the bottle.

Then she hugged me. It hurt like hell, but I was okay with that.

"Let's just sit here and rest for a while, okay?" she said. "I am tired." She yawned, then leaned her head against my shoulder.

"Are you going to stab me? If you are, I'm going to need another bottle of brandy."

"I'm through making promises," she mumbled. "Or believing them." She took another drink from the bottle.

We sat there for a long time in the sun-dappled interior of the rotting boat. I may even have dozed off. I woke when she began to tell me another story about her mother:

"Not long before she died, Momma made me go swimming with her in the big pond. I was terrified. I had been swimming in a lake before, but she was always there beside me, holding onto me. 'Won't the trout bite me?' I asked. I remember running my fingers all over her face trying to understand. Her head was nearly bald from the chemo.

"'Relax and float on your back,' Momma said. 'They won't bite you.' At first, she held onto me, but then she let go and I heard her moving away.

"I cried, 'Momma, don't leave me.' Maybe it was my imagination—I was only ten—but I thought I could feel their fins brushing my skin as the trout swam near me and it scared me. 'I can feel them!'

"'Silly girl,' she told me. 'Those are angel wings. You are swimming with the angels now.'"

I thought the story was ridiculous. Likely her mother had been close to the end and suffering from a chemo-induced fog. But if you were a young, blind girl about to lose your mother, teacher, and best friend to a deadly disease, the memory was something to hold onto.

We sat quietly, not saying anything for another half-hour or so, until Valerie sat up suddenly.

"What is it?" I asked.

Outside the boat, I could hear Patsy pacing, a low growl in

her throat.

"Is it Stu?" I figured Stu might be coming to give me another whipping. I glanced at my watch, but it was broken. "What time is it?"

"Shhh." Her hand covered my mouth. "How many would come for you?"

I scrambled up from the seat. "What do you hear?" I whispered. I could not hear anything except Patsy growling. "It's probably just your father and Vonda looking for us."

Her violet eyes were huge, but she had an oddly peaceful look on her face. "I hear screaming. Vonda's screams. There is a bit of an echo. I think they are in the barn."

I marveled again at her extraordinary hearing. Patsy's growling was louder now, too. Yet I could hear nothing. "You stay here while I check it out."

She clung to my arm. "We could stay here together, hide until they are gone. I will hear them if they come this way."

I struggled to tear away from her grip. For being so tiny, she was surprisingly strong. "I have to go, Valerie."

"Why?"

"They don't deserve this."

"Yes, they do."

I looked into her amazing eyes. She did not seem upset by her sister's screams. "No one deserves to be hurt because of me, least of all you and your family."

"Then I am going, too."

"No." I peeled her arms away. "Promise me you will not go anywhere. Just stay here, be quiet and keep Patsy quiet, too, if you can."

She nodded, a tiny smile edging her lips. "Okay, kemosabe."

I hugged her for a moment. "I will come back for you."

"Sure," she said. "I'll be waiting."

CHAPTER FORTY

I ran back the way I had come, limping from the pain in my hip and stumbling over tree roots hidden in the long grass, my heart threatening to erupt from my chest.

I hoped Valerie was wrong and that what her keen ears had heard was Stu returning in a rage to continue taking out his many frustrations on Vonda. Because if the cartel killers had arrived, there was little hope of survival for any of us except possibly Valerie, but only if she remained hidden in the Lucky Lady.

I was concentrating on trying not to trip as I ran and did not see Stu until he had a hand over my mouth and had thrown me up against a tree. "Shhh," he warned. "I think Vonda and Virgil have been taken captive. I need your help."

I nodded.

"This way."

We veered toward the direction of the shed. I was just a step behind him when we burst into its dark confines and both paused in surprise. The normally locked closet door stood wide open.

Then I heard a voice behind us, "Looking for this?"

Some things you wish you could forget. Like a sin whose stain will never go away no matter how often you repent and try to scrub it away. When I spun around, I recognized the man

I had spotted through the viewfinder of the camera as he stood on the pier aiming a gun at us on the day Heide was murdered. Now he held the shotgun with double barrels pointed at us.

"This way, señores." He motioned with the gun. He had small teeth and wore a goatee and mustache in the shape of an anchor. When he spoke, his mouth barely moved.

Catania was right. The cartel had not quit looking and had somehow managed to find me. The fear that had stalked me for several months—ever since that doomed Saturday in Newport Harbor—suddenly fled, leaving a feeling of eerie calm. All the uneasiness that had gripped me was replaced by the certainty that I was about to die. At last, the running, hiding and secrecy would finally be over. I hoped they would make it quick.

CHAPTER FORTY-ONE

The two of us were ushered at gun point into the barn. Sunlight streamed in the large doorway, illuminating Virgil who was sitting in one of the office chairs with his hands fastened behind his back and Vonda whose hands were tied to the steering wheel of the John Deere riding mower. It was obvious that she had been crying and that she had put up a fight. Her blouse was missing a few buttons so that her bra was exposed, her jeans were torn and dirty and one shoe was missing as if she had been dragged.

"Look what I found," the man called out. He motioned Stu to sit in the other chair and fastened his hands behind it with a cable tie. Then he shoved me with the barrel of the shotgun so that I stumbled and fell before the other killer. "Here is la cabron who messed up your leg."

I looked up at the woman identified as Ramona Gutierrez on her mug shot who had shot me that fateful day in Newport Harbor. She was taller and slimmer than I remembered, her skin lighter than the man's. Her hair was now blond, and a fine scar etched her cheek, but her blood-red lips were the very same. The face I recalled in my nightmares was cruel, but up close she was good looking, perhaps even beautiful once. Before she became the angel of death. She held a gold-plated pistol with a long barrel in one hand. It looked like the same one she had used to shoot me and kill Heide.

Flash. Boom.

"My goodness. Look who we have here." She laughed. She used the gun's barrel to turn my face toward hers. "Ouch! You do not look so good, my friend. What happened to your face?"

"Have you not got anything better to do than hunt for me?" I said.

"You have not answered me. Was it something to do with her?" She pointed with the pistol at Vonda. "What do you think, Arturo?"

"Probably the tall one had something to do with it," Arturo said. He used the shotgun to poke Stu in the back. "Speak up, señor."

"The bastard fucked my wife," Stu said.

"Ah, I see. How awful for you." Ramona turned back to me. "He does not like you, amigo." She smiled with perfect teeth that had either been bleached or were as false as the tone of her voice.

"Frankly, I don't like you either. What about you, 'Turo?" The other man grunted.

"Arturo does not say much, but what he can do with a coat hanger is truly inspiring." She smiled again. "I think maybe no one likes you. It seems that we do the world a big favor by killing you."

I wished now I had drunk more of the brandy. The false invincibility I had briefly felt in the Lucky Lady was long gone. "Just get it over with. Kill me and let them go."

"Not so fast." Ramona tapped her leg with the barrel of the pistol. "You see what you did?" As before, she wore a dark-colored sweat suit. Now, however, her right leg was encased in a leg brace from the thigh to the ankle.

"Think that's bad, you should have seen the boats."

Ramona swatted me in the forehead with the gun barrel, hard enough to break the skin and hurt like hell, but unfortunately not hard enough to knock me out

She shifted her weight as she studied me. "You made my life very difficult. Now I must take pills every day and night." She frowned. "You even managed to ruin my fucking sex life, not that it was ever that great."

Blood dripped into my right eye and down my cheek. "Next time you decide to kill an unarmed woman, or a little girl, maybe you should think twice."

Ramona uttered a low growl that reminded me of the inhuman scream I heard following the boat crash.

"You are very brave when you are behind the wheel of a powerful boat, but what about now, hmm?" She traced my jawline with the barrel of the gold pistol. "Not so much, I think."

I hung my head. It was abundantly clear that I was a turtle astray in the carpool lane, an instant away from death. I could envision a lonely grave marker in a county cemetery, no one knowing my real name, who I really was, what I aspired to, how I lived, and who I loved. But, if I were only half as brave as I once thought I was, perhaps I could still do something to save the others.

"You sound like an intelligent woman," I said, hoping to flatter her. "Why not let them go? They had nothing to do with it."

She crossed her arms, the pistol resting against her good leg. "*Tsk, tsk.* I do not think you understand the gravity of the situation you have put these people in," Ramona said.

Virgil's face and neck were inflamed, the cords of his neck standing out as he strained against the cable ties that bound him. "Will somebody tell me who these people are and what they are doing trespassing on my property?" He glared at me. "Was this your doing, young man?"

I wiped the blood from my eye, the better to see the injustice I was responsible for causing. "These people killed my wife and her friend and tried to kill me."

Vonda spoke for the first time. "Why? What did you do?"

"My wife stole money from where she worked. She didn't know it was theirs."

"I thought you said she was killed by a drunk driver," Stu said.

Vonda ignored him as did everyone else. "What has this got to do with us?" she asked.

"It's got nothing to do with you," Ramona said, "and everything. You helped him hide from us."

"That ain't fair," she said. "We didn't know nothing about it."

"Fair?" Ramona laughed. "What is fair? Can you please explain this concept to me?"

Vonda did not answer.

"When I was ten," Ramona said, "my mother and sister were raped, tortured and killed by members of the Mexican Navy. They used my eleven-year-old brother for target practice while I hid beneath our house. Why? Because my family would not tell them where my father was hiding. You think that was fair?" Her red lips were curled as if smiling but her eyes were black abysses.

"After several days living on the streets, begging for food, my father found me and sent me away to a private school in San Diego followed by San Diego State University. I had to beg him to let me join the cartel with him. It took more than a year before he finally gave in."

She turned toward Vonda. "I am very sorry to be the one to tell you that this day is not about being fair. No, señora," she said. "As you are about to learn, life is not fair."

"Why didn't you say something?" Virgil said. "We might have prepared for these devils."

"I told you he was a world-class fuck-up," Stu said. He squirmed against the tie that secured his hands but could not free himself.

"I know where the money is," I said. "Let them go and I'll tell you where it is."

Instead of looking pleased, however, Ramona appeared disgusted. "You expect me to believe you know where the money is now, when you are living here in this shit hole?" She waved the gold pistol in the air.

"What money?" Vonda's voice squeaked.

"Oh, dear!" Ramona laughed. "Such a bad joke you play on these poor people." Arturo chuckled.

"He never told you how his wife stole one hundred million US dollars?" Her voice suddenly changed, becoming deeper. Any pretense of civility was gone. Even the light in the barn darkened as if her evil humor had obscured the sunlight filtering through the barn doors. "Probably he never told you that I killed her. Or that Arturo killed her business partner and his family. And now, quite sadly, I must do the same to all of you."

"Jesus, Gray! How could you do this to me? To us?" Vonda red-rimmed eyes stared accusingly.

"If you don't believe I know where the money is, why would you drive all this way to kill me and these innocent people?" I asked.

"You mean in addition to this?" Ramona tapped her leg. "This is not reason enough for you?"

"It is time," Arturo said. He tapped his wrist.

"Don't rush me, 'Turo. I've waited for this moment for a long time."

Ramona smiled at me as if talking to a child. "When you have seen as much killing as I have, you realize two things. First, there is no God looking out for his people. Second, the only thing that matters in this world is keeping score."

"This isn't a fucking baseball game," I protested.

"In sports," she continued, "the team at the top does not just want to win. No, they run up the score to send a message to the other teams. That is why we go to all the trouble to find you. In addition to the Mexican Military and your own DEA, there are other cartels that would destroy us if they could find any weakness."

"Can I tell you a secret?" She leaned toward me. "Well, I confess, there is another reason. After all, in this business, I have my own reputation to protect. That is why we leave no one alive and nothing behind." She waved the gun at the others. "Nada."

"We waste time," Arturo said.

"Patience, 'Turo. Just a few seconds more." Ramona looked down at me. My knees were complaining from the concrete floor, but I barely noticed.

"I will tell you what 'fair' is. 'Fair' is when I make you watch your friends die first. 'Fair' is when I kill you last as payment for causing me so much fucking pain and for making us work so hard to find you."

I could think of nothing to say.

"Bring me the tall one, Arturo," she ordered.

"Si." The old man stood the shotgun against the office door, then grabbed the chair Stu was sitting on and wheeled it to the doorway a few feet from Ramona.

"Wait." I pleaded. It was the least I could do. "The money is in a bank in the Cayman Islands."

"No, amigo. I do not listen to you. I think you're a comedian." Ramona's ruby-red lips and beautiful, scarred face now bore the same cold-blooded visage I had spotted when she shot me. "For your amusement, you get to watch the one who injured you die first."

Arturo poured gasoline from a two gallon can on Stu, drenching him.

"Ah, shit," Stu said as he realized what was about to happen. He squirmed violently as he tried to free his hands from the plastic zip tie that bound him.

Vonda screamed. "No! Please, stop!"

"Stop this evil right now," Virgil shouted.

Arturo pulled a black handgun from his waistband, racked the slide, and placed the gun against Virgil's neck.

"Save your voice for your prayers, señor," Arturo said. "I think you are next."

"I pray that you both roast in hell!" Virgil said.

I was the only one who did not have my hands tied and was Stu's last possible hope. Before I could move, however, Ramona stuck the cold barrel of the pistol in my face.

"Don't move or I will shoot you in the testicles," Ramona said. "It won't kill you, but you will wish you were dead."

Vonda shrieked.

Ramona squinted as if in pain. "That one hurts my ears. Next time she screams, shoot her."

"You can shoot her for all I care," Stu said. "And go ahead and kill that bastard, too." Stu nodded toward me. "I had nothing to do with stealing your money. I won't say anything. Just let me go."

"What do you think, 'Turo? Shall we let him go? He says he won't say anything."

The other man smirked.

Ramona withdrew a Zippo lighter from her jacket with her free hand and flicked it open "Now no one else will dare to fuck with our money."

"Hey, bitch," came a voice from just outside the doorway. "Say something."

Ramona gaped open mouthed at the sight of a fey, naked Valerie standing just outside the barn door, blood running in rivulets down her arms and legs, fresh gashes across her forehead and stomach. "Madre de dios!"

Valerie's hand whipped the knife almost faster than the eye could track it. The blade winked in the sunlight as it turned end over end. It caught Ramona in the base of her throat. She dropped the lighter and fired wildly as she stumbled on her bad leg. The bullet skipped across the floor and disappeared out the door as a thundering boom reverberated in the barn.

There was a whoosh as blue flames scurried across the floor. Stu kicked furiously to move the chair away from the flames as they raced toward his feet.

Arturo dropped the gas can and fired his weapon, the shot knocking Valerie backward. Gasoline burped from the toppled can's opening and spread upon the concrete floor, joining the previous pool. The acrid odor of gasoline and gunpowder saturated the heated air in the barn.

Ramona made a gargling noise as blood coursed from her mouth. From my kneeling position, I dove into her legs, knocking her down.

We fought on our knees as I tried to pry the gun from her hand. I managed to trap her firing arm beneath my armpit, but Ramona would not let go. She wrenched the gun, the barrel tearing the tender skin on the underside of my arm where Stu's bat had left my skin black with contusions.

I felt my skin ripping as I fought to free the gun from Ramona's firm grip, and I grunted from the searing pain. I had become very fit from working at the farm, but Ramona's arm was strong. Her free hand shoved me away. My spine bent as I refused to let go of the gun.

The memory of my father's face suddenly appeared. When I was fourteen, I had come to while lying on the kitchen floor, blood streaming from my nose. "Get up," he ordered. "Be a man for once in your life."

My vertebrae began to twist and pop, and still I would not let go. Fortunately, she had only one good leg and, as I discovered, I had the better shoes. As our feet scrabbled for purchase on the concrete floor, my boots won out over Ramona's shoes. With one foot, I managed to find enough traction to move her backwards, while I kicked her repeatedly in her injured leg with the other.

"Kick her again!" Vonda screamed.

From the corner of my eye, I saw the blue flames reach Stu. He whimpered as they began climbing his legs.

Vonda writhed frantically against the tie that bound her hands to the steering wheel. "The knife!" she yelled. "Grab the knife!"

Through the blood running down my face and into my eyes, I saw the handle of the knife Valerie had thrown protruding from Ramona's throat. How was she not dead already? I grasped it with one hand and tried to saw at her neck.

Vonda whooped. "How's that feel, motherfucker?"

The hand that had clutched the gun so fiercely suddenly let go. Ramona clutched at her neck with both hands as blood gushed from her wound.

I yanked the revolver free with one hand. With the other, I dragged Ramona between me and Arturo, using her as a shield.

A bullet meant for me struck Ramona instead. I felt the impact as she gasped.

I took aim with Ramona's pistol at Arturo who fired at me again, the bullet whistling past my head. I began firing from where I lay behind Ramona. My first shots missed wildly, but the next shot connected, twisting the other man backward and he fell.

Arturo tried to raise his gun. I shot him again, the sound enormous in the metal barn. I would have shot him yet again, but the hammer fell on a spent round.

I pushed Ramona away and managed to stand, my legs shaking violently, the smell of gunpowder and blood making me gag.

"Gray!" Vonda yelled. "Hurry!"

I saw Virgil slumped in his chair. Stu was desperately attempting to chair hop away from the flames that were licking his chinos.

Ramona writhed on the concrete floor as the hungry flames found and enveloped her. Somehow, she managed to roll to her feet and stumble out the door. Her blond wig remained smoldering on the concrete floor.

Vonda struggled to free herself as the flames spread.

I hit the wheeled chair Stu was in and kept going, pushing it out the barn door and across the recently mowed grass.

It was a torturous hundred feet downhill to the big pond as Stu jerked and moaned. The smell of gasoline, burning clothes and flesh assaulted my nostrils. I gasped from the smoke and exertion.

The last several feet, the flames began burning my arms and hands. I picked up Stu and the chair like I was a Viking berserker. Rage and adrenalin overcame my injuries and fatigue as I reached the water and tumbled into it, drenching us both. I held onto the chair to prevent Stu from drowning until I was sure the flames were out. Then I dragged Stu, still tied to the office chair, from the water.

I needed to save the others. Before I could leave, a dark shape rose suddenly from the water and seized my leg.

At first, I feared it was a third killer. Then I saw the blade handle still protruding from Ramona's throat.

"Nada mas!" I yelled. I slammed the heel of my hand into the knife handle with everything I had. The blade bit into bone. Like a light going off, Ramona collapsed.

I left her floating face down in the pond.

Still tied to the chair, Stu was moaning and sputtering, but was alive.

"I'll be back," I said.

Valerie was breathing, but shallowly with blood bubbling from her mouth. For a moment, I saw Heide's face, a pool of blood spreading beneath her on the floor of the boat, and I begged, "Don't leave me. Not again."

"Momma said...you would...come." She blinked once and then she was gone.

I looked up to see Vonda, still tied to the John Deere riding mower. "Hurry, Gray. Help Daddy."

I cut Vonda loose with a knife. While she called 911 from the office, I pushed Virgil a safe distance from the flames that were dying out and freed his arms. The older man was either passed out or having a heart attack. When I saw that he was breathing and had a pulse, I went back to sit with Valerie.

There was no word to describe my fatigue. All the energy had been sucked from my bruised body, and I began to shiver uncontrollably.

CHAPTER FORTY-TWO

I could have laid there in the grass all night, staring at the sky as the stars came out and the frogs began their chorus, but there were people with questions.

Two sheriff deputies drove me to the emergency room to have my hands bandaged and forehead stitched. At the police station, they wrapped a blanket around my shoulders and set a cup of coffee in front of me. They wanted to know why two Mexican nationals with long criminal records, wanted by both Mexican and US authorities, would show up at an isolated trout farm intending to kill everyone.

"Got any aspirin?" I asked. It was going to be a long day.

Patsy was waiting for me when I arrived back at the trout farm. It was late. I led her to the cabin, poured water into an empty dish from a previous meal, then climbed onto the cot.

Vonda woke me the next morning wearing only a bathrobe. "You okay?" She held a glass of brandy. One breast peeked from beneath her robe.

I sat up stiffly, still wearing the clothes from the night before. They smelled of smoke and were soaked with blood and water. I felt like hell, but I was alive.

"Daddy's still at the Skagit Valley Hospital. They want to monitor his heart for at least twenty-four hours. Stu's at Harborview in Seattle. They say he'll make it—thanks to you—

but he may not walk without assistance for a long time, if ever, due to the scarring."

I nodded, too tired and too emotionally spent to speak.

"You said you knew where the money is," she said. "A hundred million dollars."

Her black eye had started to fade. Vonda was still a very attractive young woman. Now, however, she would be dealing with an invalid for however long they stayed married, which probably would not be long. As for myself, I was never going to be able to live a normal life, regardless of whether I was able to retrieve the money. There would always be another Ramona and Arturo.

"I was just trying to save lives."

She nodded. "I saw you with Valerie," she said, studying me. "You loved her?"

"Not the way she wanted. You saw her, the way she was. Those cuts were not all recent. She needed help."

She sighed. "Now I get to live with the guilt from being a poor sister, too." She studied the toe of one of her moccasins. "So, tell me, Grayson Reynolds, is that even your real name? What are you planning to do?"

"I'm leaving, soon as I can. Before any more crazy-ass killers show up looking for me."

"You're leaving me with nothing," she said. "Just a husband who's an invalid and this." She held up the glass.

"You'll be okay, Vonda. Quit selling yourself short. You are pretty and smart. And now, you'll be twice as rich."

I thought she might throw the brandy at me, but she took a drink instead.

***

Catania showed up the next day as I was cleaning up and packing my few things. There was a knock on the cabin door followed by the appearance of the agent's head. "Okay if I visit for a spell?"

My hair was still wet from taking a shower and I combed it back with my fingers. "News travels fast."

Catania sat on the chair. "It seemed appropriate to make sure I had a handle on the situation and apprise you of where you stand."

"New boots?"

Catania stretched his legs and looked down at the shiny black alligator boots. "Nice, ain't they?"

"'Ain't they'? You probably haven't been here more than an hour or two and you're already starting to talk like a local."

"Mimicry. It is a gift. Or a curse. Depends how you look at it."

I frowned. "So how much time do I have?"

"Maybe a day or two more than last time," Catania said. "The good news is you killed two of their best. The bad news is..." He paused. "They were pissed off at you before, so you can imagine how they feel about you now."

I was back to where I started. Where could I go? What could I do to escape the cartel? The task felt hopeless.

As if reading my mind, Catania said, "I might have a job for you. Driving a truck. One of those big interstate eighteen-wheelers. The kind with the bed and fridge and satellite TV so you never have to be in one place very long. I happen to know the owner. We do favors for one another from time to time."

I stared at him. "Wouldn't I need a driver's license?"

"Yeah, you would." Catania reached in the breast pocket of his suit jacket and pulled out a new wallet. He flipped it open to show a Nevada driver's license and a photo of me. "You obviously didn't get this from me."

I fingered the license. It said my name was Ray Nelson, age twenty-four, of Las Vegas.

"This is where you're supposed to say, 'What can I ever do to repay you?'" Catania said.

"It might have saved a young woman's life if you had come up with this solution earlier."

Catania grimaced. "I'd say there were trust issues. On both sides."

I nodded finally. "Thank you."

Catania held out a business card. "This is the friend I was telling you about. He's expecting your call."

The FBI agent stood. When he reached the door, he turned. "Don't forget what I said before about leaving breadcrumbs to throw them off your trail. Stay out of trouble and don't stay too long in any one place and you should be fine." He nodded and was gone.

CHAPTER FORTY-THREE

Eighteen-wheelers were lined up in the vast parking lot like a herd of wildebeests at a Serengeti watering hole and an acrid, hydro carbonaceous haze hung in the midday air. Drivers shot the breeze and topped off fuel tanks and radiators before tackling the infamous I-5 grade known as the Grapevine that I had just descended. The road immediately ahead of me, by contrast, was long, straight, and level and, as I had learned from previous trips, conducive to unplanned naps unless you were well fortified with caffeine. Which was why I was admiring the world's largest collection of automotive deodorizers while I poured liquid that smelled like burned brakes and resembled used, thirty-weight oil into a Styrofoam cup.

"Watch yourself, son," cautioned a tall, sixty-ish guy with brush-cut hair who wore a denim vest, jeans, and a brass belt buckle the size of a dessert plate. "That'll grow hair where you don't need it and lose it where you do."

I stirred in the contents of a little plastic tub of flavored cream to improve the viscosity. Over the past few months, I had let my hair grow to cover the fading scar on my forehead and added a beard. I was in no immediate danger of losing hair anytime soon unless I discovered a barber in a truck stop, which was not out of the question. Some of these modern-day oases were like a miniature town with their own bank and post office.

"That your long-nose Pete I seen in the back?" the older man asked. Long distance drivers, as I had quickly learned, were an inherently curious bunch.

"Yep." Another minute of this guy's dialect and I would be back in West Texas, delivering newspapers before my junior high social studies class.

"Nice rig. Where you pointed?" He emptied the pot into a metal coffee mug the size of a large thermos.

"Portland. What about you?"

"San Diego, Ft. Worth, Bozeman. Won't see home for a good while yet."

"And where's that?"

"Got a forty-acre spread up near Wenatchee. Now that is God's country, for sure. But for the past thirty-three years," he hooked a thumb over his shoulder in the direction of the parking area, "I have slept in a cab more than a real bed. This might be my last year though. Wife says it's time to call it quits, or she's going to find a real husband." He chuckled as he extended his right hand. "Name's Tom."

"Ray." I shook the hand that was offered.

"What about you? Where's your home?"

"The truck."

Tom's hazel eyes looked deep into mine. "Forgive me for being nosy. Other than Facebook, this is about the only time for socializing I get." He pulled a battered leather wallet out of a hip pocket and dug out a business card whose paper resembled a bit of rag and whose type was faded and split by creases. "Don't get a lot of requests for these, but a feller needs to have a phone number he can call in the dead of night, or a place he can just show up without an invite. The wife bakes a mean lasagna. Makes her own tomato sauce. You ever get up our way, give us a holler."

He paid, then waited while I did the same. Together, we

re-entered the metallic glare and deafening exhaust of a departing Trailways bus. As I walked toward the truck, I wondered how much longer it would be, if ever, before I did not look like I needed a hand on my shoulder and a word or two of advice.

***

I had been throwing the gym bag with my belongings in the back of the Toyota when I saw Virgil walking down the hill toward me. He had Patsy with him.

"Was you thinking to just slide out of town, not saying nothin'?"

"To tell you the truth, Virgil, I was trying not to think."

"Still 'trying to just get by,' I expect."

I recalled that first day, the tractor test, and the rain that pock-marked the ponds.

"Listen, son. Can I still call you that?"

"I don't deserve to be called that. I cost you your daughter."

Virgil held up a hand for me to be silent while he fought back raw emotion. I waited, not having adequate words to begin to apologize for Valerie's death.

"You were right about Valerie needing help," he said. "Just like you were right about a lot of things. Fellow at the morgue said she had been hurting herself for a long time. I missed seeing it, just like I missed seeing what was happening with Stu and Vonda. They wanted out of here so badly, they didn't care who got hurt."

I couldn't think of anything to say.

"How are you doing with all this?" he asked.

"I have to admit, I don't understand." My voice quavered a little which embarrassed me.

High up in the mountains, the leaves of maples and alders were already beginning to turn red and yellow-green and an occasional larch tree blazed with gold fire. Fall would come early this year.

"I thought it was just me," I nodded at the sky, "but he doesn't care about anybody."

Virgil spat on the grass as we stood by the small concrete pond, empty now, where he had first told me about the trout that lived there. "Young man, you have a great deal to learn." He turned to look at me with pale blue eyes that had aged at least two decades in the past twenty-four hours.

"She's with him now." He paused to wipe his eyes with a sleeve. "And her momma."

Virgil gripped my shoulder with one large and heavily veined hand. "Vonda says you got a job as a truck driver. A piece of advice. The road is long. It has got its treacherous, rocky parts with no shoulder or places to pull off and rest. And it has got other parts so pretty and sweet you will forget the painful ones. Stay awake. Learn from both the good and bad. Do not go blaming God for what you do not understand. His ways ain't our ways. And remember, the Good Book is the only road map worth its salt."

***

On the way out of town, I stopped at the Burlington Library. By now, the librarian was used to seeing me. He took one look at my face and froze.

"What happened?"

"Car accident." According to Vonda, the bloodshed at the trout farm was all over the news and the last thing I wanted was any additional notoriety. "I need to use one of the computers."

I had written down a short list of passwords that I had thought long and hard about. If I was right about Heide and her fondness for Istanbul, the cultural center of Turkey, there were several ways to disguise it so it would not be obvious but would be easy to remember. First, I opened an account on the

TOR network to disguise the computer's IP address and its location. Now no one would know if the computer I was using was in Burlington, Washington, or Bangalore, India. After logging on the bank's web site, I hesitated. I had only three chances to get it right, because once I called up the bank's login page and attempted to sign into the account, it would set off alarm bells if I failed. I looked at my short list of possibilities, took a deep breath, then typed. If ever there was a longshot, this was it. But what the hell.

The great thing about hiding money today is that there are many ways to do it. I might not be as smart as Heide or her friend, Jeff, in IT, but I knew a little about cryptocurrency from reading up on the latest technologies at the Burlington Library. Bitcoin was just one example of a blockchain ledger protected by cryptographic algorithms.

Within an hour, I had created an anonymous digital wallet and sixteen-character private key. To make it even more impossible to track, I opened an account in a third-party service that, together with my TOR account, would guarantee my privacy by combining my transactions with dozens of others so that no one, including the IRS, FBI, or Sinaloa Cartel, would be able to trace the account or track the amounts being transferred. The problem with digital currencies is its limited purchasing power until it is turned back into cash or something else of value—which risks exposure. But that was getting easier every day as more and more banks and businesses accepted them.

I left Burlington one hundred million dollars richer than when I had arrived. The irony was that I could now afford to finish art school but could not do so without endangering not only myself, but the faculty and other students. On the plus side, I might never be able to spend large sums of the money without inviting unwanted scrutiny, but neither would the cartel or anyone else.

***

I opened the door to the truck cab and climbed in. A shaggy head rose from the passenger seat and licked her lips hopefully.

"Don't worry. I didn't forget." I opened the box of dog biscuits and offered Patsy one which she instantly inhaled. "Some dogs actually enjoy chewing them." After a few more biscuits, it was time to roll.

The engine started with a deep-throated rumble that vibrated throughout the cab. I checked the water and oil gauges followed by a glance at the mirrors, then let out the clutch and pulled out onto the easement road.

I had earned the right to drive the Peterbuilt after passing all the tests and agreeing to the terms for freelance long-haul drivers. It had a bed, a compact refrigerator, a microwave oven, and even a satellite television—all the comforts of home in a space the size of a large closet. It made my previous home in the cabin feel like a mansion.

I merged behind another tractor trailer. A minute later, we were headed north on the I-5, the windows open so Patsy could enjoy the breeze.

We rode in silence, Patsy thinking about food, or whatever dogs think about, and me contemplating regrets, as I often did, and lessons learned as Virgil had advised.

According to the last phone call from Vonda, plans were already being drawn up to convert the trout farm into an exclusive neighborhood of estate homes for the upper-middle-class who continued to flee Seattle, San Francisco, Los Angeles, and a hundred other cities where there is too much crime, too many incidents and accidents filling the television and newspapers, too many homeless with their afflictions and addictions, too many lost and angry refugees seeking the promised land, and too little space. It was hard for me to imagine the trout farm turned into yet another cul-de-sac, and

I was glad I wouldn't be around to see it. Nor had I been able to stick around long enough to see Valerie's body laid to rest. Catania had warned me there wasn't time.

Do places have memories? Once it became a neighborhood of new homes and families, would the land remember the pastoral beauty of the trout farm, the crowds of people that visited, or the legendary fish called Moses that once lived there?

I passed a Ryder Rent-a-Truck headed north and towing a subcompact. Beneath my sunglasses, I felt my eyes blur for a moment, and I pinched the bridge of my nose to clear them. Once again, I was on my own and not by my own choosing.

I had not loved Valerie in the same manner I had loved Heide. Nor had I been attracted to her sexually like I had been to Vonda. I had not even realized how much I cherished her music, her beauty, and her ability to hear what I was thinking until she was gone and the ache in my heart threated once again to capsize me.

Love was not always about passion or romance. Sometimes, love was having someone committed to standing by you, even when you failed. Even though she knew about my having sex with Vonda, Valerie still gave her life to save mine.

The guy I see in the rearview mirror looks familiar, but not the same. In addition to the long hair, he is a little heavier in the face, filled out in the shoulders and chest. But he rarely smiles. And the eyes. The eyes look haunted.

Valerie said you can't hide from your fate. I was not sure what I believed in anymore, but I was trying to keep an open mind. If believing in God helped Virgil cope with the loss of his youngest daughter, perhaps it could help me, too. Maybe her mother was right, and Valerie was now swimming with the angels.

Lately, I had begun listening to religious radio programs. I suspected it was part of the loneliness and the search for something to sink roots into, a state that wasn't listed on any map. On the radio, they called it Grace. It sounded like a place I needed to find, especially now that my Eden no longer existed.

Except to pass a slower vehicle, I stuck to the right lane, keeping one eye on the road and another on the landscape. The warm air tasted of dirt, fertilizer, and sun. A hundred-thousand acres of farmland, already brown, rippled in the noon-heat like the muscles of a reclining dancer, retired from some great, early caravan back when the world was new.

It occurred to me, as I sipped the bitter coffee, that it was a fine day for taking pictures.

END

ABOUT THE AUTHOR

Colin Kersey enjoys writing exciting stories peopled with unique, handicapped characters and their dogs and taking place in colorful locations. His first novel, *Soul Catcher,* was published by St. Martin's Press. A former Washingtonian and self-described rainophobe, Colin now lives on a sunny island in Southern California where he is employed as Global PR Manager for a Japanese company. He is a graduate of the University of Washington, Western Washington University and the novel writing program at Stanford University. He is currently working on a third novel.

ABOUT ATMOSPHERE PRESS

Atmosphere Press is an independent, full-service publisher for excellent books in all genres and for all audiences. Learn more about what we do at atmospherepress.com.

We encourage you to check out some of Atmosphere's latest releases, which are available at Amazon.com and via order from your local bookstore:

Saints and Martyrs, a novel by Aaron Roe

The Recoleta Stories, by Bryon Esmond Butler

Voodoo Hideaway, a novel by Vance Cariaga

The Weed Lady, a novel by Shea R. Embry

A Book of Life, a novel by David Ellis

It Was Called a Home, a novel by Brian Nisun

Grace, a novel by Nancy Allen

Shifted, a novel by KristaLyn A. Vetovich

Because the Sky is a Thousand Soft Hurts, stories by Elizabeth Kirschner

Stronghold, a novel by Kesha Bakunin

Unwinding the Serpent, a novel by Robert Paul Blumenstein

All or Nothing, a novel by Miriam Malach

Lightning Source UK Ltd.
Milton Keynes UK
UKHW042341260721
387780UK00004BA/911